QUINN'S BOOK

WILLIAM KENNEDY

Quinn's Book

VIKING

VIKING
Published by the Penguin Group
Viking Penguin Inc., 40 West 23rd Street,
New York, New York 10010, U.S.A.
Penguin Books Ltd, 27 Wrights Lane,
London W8 5TZ, England
Penguin Books Australia Ltd, Ringwood,
Victoria, Australia
Penguin Books Canada Ltd, 2801 John Street,
Markham, Ontario, Canada L3R 1B4
Penguin Books (N.Z.) Ltd, 182–190 Wairau Road,
Auckland 10, New Zealand

Penguin Books Ltd, Registered Offices:
Harmondsworth, Middlesex, England

First published in 1988 by Viking Penguin Inc.
Published simultaneously in Canada

A portion of this book first appeared in *Esquire*.

Quotation by Albert Camus on page 1 is used
by permission of Alfred A. Knopf, Inc.

Illustrations on pages 185 and 237 (figure on left)
courtesy of the Bettmann Archive.

LIBRARY OF CONGRESS CATALOGING IN PUBLICATION DATA
Kennedy, William, 1928–
Quinn's book.
I. Title.
PS3561.E428Q56   1988   813'.54   86-45858
ISBN 0-670-80437-1
ISBN 0-670-82213-2 (Limited Edition)

Printed in the United States of America by
Arcata Graphics, Fairfield, Pennsylvania
Set in Old Style Number 7
Designed by Francesca Belanger

The author would like to acknowledge with gratitude
the support of the MacArthur Foundation
during the years that this book
was being written.

This book is for
Dana,
By Herself

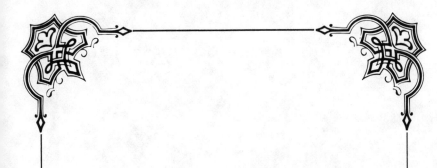

Book One

. . . a man's work is nothing but this slow trek to rediscover, through the detours of art, those two or three great and simple images in whose presence his heart first opened.

—ALBERT CAMUS

A CATACLYSM
OF LOVE

Albany

Winter & Spring
1849–1850

I, DANIEL QUINN, neither the first nor the last of a line of
such Quinns, set eyes on Maud the wondrous on a late December
day in 1849 on the banks of the river of aristocrats and paupers,
just as the great courtesan, Magdalena Colón, also known as La
Última, a woman whose presence turned men into spittling,
masturbating pigs, boarded a skiff to carry her across the river's
icy water from Albany to Greenbush, her first stop en route to
the city of Troy, a community of iron, where later that evening
she was scheduled to enact, yet again, her role as the lascivious
Lais, that fabled prostitute who spurned Demosthenes' gold and
yielded without fee to Diogenes, the virtuous, impecunious tub-
dweller.

This crossing was vexatious to all logic, for earlier in the day,
before the wildness came, she might have crossed far more safely
farther north via the dependable, strong-hulled ferry that would
have carried her over a narrower and calmer band of the Hudson
without incident and deposited her upon the steps of the Troy
wharf. But recklessness was far likelier to send the shiver of lust
through the spines of men, fire envy in the livers of their wives
and daughters, and set tongues to gossipaceous clacking that
would pack the hall for La Última's next performance; and so
she had advertised in the *Albany Chronicle* that she would pay
one hundred dollars, a bloody fortune, to any boatman who
would, at four in the afternoon, take her, her luggage, her serving
maid, and the child who traveled with her across the river from

Albany to Greenbush, where she would board a carriage bound overland to Troy.

Her advertisement appeared at the end of a week's spell of unseasonably balmy weather. She'd been in Albany five days, enthralling theatergoers with her acting and dancing, her beauty and sensual aggression. (Indeed there were some in the city who blamed her not only for the warm spell but even for the evil and grief that would befall us all on the day of her leave-taking.) The balminess had brought on the partial melting of the river's heavy ice, and had also halted all crossings by sleigh. A sizable channel opened in the river's center and a few sloops went straightaway downriver with little trouble. But cutting cross-wise into that current and its ice floes with a skiff was another matter.

The skiffmen had come out in number at the hour specified in La Última's advertisement and clustered under the Great Albany Pier with their craft, at rest on the shoreline's ice. But as the warmth of the day deepened, those wary Albany water rats (I include my master) were in agreement that the floes' growth in size and frequency, indeed the whole river's present nature, which was one of mild flood, argued that skiffs had no function on water such as this; all agreed, I say, except Carrick, the rotten Scottish hunchback of syphilitic mien, no longer welcome in the brothels of Albany, who had reached no such decision and was firm in his life's role as Albany's undauntable ferryman, ready to carry the urgent mail, the woeful news, or the intrepid passenger across the waters during storm or flood, and now the only soul at the pier willing to transport this plumed cargo to the far shore.

La Última's crossing had attracted such crowds that the bridge from the Quay Street shore out to the Great Pier (which paralleled the quay thirty yards from the shore) creaked with the weight of hundreds as La Última, her maid, and the child arrived in their carriage. A dozen men on the quay shoved aside the mob of ill-clad urchins who were vying for the right to carry La Última's trunk and to escort, hand-by-glove, the grand señora (for she had lived through three legitimate husbands, plus several hundred lovers). As she dismounted from the carriage she took command of the raffish disorder, singled out two muscular men, and gave them five dollars each (thus ensuring the security of two families, or at least the slaking of two thirsts, for the ensuing fortnight) to carry her trunk and hand luggage. She strode ahead of her entourage straight into the crowd, which parted at her advent to allow her entry to the steps leading down to the boats. There, standing on the ice in front of his skiff, Carrick greeted her, scraping obsequiously and explaining that only he was willing to cross these waters with her valuable self, prompting La Última to sniff in the direction of the other boatmen and give us all the flick of her chin in contempt for our lack of courage.

"It eees a pleasure to meet a rrreal mon," she said in her fraudulent, Hispanicized English (she was of Hibernian stock and spoke the language perfectly). She lifted Carrick's woolen hat and kissed him on his lumpy forehead as she might a pet piglet, then handed him, most ostentatiously, the promised one-hundred-dollar bill. The crowd cheered the hunchback, who flashed his toothless smile, pocketed the bill, and then gave La Última his hand to help her into his craft. The child and the maid followed (the maid in height, facial contours, and hair color being very close to a duplicate of the actress, it being commonly known that for special suitors the women dressed like twins). Carrick and his helper then lifted the skiff's line from its mooring post and pushed off from the shoreline's ice out onto the water. The boatmen stood up in the skiff and poled like gondoliers past the end of the Great Pier, Carrick poking the water ahead of the bow, seeking the floes, guiding them out of the way with the poling oar. And thus did the crossing begin and the skiff move out into open water on this dusky afternoon of high tragedy.

The skiff had reached the center of the river when we saw it wedge into a floe that would not yield to the prickings of the poles, saw it go crooked in the current and move slowly downriver backward, out of the hunchback's control. I could see La Última tightly gripping the side of the skiff with one hand, holding her hat with the other. The great, unseasonal feathered and amber plume in that hat, a match to her amber coat with the beaver collar, is as indelible in my memory as is the vision of her maid holding tightly to the child, and of Carrick and his helper poking the ice with their long sticks, a pair of needles attacking an iceberg, as the boat floundered like a toy.

My master and another boatman, named Duff, immediately shoved off into the water—I was sitting in our craft but not consulted—and we headed out for the rescue, proving, I thought, that virtue needs only a challenge to be awakened from dormancy. But my master was moved for quite another reason, and we were halfway to the trapped boat because of that reason when we saw a large hillock of ice smash into Carrick's craft and stove in its side, causing it to instantly list and take in water. We reached it too late to save Carrick, his helper, or the maid, who were knocked out of the boat when the hillock struck. It was I, however, who reached the child about to go under and hoisted her into our own skiff, while Duff behind me held off the flowing ice to guard my flank in the racy waters. And then my master, John the Brawn, caught the beaver collar of La Última's coat with his boat hook, and with one mighty lift, hauled her and her sodden plume up from the current, alas beyond our help.

"One dead slut," said my master as he also hooked La Última's floating trunk and lifted that aboard, too, that being the true focus of his concern. The child's countenance was as frigid in the face of death, loss, fright, and strangers as were the river's wicked waters, which were just beginning their avaricious devouring of human life. Not until springtime would the maid and Carrick turn up, sixty miles downriver, locked in grotesque, inverted embrace on the eastern shore (Carrick's pockets turned out), as if they had been out for an orgiastic swim and had died submerged in perversion.

We made our way back to the pier, I full of such fears as might have paralyzed me had I not been in thrall to the vivid young girl who held my hand with the same tenacity a starving wolf might grip with peerless jaws the flank of a vagrant deer. In truth, her grip was more memorable by double than the frigid bite of the river, which would leave me forever with fingers that only the summer sun could ever truly warm.

The crowd had grown ever larger on the bridge as word spread of our rescue effort, and as we moved onto the shore ice with our boat and our salvage, those crescive masses began struggling for greater vantage, shoving rudely among themselves, when suddenly, with a flagitious roar and an agonized whine, the old wooden span collapsed in twain, plunging a hundred or more of our citizens onto and through the fragile ice and into the deadly bath, while another hundred saved themselves with desperation leaps and wild clutchings to the fractured boards and railings; and there ensued then a mad scrambling upward and sideward by that doomed and threatened clot.

Their shrieks were the saddest sounds of my young days and instantly we all moved in our boats to help those we could. We saved about forty and lost we'll never know how many in those first few minutes before the onset of the even greater cataclysm, which, when we perceived it (I say we by way of collecting the common perspective we arrived at in a later and calmer moment), generated in us such fear of the Lord, of nature gone wild, of cosmic, mythic rage against our vulnerable puniness that we were negated as individuals and became as grains of sand, as desiccated leaves. We survived only because we survived. There is no other ascribable reason or logic behind who was saved and who wasn't, any more than there was logic in the way I alone of my family had come through the cholera unscathed.

The torrent came while we were frantically rescuing the drowning hordes from the bridge, roared down upon us from the northern river—a rush of ice like none in Albany had ever seen, even the eldest. It came, they later said, from the Mohawk River, careening with tumbling, tumultuous dudgeon into the Hudson, dislodging more and more of both rivers' heat-weakened blankets of ice, crunching and cracking and pushing more and more of its own fractured surface until, reaching Albany, the glut bedammed itself, clotted the whole transverse of the river's channel with chunks and prisms of ice in a sudden upthrust, a jagged wall built so quickly and with such superb natural engineering that had we not been hauling in the wet and the dead we would have given it the same attention we give an eclipse of the sun, for it was equivalently awesome.

The wall of ice grew from a relatively small, fencelike structure, say five feet high, across the thawed center of the river, continued building upon that fence a pyramid, a mountain, an instant Albany iceberg that never was before and probably never will be again. It rose to what some calculated as the height of ten men. Others said twenty. It grew swiftly upward with boundless force, brilliant chaos, and just as we thought it would never cease to grow, it was struck from within and below by some central power we could neither see nor understand, even now, but which exploded that mountain into a Vesuvius of crystal, showering the shores of both Albany and Greenbush with fragments, wounding an unsuspecting half-dozen people, killing two horses and a pregnant cat on the quay, and loosing a tidal wave that swept every object storehoused on the Great Pier, including barrels of coffee, piles of lumber and staves, and another dozen men, tumbling them into the torrent as if they were the river's own algae, which they would very soon become.

That wave would raise us all, the drowning masses, the handful of salvationists, to its stunning crest, then settle us back into a trough, rocking us on a slowly rising flood tide that would, half an hour after our departure, spill over the quay and crawl into storehouses, and, worse, into the plaster works and lime kiln, there mixing with and slacking the lime into chemical combustion that would set fire to a block of stores along the quay frontage: fire rising out of flood—the gods gone mad.

Because there was such panic, such fear, I focused finally on what was possible for us alone to do: save the child, this orphan of the river, who was shivering and unable to walk when I lifted her out of our skiff onto the shore and led her up the steps to dry ground, knowing, as we threaded our way through clusters of desperation, that this frail creature would die of frozen blood if I did not soon warm her. My master, meanwhile, lifted the corpse of La Última from the skiff and plopped it down on the shore ice, far more concerned with the contents of her trunk than with the disposition of her person. Even as the child and I were saving ourselves from water, John the Brawn, under the eyes of heaven and all the bereft, was hammering at the latch of the trunk with the end of his oar: a vision of how the fear of death easily yields to the power of greed. But the trunk would not yield, and so John turned again to the dead Magdalena Colón, clutched her under his left arm, and, gripping the trunk handle with his right hand, ascended the quay's steps, bumping both the actress's toes and trunk on every step as he came, but rising willfully up from the water to dry turf, a Palaemonic figure bereft of sanity.

On the quay the kin and kith of the lost were loud in their lamentations, while at least twoscore people were still clinging to the far segment of the fractured bridge, some of them failing of purchase and falling through the broken ice, either emerging by splash of will and main strength or vanishing in frozen weakness beneath the rising tide of ice and blood.

John stood the trunk on its end and gave both his hands to the dead Magdalena, lifting her into a semblance of womanly order, however dead, and laying her down again so as to catch his breath and consider the immediate future. He turned his gaze to the child we would soon know to be Maud, and he asked her, "Have ye family?" Maud only stared at him as an answer, and then he cast an eye at Magdalena.

"Is that one your ma?" he asked, and that roused Maud.

"She was my aunt," said Maud, "and vastly superior to Mother as a human being."

"Where is your dastardly mother?"

"She is with the King."

"Ah, the King," said John. "She's a queen, is she?"

"She's the King's companion," said Maud.

"And which king might it be that's keen on your ma?"

"The King of Bavaria."

"Bavaria, a grand little place, so they say. And is the King, like yourself, stopping here in Albany for a bit of a visit?"

"They are both in Bavaria. The King has gone into exile," said Maud, whose want of childish speech was giving me the image of myself as a tongue-tie, and I being almost fifteen, two years and three months older than she.

"Your auntie's fair croaked and your ma's in bloody exile. So where might your da be, then?"

"My mother always said she didn't know for certain where he was. But she's a liar."

Just then, with those poor souls who were clutching the bridge's far segment sending up their continuing chorale of dangling doom, and with the living onshore throwing themselves into furies of grief over the dead and the missing, a woman whose husband, or perhaps brother, lay inert on the quay looked at us and recognized the corpse of Magdalena, her amber plume, sodden and bedraggled (but a swatch of autumn nevertheless), still jutting markedly from that dead skull. And that woman then rose up from beside her inert man, let seethe through her teeth a single word—"Herrrr"—and, following upon this with the maddened and throaty growl of a jungle feline, flew across the space that separated us, pounced upon the courtesan's lifeless body, sank her teeth into that pallid cheek, and came away with a blooded wad of flesh in her mouth, which she savored with a bulging smile and then spat onto the dead actress's chest. Stiffened with loyalty to our corpse, I leaped into the tableau and yanked the toothy bitch by the arm, flinging her aside so that John the Brawn might lift our dead lady out of more harm's way.

John carried her to where a policeman stood guard over the lengthening row of the congealing dead, while other police pressed cabmen and private carriages into hauling the freezing victims to the city's clinic. My master lay the dead woman down, straightened her dress over her legs with a show of modesty I would not have predicted, and gently stroked her hair out of her face with two fingers.

"They mean to eat her like wolves," said my master to the police officer.

"Move along, don't handle the dead," the policeman told him.

John tipped his hat and smiled through his light-brown teeth, not one to argue with the law; for indeed John was fugitive from trouble in a dozen towns along the canal, his last excursion with the bottle ending in the destitution of Watervliet's Black Rag saloon, even to the felling of the four pillars that supported the tavern's second-story porch.

We went back for the wardrobe trunk, and only when my hands were full did Maud release her grip on me. She had watched the cannibalizing of her aunt without a word and offered nothing but a mute stare at that supine form, one among many. But as we walked from the edge of the quay with the trunk (I knowing nothing of John's next intentions), Maud halted and said, "We can't leave my aunt lying there in the cold. It isn't civilized behavior."

"We'll not leave her," said John, who hailed a close carriage that was moving toward us. As the driver slowed, John grabbed the reins of the horse. "We're sore in need of your service," he told the driver.

"I've orders to do what the police want, them and none other," retorted the driver.

"You'll succor us or I'll maim your horse and splinter your backbone," said my master, and the driver grumbled his comprehension of the priorities. With the cabman's help I put the trunk on his luggage rack and helped Maud into the cab, thinking John would enter with us. But he called to the driver to wait and went back to the quay's edge, returning with the limp form of Magdalena Colón across his outstretched arms. I had a sudden vision of my sister being so carried in from the street by my father, she then dying from the same cholera that would strike both him and my mother within a week, thus setting me on the road toward my rendezvous with John the Brawn. John was a man I thought I knew after my time on the canal under his heavy hand. I even once thought I was rid of him when his rotted canalboat sank in a storm near Utica, and glad I was of it. But I was not rid of him, and as he walked toward me now with the dead woman in his arms, I realized how little I really knew about him, or about any man. I especially could not find a place for the tenderness he displayed in stroking the hair out of La Última's eyes with his two callused fingers.

"Is she dead?" the driver asked him.

"Dead as dead ever gets," said John. "A dead slut with a hole in her face."

And he thrust La Última into the carriage with us, sat her across from Maud, and flopped into the seat opposite mine,

holding the corpse upright with his arm around her shoulder.
Had she not been so wet they might have been taken for lovers
bound for an escapade. Maud had taken my hand as soon as we
sat beside each other, and I'd smiled at her. But she had only
fired her eyes and turned her head, keeping hold, nevertheless,
of my hand.

"Well, Miss, what shall we do with her? Take her up to Congress Hall and auction her off to the politicians? Put her on view
at The Museum? Or is hers a Christian body crying for six feet
of holy dirt?"

"Mrs. Staats will know what to do," Maud said. "My aunt
was fond of her."

Maud looked intently at La Última's face, then reached over
and touched the dead woman's cheek near where it had been
bitten. "It's so sad," she said. "She cared about her face above
everything."

"She had a pretty little face," said John. "We couldn't let them
have it all." He stroked around the raw wound with a single
finger.

"Did you know her?" asked Maud. "I never saw you with
her."

"I knew her," said John. "Saw her in New York, months ago.
She acted, danced, sang. I saw her do her Spider Dance. Now
there was a picture. A woman to remember, she was."

"You would probably want to kiss her. Men always wanted
to kiss her."

"You're a bright-spoken, savvy child," said John, and he turned
his face to La Última, gripped her jaw between the thumb and
first finger of his right hand, and kissed the dead woman long
and vigorously on the mouth.

"You're a wicked man," said Maud.

"They've told me that," said my master, smiling and settling
back into his seat. "But have ye never seen anyone kiss the dead?
They all do it."

We'd ridden two blocks off the quay when the carriage driver stopped and called down to us, "Where do we be goin'?"

We all then looked to Maud, who said staunchly, "To the home of Mrs. Hillegond Staats."

"Do ye know that place?" John asked the driver.

"There's none in Albany doesn't," came the ready answer, and the driver sped away toward the Staats mansion, a dwelling place of exalted lives, and a safe harbor as well for certain desperate souls who'd been chilled, like ourselves, by the world's bitter ice.

As we rode, Maud fixed silently on the face of her aunt, occasionally looking to me for solace, or perhaps wisdom of the instant, as if I and not my master were the source of power in this quartet of misfits. Maud took my free hand in her own (we now holding both each other's hands) and whispered to me, "We must patch her cheek before we bury her, for she'll have no luck in the next world with her face like that." And then she added after a pause, "And we must bury her beneath a tree, for she loved trees almost as much as she loved men."

I nodded my agreement and Maud smiled, the first smile of hers I had ever seen, and I have remembered it all my days. But I knew nothing of patching flesh. With what did you patch it? As to burial, it had not crossed my mind that any portion of the task would ever fall to me. But I had already twice assented to Maud's will, which, I would come to know, was an element very like Roman cement once it had assumed a shape.

Our driver turned onto the carriageway that led to the Staats mansion and called to us that we'd arrived. Maud and I held silence. John the Brawn grumphed and let Magdalena fall sideways, her head striking the carriage wall with a memorable thump; and he said he'd see who was at home.

"You're sure she knew this Staats woman?" he asked Maud.

"We were her guests for two evenings," said Maud.

John opened the carriage door and the encroaching night reached in for us with a profound chill, a blast of northern air that had dropped the temperature perhaps twenty degrees in as many minutes. As John walked off in the half-darkness our eyes played the night's game and we saw that a half-moon was sending a straying gleam into one of La Última's eyes, now fully open and staring at us.

"Close her eye," said Maud, gripping my hand as if she felt herself still in the wild river. "You must never let the dead look at you."

I dutifully moved the eyelid down over the eye, feeling the flesh soft, pliable, and without warmth, but not yet chilled, somewhat like the loose skin of a chicken dead thirty minutes.

"What can the dead see?" I asked Maud when I'd done her bidding.

"If you look in their eyes you see your fate. And one must never know one's fate if one is to keep sane."

"I wouldn't mind seeing my fate," I said, "for then I'd know how to avoid it."

"You can't avoid your fate, you goose. That's why they call it your fate."

I let her have the argument, for I noted that Magdalena's eye was quavering, and I grew fearful. Slowly that same eyelid slid open, back to the point from which I had closed it, and the eye again fixed upon Maud and me. I leaned forward for a look but Maud tugged me back with her urgent bulldog grip. I broke her hold and looked squarely into La Última's eye by the light of the brilliant half-moon, at first seeing the conventional human orb: the maroon iris, the deep-brown pupil, the soft white transparency of the conjunctival membrane striped with the faintest of frigid purple rivers and tributaries. And then in the center of the suddenly luminous pupil I saw a procession of solemn pilgrims moving through a coppice: night it was, but snowing, and as fully bright as this true night that surrounded us. And there was Maud, her hand held by an old woman. There, too, moved John the Brawn, ahead of a figure wrapped in furs. I myself trudged forward alongside a black dog and I sensed that this was the funeral procession of Magdalena, made visible for us by her own dead eye. Her body, however, was not in portage, nor was it anywhere to be seen.

I intended to say nothing of this to Maud, having no wish to confirm the superiority of her mystical knowledge to my own. But she knew from my steady gaze into that dead eye that I had indeed seen something queer, and so at her earnest tugging of my sleeve I reported the scene to her, was narrating the cortege's route, when the vision abruptly changed to an even darker night, with a ragtag troop of men swarming down a city street and smashing the windows of a newspaper office with stones and clubs. It changed a second time and a young man, his face familiar but to which I could attach no name, emerged from the same building in bright daylight, talking soundlessly but volubly to two men who held him by the arms as they walked. Suddenly he was thrown into a carriage, which swiftly wheeled off behind a matched pair.

I had no time to speak of this to Maud, for John the Brawn opened our own carriage door with a bravissimo shout: "Out and down with you both. We are welcome guests of the mistress of this grand place." And when he hauled both of us out, he lifted the trunk off the luggage rack, plucked Magdalena out of the cab, and threw her over his shoulder like a sack of barley. Then, with a dismissing wave to the carriage driver in lieu of a gratuity, he led us up the gravel pathway to the house, dragging the trunk. Maud held me back a few paces and whispered to me in a desperate tone of voice, saying I must always remember she was never going to marry anyone, was never going to grow up to be like her hated mother, or even like her saintly whore of an aunt, and that I must promise to steal her away from this house if it should come to pass that the Staats woman, or some other hateful adult, should try to take charge of her life.

"It's you who have first right to my life," she told me, "for it was you who kept me from sliding to the bottom of the river. Will you promise me—promise on your heart's blood—that you'll steal me, whatever the cost?"

Her vehemence took me over, and I swiftly and foolishly promised: I will steal you, if need be, no matter what the cost, no matter how long it takes.

"Now kiss me," she said, and I kissed her on the cheek, the first female flesh other than my mother's and sister's to ever brush my lips. I also tasted a wisp of her hair and found the whole sensation surprisingly exciting to my mouth and lower intestines.

"Hurry along," John said to us, and we mounted the steps of the canopied porch to see him with Magdalena slung over his shoulder, standing now beside a strapping woman whose stature seemed not to pair with the wrinkles of her skin: as if she had not shrunk with age but had grown muscular. Her cheeks were rosy coins of paint and from her naked ears dangled earrings that looked very like church bells. She was still formidably handsome despite the wrinkles and the grotesque nature of her adornments, and as we stepped into the first warmth any of us had known in what seemed like an age of icy blasts, she squatted to greet us. This hothouse crone—Hillegond Staats was her name— embraced both Maud and me together with those powerful arms, pulled us to her wrinkled, half-draped, and formidable bosom, which smelled of corn powder and myrrh, and wept rhinoceros tears of gratitude that an adventure of the heart was entering into her life. She said as much in words I cannot precisely recall, for the degree of their welcomeness crowds out their sound and shape in my memory. This giant creature, Hillegond, had us in her power, which was very old power and reeked of money and leisure and exploitation and looked for its deeper meaning

[19]

in the eyes of madmen, dead whores, and children of the wild river.

"Come in, come in, my frozen dears," the great crone said to us. John the Brawn shoved the door closed behind us and we stood in that grand entrance hall, dwarfed by the unknown, which billowed crazily through that mansion like the lovely heat that was already warming our souls.

WHEN HILLEGOND CEASED to squeeze the frigidity and the breath out of Maud and me, she shooed us into the care of a black man named Capricorn and a black woman named Matty, both of them slaves in their youth. Capricorn wrapped me in a blanket, took me to the kitchen, sat me in front of the huge gray brick kitchen fireplace, and fed me Dutch soup with apples, potatoes, carrots, and the livers of certain undesignated creatures, unarguably the most important meal of my life, while Matty took Maud elsewhere for a change into dry clothing. Capricorn, who as a freed slave thirty years earlier had been a man of social eminence among Negroes, was kindly toward me without undue deference. Meanwhile, Hillegond, my master, and the residual elements of Magdalena found themselves together in the *Dood Kamer,* or dead chamber, the room set aside in substantial homes of the old Dutch to accommodate death.

Hillegond's house was indeed old Dutch, and substantial. She was born Hillegond Roseboom, daughter of an Albany tavern-keeper of bibulous repute; and it is known that she said farewell to maidenhood at age sixteen (some insist she voyaged out years earlier) by marrying Petrus Staats, son of Volckert Staats, grandson of Jacobus Staats, great-grandson of Dolph Staats, great-great-grandson of Johannes Staats, great-great-great-grandson of Wouter Staats—all of these descended from a pre-Christian or perhaps even a primal Staatsman, though the voluminous family records (initiated by Volckert, preserved by Petrus) trace the family only to the sixteenth century, about the time Holland was declaring itself independent of Spaniards and preparing to shape the New World in the image of Dutch coin.

The first to reach the New World was Wouter Staats, who gained renown as a trader by perfecting counterfeit wampum (polished mussel shells with a hole in the center, strung on a string). Wouter arrived with his wife at Fort Orange, the early name of Albany, in 1638, and in 1642 fathered Johannes, the first born-American Staats, a noble-headed youth who grew up to serve in the militia as an Indian fighter, gaining knowledge of the wilderness and its inhabitants to such a degree that upon leaving the military he entered the fur trade (beaver pelts) and earned the wealth that began the family fortune.

Johannes was everywhere praised for his honesty but suffered the taint of a curious wife, Wilhelma, who worked as a produce trader during Johannes's long absences in quest of furs, and incorrigibly sold her customers spotted oats and blue wheat. Johannes retired Wilhelma when his wealth permitted, and through his charities erased her stain from the family reputation. He also became a zealot of religious liberty, championed the right of Lutherans, Huguenots, and Jews to worship in Albany, and, upon the appearance of Newton's comet, arranged the day of prayer and fasting that was credited with persuading the Deity to banish the dread missile from Albany's skies.

Dolph Staats, eldest of Johannes's six children, was born in 1664, the year English military might sublimated Dutch power without seriously altering the daily life of Albany Dutchmen. Commerce proceeded apace, pigs roamed the streets, and the old burghers in their cocked hats and worsted caps still filled the air of the town with pipe smoke and, as one English visitor noted, with phlegmatic gravity as well. Dolph Staats came to enjoy the energetic English and traded profitably with them, expanding his father's moderate fortune through mercantility, selling the productions of Europe—Bibles and snuffboxes, fiddle strings and China teapots, love ribbons and dictionaries, satinets and shalloons—to his townfolk. His concern with garmenting impelled him to ask the governor of the province to take pity on the ill-clad English soldiers garrisoned in the town, their tatters so advanced that ladies were advised to avert their eyes when passing lest their gaze intersect with the soldiers' private physical portions. It was also Dolph who left the family signature on two stained-glass windows of the old Dutch church: one the family coat of arms in four colors, and, uniquely, the glazened image of a supine infant whose physiognomy combined the blond ringlets and eyebrows of a Dutchified Jesus, with the crossed eyes of Dolph's only son, Jacobus.

Jacobus, as he grew into ascetic adolescence, loathed his father's mercantile life; loathed also the town's wandering pigs, which he saw as an image of fattable Dutch desire. And so he apprenticed himself to his grandfather Johannes, with whom he sat for long hours, listening while the old man curled pipe smoke around his balding pate and recollected his days with canoe, blade, and rifle, abroad in the land of the red maple, the redwing, and the redskin.

Jacobus married Catrina Wessels, the wall-eyed niece of the Patroon, that absentee landlord who by the fourth decade of our own nineteenth century had held for two hundred years, along with successive heirs, an estate of seven hundred thousand acres, an entity so all-encompassing that arguments prevailed as to whether the Patroon's demesne was within the bounds of Fort Orange, or whether Fort Orange trespassed upon the Patroon, and on which some one hundred thousand tenant farmers and lesser vassals paid rent and servitude *in perpetuum;* and while this colonizing was doubtless the great expansionist stroke that created our present world, it was also the cruelest injustice American white men of the New World had ever known, and would precipitate warfare that itself would continue for decades.

The marriage of the wall-eyed Catrina to Jacobus, who remained cross-eyed into adulthood, was a matter of considerable discussion in Albany, and it was speculated they would give birth to children who could look both left and right at the same time they were looking straight ahead. Social conversation with Catrina and Jacobus together was also said to be a nerve-racking experience since one never knew to which of the four eyes one should properly send one's gaze. But the union was blissful, and the Patroon, mindful of the boon to the family in Catrina's marriage to even a mal-orbed primitive, bestowed a wedding gift of land on the couple, whereupon Jacobus immediately moved out from the town, taking with him the hybrid image of himself and Jesus in stained glass, installing it in the cabin he built in his new and personally owned wilderness three miles to the north in the midst of a primeval forest, and leaving his father to fill the hole in the church wall and to make moral amends for his son's profane deed. On his land Jacobus felled timber, burned it in an ashery, extracted lye from the ashes, boiled the lye into black salts, and then sold the salts to the town's only soapmaker for melting into potash.

He built then (this being the mid-1730s) a sawmill alongside the erratic creek that took his name, the Staatskill, a stream with wellsprings in the western plateau beyond the town, and which, at normal flow, coursed placidly eastward toward the river. But the creek was given to flooding after heavy rain, which Jacobus discovered as the water rose over its banks and diluted into uselessness his large holding of black salts. Jacobus thereafter focused his salvation on his sawmill, which he built on the edge of the stream's lone cataract, Staats Falls, where the waters collapsed with great aesthetic gush and spume into an effervescing pool and then ran for an arrogant mile down the slope of Staats Hill to meet the river at a point by the Patroon's Manor House, near where a handful of Irish immigrants in the employ of the Manor were throwing up one humble dwelling after another in what would eventually be called The Colonie.

Catrina bore Jacobus two sons: the elder called Volckert, a pleasant, boring child of surprisingly normal eye structure; the younger an infant boy whose birth brought about Catrina's sudden demise, but who was himself baptized in time to join his sinless mother in the Dutch Reformed parlors of heaven. With the help of Volckert, Jacobus spent the next decade building the earliest frame building of the mansion in which we fugitives of the wild river would find refuge a century later; and he lived there with Volckert in celibate isolation, an irascible, pointy-headed, and spindly terror to the Irish children who spooked his footsteps on his daily walks through the slowly vanishing wilderness on the mansion's periphery.

Then, in his dotage, the old dog Jacobus kicked up his fleas, traded a pint of gin for an Indian squaw named Moonlight of the Evening, who had been a house servant of the Patroon in her adolescence, installed her as mistress of the Staats ur-mansion without the benefit or liability of wedlock, and with that single act translated his own eccentricity into public depravity and his mansion into a house of miscegenational vice. The affront was not only to white purity but also to the red nations of the New World, for Moonlight's eldest brother had been halved by an ax wielded by a white woman he had sought to rape while drunk on white man's rum. The killing of his favorite son undid Taw Ga Saga, the father of Moonlight and a sachem of one of the five Indian Nations; and yet Taw Ga Saga tempered his hatred of whites with an eloquent plea to the Governor of New York, ponting out that when Indians brought beaver skins and other peltry to Albany for sale, the white men first gave the Indians a cup of rum. They did the same when the Indians sat down to sign a bill of sale for a piece of land. And in the end, said Taw Ga Saga, the peltry and the land always went for more rum: "For it is true, O our father, that our people crave rum after they get one taste of it, and so long as Christians sell it, our people will drink it. We ask our father to order tap on rum barrel to be shut."

But it was never shut and Taw Ga Saga, ousted from power because of his son's act, took to drink himself, lost all pelts and all land, and finally died in abject disgrace after selling Moonlight of the Evening to Jacobus for the infamous pint of gin.

Jacobus's son Volckert was thirty when Moonlight of the Evening became his unlawful stepmother and he left home the same day, becoming peerlessly Godful in mortification for the family shame and earning the sobriquet Venerable Volckert. The year after she moved in, Moonlight of the Evening bore Jacobus a son, called Amos after the rustic Hebrew prophet. Amos became the first chronicler of the Staats family, keeping voluminous journal notes of his father's and his mother's memories, from the time he entered adolescence. But Amos lived only to the age of sixteen, dying a young hero, the first soldier of the Continental Army to bring the glorious news to Albany that Burgoyne had surrendered and was no longer a threat to the city. Amos's valiant thirty-mile ride was accomplished with a wound that proved fatal, but he was made an immediate legend. The switch with which he had whipped his horse was salvaged by a woman after he dropped it when toppling from his saddle, and she planted it in her front yard on Pearl Street, where it grew into an enormous tree that for several generations was known as Amos's Oak. Jacobus buried the boy under the floorboards of the cabin he himself had built when he settled the land, and placed a marble sarcophagus in the middle of the main room, which had been long empty but was still of sound construction, and into which the sun beamed at morning through the crossed eyes of the Jacobus-Jesus window.

Thrown into despair at the loss of his son, Jacobus brooded for three years, suffered an apoplectic fit in 1780 while chasing a family of brazen Irish squatters off his land, and died of splenetic outrage. Volckert immediately began proceedings to oust Moonlight of the Evening from the Staats mansion, which Ja-

cobus had left to her alone in his will. But the will was flawed
and easily tumbled, and Moonlight of the Evening spent her last
year of life in the sepulchral Staats cabin, using her son's sarcophagus as a dining table. Volckert had buried Jacobus with
as much restraint as was seemly in the Dutch church, and while
maneuvering to take over the land and house from Moonlight
of the Evening, he also saw to it that the name of Jacobus became
anathema in any society that coveted the presence and probity
of Venerable Volckert. Within a month Jacobus's name was only
on the tongues of cads and vulgarians, and within a year in the
most proper social groupings, Jacobus had faded into a shadow
figure of doubtful legend, one who, like the silver-tailed shoat
and seven-titted cow, may or may never have existed.

Volckert's wife, Joanna, a woman of mindless piety, bore twin
daughters, Trynitie and Femmitie, and they, raised in cloying
righteousness, wed men of means from the outlands as soon as
it was in their power to do so, and moved to New York and
Boston, well out of probity's clutch. Volckert's wife also bore
him a son, Petrus, who, as we have said, saw fit to wed and
woo the bounteous and bawdy Hillegond in yet another reversal
of the moral order in the Staats family, which, in matters of
sensual predilection, exhibited all the stability of a Bach ca-
denza.

Petrus, inspired by the mercantile success of his great-grand-
father Dolph, whose early investment in an overland stagecoach
line had been passed on to Petrus as a legacy, proved to have
economic genius in his makeup. He octupled the Staats fortune,
becoming Albany's richest man as the new century began. He
also proved the most benevolent of all Staatses, and was loved
by his contemporaries, who honored him by naming both a short
street and a public water pump after him. He branched into
hardware, joining the Yankee Lyman Fitzgibbon in an ironworks and foundry, and was also an investor in several canals

[27]

(including the Erie), which his peers found quixotic, since canals offered stagecoach traffic its principal competition. But Petrus found such thinking benighted, was in time hailed as a pioneer of transport, and was buried beneath a tombstone bearing a carving of a canalboat.

Petrus died in 1835 at age seventy-two, a nobleman of the spirit and the purse, having built a marble mausoleum around the grave of his uncle Amos, the half-breed (who was only two years his elder), and having also transformed the Staats house into a Federal mansion of such vast dimension that travelers came to Albany expressly to see it. His wife, Hillegond, bore him a stillborn daughter and a son, Dirck, who was destined to play a most significant role in my life, and who, at the time of our arrival at the mansion, was in disgrace with his mother, who had turned Dirck's two full-length portraits, painted when he was twelve and nineteen, to the wall. In the years after the death of Petrus, Hillegond had refused all offers of marriage, certain that her knowledge of men, despite her uncountable intimate encounters with them, was seriously bescrewed. Further, she grew certain from a recurring nightmare that should she ever consider a man as a second spouse, he would strangle her in her bed with a ligature. And so, when she imposed her bosom on Maud and me and welcomed us into her life, she was also keeping one wary but wavering eye clearly fixed on the most virile man to have crossed her doorstep in years, my master, John the Brawn.

How virile he, how wavering she, is the matter next at hand, for when I felt myself fully cooked by the fire in Hillegond's kitchen I stood up and found myself (still wrapped in the blanket) face-to-face with Maud, who was dressed most curiously in clothes that had belonged to Hillegond when she was Maud's size. The dress was drabness itself, but Maud was glad of the gift, and I was exuberant, both from the warmth the fire had kindled in my blood vessels and from being reunited with this magical child.

"What do we do now?" she asked me.

"I couldn't say. Perhaps we should find the mistress."

"She's ever so frightful-looking, but I am fond of her," said Maud.

Matty, the Negro woman, breezed by and waved us in the direction of the front end of the house, then went about her business in the kitchen. Maud and I stepped gingerly toward the main salon but were caught by the sight of Hillegond's full-body profile standing just inside the door of the *Dood Kamer,* which gave off the foyer. Hillegond was rigid, both her hands gripping the insides of her thighs. We looked past her and saw my master attending to the corpse of Magdalena, which lay supine on the room's catafalquish bed, to which one ascended by climbing two steps. John the Brawn, in shirtsleeves and trousers, was, with notable delicacy, raising the chemise of the dead woman from her knees to her thighs, having already raised and carefully folded her skirt above her waist.

"What is he doing?" Maud asked me in a whisper.

"I can't be sure," I said, though that was a canard. I knew very well what he was doing, as did Hillegond, who stood wide-eyed as John exposed Magdalena's nether regions and then undid the cincture at his own waist.

"You mustn't look at this," I said to Maud, and I interposed myself between her and the brazen necrophile. But she shoved me aside rudely and barked in a whisper, "Get out of my way, you ninny, I've never seen anyone do this before," which I came to know as Maud's battle cry in her witnessing of this life. And so we squatted in the doorway, unnoticed by the principals in the vivid scene unfolding before us.

John the Brawn climbed aboard Magdalena Colón and began doing to her gelid blossom what I had heard him boast of doing

[29]

to many dozens of other more warm-blooded specimens. The sight of his gyrations aroused Hillegond to such a degree that she began certain gyrations of her own, uttering soft, guttural noises I associate solely with rut, and which grew louder as her passion intensified. Magdalena looked vapidly toward us as John gave her the fullness of his weight, her one eye still open and staring, her hair fanned out in handsome peacock show on the pillow.

Hillegond's moans came forth with such uncontrolled resonance that when John turned and discovered her pelvic frenzy he pushed himself away from the inert Magdalena and bobbed brazenly toward our hostess, who swooned into a bundle; whereupon my master did to her skirts precisely what he had done to Magdalena's and, with what seemed to me magnified elevation (proving the truth of the adage: fresh comfort, fresh courage), crawled aboard the supine Hillegond and renewed his roostering. This taking of her infernal temperature restored Hillegond to consciousness and she threw her arms around John and yielded herself with a long crescendoing moan that concluded when our lady of the catafalque opened both her eyes and said aloud from the frigid beyond she had been inhabiting, "Why did you stop doing me?" raising her arms and stupefying us all, not least my master, who backed outward from Hillegond and, with undiminished extension, walked to the unfinished Magdalena, inspected her center (whose visibility she heightened at his approach), and then clambered once again aboard this abused flower, now resurrected from wilt by the sunny friction of joy. The spent Hillegond rose to one elbow and studied the sight as she might the resurrection of Lazarus, her sensual zealousness giving way to a vision of the miraculous. She covered herself and bore witness while my master, having quickly moved beyond amazement, resumed the thumping of his newly sanguinolent slut with vile laughter and swollen vigor, creating a triadic climax, not only in his own member and its hostel, but also in the bite wound of La Última's face, which, as she bent herself upward to John in consummation, began to ooze the blood of her life, demonstrating that she was again at corpuscular flood in every vein and vessel of her being.

When the orgiasts ceased to move they looked pensively into the glut in their own psychic interiors, Maud and myself perfectly invisible to their eyes. But I sensed they would see us soon enough and know by our expressions what we had seen, and I could not be sure what they might do to us for such knowledge. I pulled Maud away and led her to the front parlor, where we sat upon a green velvet sofa very like the color of Maud's eyes in subdued light. I did not know what to say to her about what I felt, but she, never at a loss for comment, announced:

"He is a low beast, and they are both fools for a man. Would you want to do that to me?"

"I think so," I said, though I had not considered it in such an individualized context.

"I'm not at that stage yet," said Maud.

"I guess I am," I said.

"It seems to be very affecting, what happens to one."

"That's what I've heard."

"I should have thought you'd have already tested it."

"I've not had the opportunity," I said.

"When I'm ready to do it," Maud said, "I shall seek you out."

"I look forward to that," I said.

We were both utterly calm—a great lie, of course, for the agitation we felt was not only beyond words but would take decades to be sifted of significance. An image recurred for years in Maud's mind of a voluptuous woman giving birth to an infant skeleton; and I, for years, dreamed of a woman who owned bilateral pudenda. We sat on that vernal sofa staring at a primitively painted portrait of a child wearing a white dress with a lace collar, holding a hoop in one hand while her other hand rested on the neck of a gander two-thirds her size.

"I never want to be old," said Maud. "I want to be young forever and ever, and then, when I'm of a certain age, I want to be very suddenly dead."

"You can't be young forever and ever," I said.

"Yes I can."

"No you can't."

"Yes I can."

"Not anymore," I said; for ignorant as I was, I knew.

I HAD NEVER SEEN anyone return from the dead before Magdalena Colón was resuscitated by love, the same commodity used by the Christ to effect a similar end. I draw no blasphemous parallels between John the Brawn, the amatory instrument, and Jesus; or between Jesus and Magdalena, especially in light of what she reported to us about her deathy interlude. But the power of love is more various and peculiar than we know.

Once out of the orgiastic moment, Magdalena became the cynosure of our curiosity, for what usually follows the enactment of human improbability is the quest for proof it has really occurred. And, indeed, we all craved the gossip of her soul. And so after Magdalena had dressed herself in dry clothing, after John's tucking of cincture, after the smoothing of all skirts and with the dissembling smiles that follow satiety, the adults gathered in the east parlor, where Maud and I were sitting, I amid a personal rapture that intensified with every moment spent in her presence, awash in desire for I knew not what; not, certainly, the simple raising of her skirts in emulation of John the Brawn. Such vulgarity (though I have since learned not to demean it) was insufficient response to my yearnings, which were destined to intensify even further during this singular evening.

Hillegond took maternal control of Magdalena's bite wound, bathing it, bandaging it, sitting the patient close to the fireplace, whose fire Capricorn faithfully stoked. Then we huddled in front of the flames as Magdalena relived for us her time in the underworld.

"When I first died," Magdalena began, speaking with a dramatic fervor befitting her thespian nature, "I saw a child looking up at me from the bottom of the river as I was slowly sinking from above. She was a pretty little thing, and she looked like a doll I used to own. I remembered the dress, a blue gingham."

"Did she speak to you?" Hillegond asked. "They like to speak, dead children do."

"She gave me a welcome, is how I'd put it," said Magdalena.

"I knew it," said Hillegond.

" 'I welcome you,' she said, 'to the birthplace of dreams, where even dolls live forever.' "

"Isn't that just like a child?" said Hillegond.

"Do you mean," asked Maud, "that you remember those words, just as the little girl spoke them, and you were both under water?"

"Not only under water," said Hillegond, "they were both dead too, weren't you, dear?"

"Well, I think so," said Magdalena. "I mean, you never get to hear that sort of thing when you're up and about."

"Never," said Hillegond. "It's a special event, being dead and then coming back. I never thought I'd see it with my own eyes."

"But here I am," said Magdalena.

"Here you are," said Hillegond. "Aren't you the wonder?"

"Was there anything at the bottom of the river except the child?" asked Maud. "I should think there'd have been dead fish and lots of muck."

"Dead fish rise to the top of the water," I said, expert at last on something.

"I don't remember any muck," said Magdalena. "The most I remember is how bright it was. 'It ought to be dark at the bottom of the river,' I kept saying to myself, but it was like the light of a thousand lamps. It was ever so cozy."

"Were you in heaven or hell?" Maud asked.

"I really couldn't say, Maudie, but I think it must've been heaven."

"You in heaven?" said John the Brawn, and he let out a great guffaw. "That'll be the day, me love. I'll show you how to get to heaven," and he guffawed again.

"You are too crude for words," Maud told my master, stamping her foot as she addressed him. "You are the piggiest man that walks the earth and I hope you rot so awfully that your feet fall off."

"Now, now, dearie," said Hillegond. "He's only making a joke to lighten the subject. Your auntie was dead, you know."

"I rather doubt it," said Maud. "I believe the symptoms of her life vanished, but not life itself."

"She's a savvy little brat, ain't she?" said John. "She'll grow up to drive men batty, is what she'll do."

"I was *very* dead," said Magdalena. "Don't tell *me* I wasn't dead. You think I wouldn't know it if I was dead?"

"Of course you wouldn't," said Maud. "Nobody knows anything when they're dead."

"Oh, that's very wrong, child," said Hillegond. "All sorts of people come back from the dead to tell what it was like. I've heard of folks who saw dead women with their feet on backwards, and dead dogs climbing trees, and dead men covered with feathers. You mustn't be too smart about the dead, child, or they'll catch you out when you don't expect it. Be friends with the dead is what Hillegond says, and it's served her well."

"Anyway, I'm glad I'm not dead anymore," said Magdalena, who saw Hillegond usurping her stage.

"What'll you do now, dear," asked Hillegond, "now that you're not dead?"

"Oh, I have plans," said Magdalena. "I've got bookings to dance all the way to Buffalo. They'll want me more than ever, now that I've died and come back."

"You'll want bodyguardin' for certain," said my master, "or

[35]

the crowds'll tear you apart. A strong man's what you'll need."

"I imagine I will," said Magdalena, nodding, and when I saw the way Maud looked in that very moment, I knew she felt trapped and that she would soon remind me of my promise to steal her. But before anything of that order could happen, a fierce knock came at the door, and as Hillegond opened the portal to the arctic night, a tall, cadaverish man, his hat and greatcoat covered with snow, stepped across the threshold to utter the single word "Lunacy."

"Lunacy?" echoed Hillegond.

"Prisoners," said the stranger, and he doffed his hat, revealing a thick head of hair, white as the snow that spattered about the foyer when he whacked his hat against his leg. "Wrap yourself up, Hilly. Your mansion has been defiled by madness and I need help in coping with it."

The man who brought us this grim news was Will Canaday, one of Albany's most powerful citizens, the founder and editor of the *Albany Chronicle,* a sheet of considerable power and political brash. His newspaper had brought us to this house, for it was in the columns of the *Chronicle* that Magdalena had placed her notice about crossing the river. And now here appeared the owner of those columns, bringing us news not only of the prisoners he had been tracking but also of the ongoing madness of nature and its consequences to all forms of life.

The cold had descended upon the city so suddenly after the flooding of the riverbanks that men were forced to bring their livestock to high ground. Canaday mentioned one man who brought his horse into his front room, and wisely so, for horses tethered untended in water found their legs frozen in the instantaneous ice that rose 'round their bones. Before the night was out, one man in Greenbush would grow furious at his inability to extricate his horse from deep ice and, in watching the horse dying standing up, the man himself would die of a con-

gested brain. Carriages would become ice-locked, birds would
freeze to the limbs of trees, and not only ice but fire would ravage
the city wildly and indiscriminately. The bonnet of Bridie Conroy, an Irish washerwoman, would catch fire from sparks on the
burning quay and Bridie would run crazed into the night, tumbling headlong into a shed full of hay, and igniting what history
would call The Great Fire—six hundred buildings, many of them
shops, all burned to cinders: five thousand people without lodging
from the blaze that would yield its fury only to the heavy fall of
snow that was just now beginning.

None of us, not even Will Canaday, knew of this new curse
sent down upon Albany by the maddened gods on this day of
hellfire and ice, for Bridie Conroy was not yet aflame when Will
cast his glance upon our comfort near the fireplace. He spoke to
us with such solemn intent that we were all moved outside of
ourselves.

"I would not normally recommend that any man, woman, or
child look upon what I am about to show to Hillegond," he said.
"But by all that is holy in this world, I feel that everyone alive
should see this sight, so that its vision may endure for as long
as we are able to hand it on."

As if summoned by Mesmer himself, we all slowly arose and
wrapped ourselves in heavy garments to fend off the night, and
we trekked single file through the new snow into a coppice in
what I, from my vantage point at the rear of the column, saw
to be the same procession of pilgrims I had witnessed in the once-
dead eyeball of Magdalena Colón, even to the presence of Will
Canaday's black dog at my heels.

Carrying a torch, Will led the way to where Amos Staats,
adolescent hero of the Revolution, lay buried in his marble mausoleum, and where his Indian mother, Moonlight of the Evening,
had spent her final days eating meals off his sarcophagus.

Hillegond entered behind Will and John, and she gave a shriek that bespoke the power of this madness Will had invited us to witness. One by one we entered, Maud again clutching me in her passionate way.

What we first saw when we edged around the sarcophagus was a dance of light and shadow from the torch upon an image I could not discern with certainty. In truth, its abnormal position was such that no man would have understood the sight at first glance. What was clear was the head of the hanging man. The light revealed his crooked neck, and the rope around it suspended from a decorative protrusion of marble. But the top half of the corpse was awry, in a way no hanging man's logic would recognize, angled unnaturally, as if he were lying asleep on the very air.

In time our eyes perceived that the dead man's arm was pulled earthward by something unseen, and what lay at the end of that arm proved to be another being in total shadow. Only when Will Canaday moved the torch closer to the tableau did we see the dead arm manacled to the living arm of a Negro, a man in such debilitated condition that he looked more dead than the corpse above him. Yet his eyes were open and staring.

"He's alive," said Maud.

"It's Joshua," whispered Hillegond, leaning close to the man.

"It is," said Will. "That's why I tracked them."

"But who is the other?"

"A Swede who spoke no English and whose name I don't know," said Will, handing me the torch and moving a wooden box to use as a step stool. "He was driven wild when he lost his wife in a throng at New York. Swindlers put him on a boat to Albany to find her, then abandoned him and took his life savings. Once in Albany, realizing he was lost and in penniless despair, he dove headlong into a well to kill himself, and when a good samaritan pulled him out before he drowned, he brained the samaritan with a club. Constables shut him in prison and he grew ever more demented, screaming constantly of his losses."

"God save us from madness," said Magdalena, and she blessed herself with the sign of the cross.

"Only a madman could understand what has happened today in this mad city," said John the Brawn, his first admission in my hearing that he was not equal to all that passed in front of his face. Will clambered atop the tomb of Amos to cut down the Swede and I noted then that the covering slab of marble atop the tomb was already dislodged from its straight angle. As Will stood on tiptoe to cut the rope his foot moved the slab farther and it fell to the floor, marble onto marble, splitting into four irregular pieces as neatly as might a well-cut diamond. For an instant Will dangled in air, his arm around the dead man's waist. Then, with full awareness of his position, he deftly sliced the rope and, quite agilely for his fifty years, leaped to the floor clutching the corpse, avoiding the violation of Amos's exposed coffin by either his own or the dead Swede's heavy feet.

Certainly our priority now was the rescue of Joshua from his torture: removal of the manacle that was still tearing his flesh. With the dead man's weight it had cut into the bones of Joshua's wrist and hand, and he had lost such blood as would bestow death on most men.

Will and my master tried ways of carrying him so as not to injure him further, but whichever way they lifted, the Negro's pain was compounded. And so I spoke up.

"If each of you support one man, I can walk between them and hold up their arms. That way there won't be any pressure on the wounds of the man called Joshua."

"That's good thinking, lad," said Will.

"He's a ready one," said my master.

"We can't leave the tomb open like that," Hillegond said. "I'd be afraid some animal would come in."

"We'll put boards over it," said Will.

"I'd be afraid of rodents. No, he's got to come into the house."

"You want the coffin in the house?" said Will.

"In the *Dood Kamer*," said Hillegond firmly, and she turned to leave.

"Come, Maudie," said Magdalena. "Back to the house."

"I prefer to go with Daniel," said Maud, the first time she had pronounced my Christian name. "I can come to no harm in the company of three men, and I shall carry the torch to show them the way."

"She has a mind of her own," said Hillegond, who then took the arm of Magdalena; and with heads bowed against the billowing snow, the two compatriots in lust strode out into the night toward the mansion.

Will led us to a secondary entrance of this enormous house, where we were met by Capricorn, who expected us. We followed him through a long corridor, down two dozen steps to a basement, and then, by the light of Maud's torch and Capricorn's lamp, we walked the length of the enormous cellar to a cavelike room whose existence became obvious only after Joshua moved two foundation timbers, which were, in fact, a door.

We lowered Joshua to a padded pallet that lay ready on the floor, and the manacles cut again into his wrist, shooting agony even through me. Capricorn squatted beside Joshua to study his condition, then rose and spoke to us.

"I thank you gentlemen, and you, too, Master Daniel," he said. "I'll take care of him now."

He turned back to Joshua, and as he did so, his lamp cast a beam into the deeper region of the cave and I caught sight of three forms, one a female, all Negro, all crouching in the darkness. I gave off a startled grunt and Will saw my surprise.

"Whatever you see, boy," he said to me, "you see nothing," and he shook a finger in my face. "Nothing."

I nodded at this and he added, "I'll join you in a few minutes at the mausoleum to bring in the coffin," and Maud, John, and I retreated from the cave while Will conferred with Joshua. As we went my master remarked, "They got themselves a regular nigger factory in there."

"You mustn't use that word," said Maud.

"What word might that be?" said John.

"You know what word I mean," said Maud, "and if you use it again in my presence, I shall find a hatpin and stick you with it."

John shut his mouth at that, the first of his many silencings by Maud, and we retraced our steps to the mausoleum. Will eventually enlightened me on Joshua, an intrepid fugitive from Virginia who had escaped from slavery, later returned to Virginia by stealth to free his woman, and on subsequent trips led six other slaves through the night forests to freedom in the North. He had been recently captured near Albany by slave hunters, the quest for him sweetened by a three-hundred-dollar reward, and he was jailed under the federal law that honored the property rights of Southern slaveholders.

News of a fugitive slave's capture reached Will Canaday at the newspaper and he discovered it was Joshua in custody. A conspiracy among antislavers to snatch Joshua away from the law was plotted, but the day's madness intervened yet again: the driver of the carriage transporting the prisoners to a southbound train was struck by a flying prism of ice, and before Will Canaday and his conspirators could intervene, Joshua and the Swede to whom he was manacled took the reins themselves, fled from both captors and liberators, lashing the horses into such furious flight that at one turning both men were thrown off the carriage, whereupon they fled by foot to the sanctuary offered by the mausoleum of Amos Staats, where Will found them. Once inside the tomb, which over the years had become as much a storage shed as a burial site, the Swede decided that death was his destiny. He choked the weakened Joshua out of his lights with a single hand, and then, with a length of rope, hanged himself with great skill and effectiveness, full certain, I conclude, that no horrors of the beyond could match those of this world.

We waited in the mausoleum and Will returned presently. Then we three, two men and a boy, with Maud lighting our way, lifted Amos from what proved not to be his final resting place, carried him up from the earth and into the *Dood Kamer,* which was thereby hosting its second resurrection of the evening, and placed his coffin on the same raised platform from which Magdalena had arisen. The coffin was remarkably clean and dry in spite of its years of burial, and the odor of its occupant's decay had been banished by time.

The entire household, servants included, gathered in front of the coffin when we set it down, witnesses all to sanctity disturbed, a hero encased, though I knew nothing of Amos's history in the Revolution at that moment. The coffin had been hand-hewn by Amos's father, Jacobus, who had also sealed its edges and sur-faces with a substance waxen to the touch and which seal I now could see had been broken, an infinitesimally fine crack running the length of coffin where the lid closed.

"I would like to see what he looks like," Maud said.

"Dead these seventy-odd years, he wouldn't be a pretty sight, child," said Hillegond, more amused than affrighted by Maud's suggestion. But Maud did not wait for approval. She walked to the coffin and lifted the lid on a stunning sight: Amos in his soldier's cap and uniform, arms crossed on his chest, a warrior's medal over his heart, lying as if asleep. His skin was a gray transparency, the color of exhausted night, the perfection of his death exuding a radiance that awakened swooning sounds in the onlookers.

"He hasn't decayed," said Will. "An amazing achievement. It must be the way the coffin was sealed."

"I always thought corpses rotted from the guts out," said my master.

I moved alongside Maud, and as naturally as breath itself we

[42]

intertwined our hands and stared at Amos from the end of his coffin.

"He's so beautiful," Maud said. We stared together at his beauty until she turned her gaze to my own face. "And you are beautiful as well," she said, and she kissed me with her mouth upon my mouth. She kept her mouth there and my arms went 'round her. We kissed under the spell of death's beauty, then stopped kissing to gaze again at Amos.

"Oh my God, look what's happening to him," said Magdalena. His face had begun to swell: cheeks, forehead, neck, eyelids all rising as might a loaf of leavening bread, a shocking sight from which we could not take our eyes. And then he exploded—his perfection, I suggest, rent by the air of our pernicious age— exploded upward and outward, his hands and face disappearing beneath a great grayish puff of dust tinged with pale blue, a puff that ascended fully six feet above the coffin and spread over us all in a melancholy haze. The dust demarcated the end of some-thing, the final burst of heroism, perhaps, whose like was no longer accessible to our commonplace lives. The sadness of lost glory was implicit, most especially to Maud, who cried as if a demon held her in its jaws. She clutched me, threw her arms about my neck and kissed me again with passion and energy, ground her pelvic center against my own and kissed all of my face with a ferocious gluttony.

She kissed me, she kissed me, and I kissed in return, quite well, too, I thought; for in one sweet instant she had taught me the true purpose of the lips in matters of profound affection. The dust was falling onto our heads and shoulders, the air slowly clearing; and though we did not interrupt our kissing, I could see from my eye's corner that the face of Amos was gone, as were his hands. His chest had collapsed, as had his legs, so that the uniform seemed to have lost its inhabitant entirely, replaced by a skeletal stranger. Having seen this and understood none of it, I returned my eyes to Maud and kissed on until we were pulled apart by angry hands and a wild woman's scream; and I turned to face Magdalena, who slapped me viciously across the cheeks: front of the hand, back of the hand.

"Loutish child," she yelled.

I forgave Magdalena her anger but I ripped myself away from her and again thrust my face against Maud's, kissing with all my soul until they rent us yet anew. In the frenzy that followed I remember uppermost a remark by Hillegond. "They are fortunate children," she said. "They know love."

But fortunate was not the word for what was to become of us.

THEY SEPARATED US that night, Maud and me, and we slept in isolation with our newborn love. I made no protest. I had no rights where she was concerned, though I cared nothing at all for rights when it came to her presence in my days. She, contrarily, complained vigorously about her aunt's behavior toward me, argued that I, more than anyone else alive, had the right to her company, for without me she would have been on the river bottom with Magdalena's doll. In outrage over the situation she refused to eat.

I came to this information belatedly, for no one told me what was afoot. Hillegond spoke sweetly but inconsequentially to me, Magdalena was remote and growing more ill, and John the Brawn sold his boat and told me he was done with the river. I asked if that meant I was out of a job and he said, "We'll see." He patted my head and said, "Don't worry, lad. You'll get your crust of bread."

Magdalena grew so monstrously ill from her wound that she ceased coming to table and remained abed. Feverish, and in hellish pain, she was the belated victim of her attacker's vile mouth. Her room's door was ajar when I once passed it and I peered in to see the wound, having only heard of its festerment second-hand. The bite had swelled into a yellow-and-purplish horror and was oozing a green slime that filled the room with a repellent odor. Hillegond took to burning incense of two kinds in the room: one to keep down the odor, another to ward off the blood devils that threatened Magdalena. But the combination produced a new mélange of smells that was miasmic in its effect on the patient, and so out went the incense, worse grew the stink. The wound was a menacing sight and made me wonder how any of us ever survive our own interior poisons. With ghastly speed the beauteous Magdalena had been transmogrified into a rancid hag, sister death beginning yet again to take residence in her eyes. My brief glances at her satisfied my inquisitiveness, for none but the perverted could have long fastened an eye on that befoulment.

It fell to the Negro servant, Matty, to bathe and dress the wound according to the doctor's instructions. But when the treatment failed of healing, Matty began a treatment of her own: a poultice of herbs, flowers, dried goat dung, minced crickets, and other improbable ingredients, all boiled, strained, reduced to a powder, mixed with the whites of two duck eggs, and then applied to the infection beneath a bandage made from a fresh bedsheet. Within two days healing began. Within a fortnight Magdalena was growing new tissue, which would in time leave only the slightest evidence of what had once prevailed beneath her skin. I saw the miraculous improvement when I eavesdropped on her lecture to Maud about the evils of Maud's fast (which I persuaded Maud to rescind, for my sake as well as her own; for of what value would my love be if it had no object upon which to resplend itself?). I saw the radiant Maud standing attentively by the sickbed and my heart sped.

"How dare you put your life in such jeopardy?" said the angry Magdalena. "How dare you, when I am so hounded by fate. Clara, my own sweet serving girl, uselessly drowned, my face almost the ruination of us all, for where would any of us be without it? And you, spiteful child, you take it upon yourself to starve your body, your only salvation. Do you think men care for a woman's mind, especially the mind of a wicked twelve-year-old like you? Do you think you can live by your wits alone, with no help from the talents you inherited with your flesh? Do you think that silly canal boy can save you from ruination, when he cannot even save himself? He's a penniless orphan, seeking to steal you away from me with his urchin ways." (This remark cut me deeply.)

"You fail to see in him the high quality I see," said Maud (and I recovered immediately from La Última's cut).

"Child," said the courtesan, "you have a strong mind, but you are little schooled in the ways of men. And now it is *you* who must take Clara's place as my social companion. It is *you* whom I must dress as I dress myself. It is early for you, but this is an inheritance we must learn to accept."

"You want me to love men for money?" asked Maud.

"I shall teach you to talk to men, to disarm them of their harsh moods, to entice them into sweetness, to pleasure them. I shall turn you into a songbird, a dancing swan. I shall teach you how to survive this life, child Maudie."

"Dear Auntie," said Maud in a tone of affectionate iron, "I am your niece of blood and I love you more than I ever loved my mother. But I won't be a carnal woman for you, or for us, or for me. I love only Daniel Quinn and I want to give him half or more of my life."

Was ever a more precisely self-apportioning line uttered by woman? But Magdalena was not as impressed by it as I. "Oh pish, child," she said. "Pish, pish, pish."

I saw that I was not a consideration in Magdalena's plans. John the Brawn continued his dalliance with Hillegond, their periodic thumpings a comic ritual to the entire household, and he paid me small heed. I gravitated to our neighbor Will Canaday, who visited us often, first to rid us of the dead Swede, then to aid in the reburial of Amos's dusty skeleton, and more mysteriously to spirit away Joshua from his hiding place in the netherworld of the mansion, an event I witnessed without Will's knowledge during my exploration of the great house (an entity

[47]

of such enormousness that one needed one's wits always at full brim to avoid being lost in the maze of corridors, tunnels, staircases, chutes, dropaways, cul-de-sacs and other oddities—unopenable doors without handles or locks—that abounded in the multiple wings, towers, and catacombs of the place).

"Where did you take Joshua?" I asked Will the day after I saw them leaving. "Did you take him to the doctor?"

"Master Quinn," Will said to me, and I knew from this formality, as well as from his tone, that seriousness was about to descend upon me, "you will put Joshua out of mind and forget you saw him here if you want to preserve his life."

I nodded instant agreement to this and Will smiled at me. He inquired of my family, which was the beginning of my friendship with this splendid soul, an irregular man of this world, cut to no cloth save his own, neither in his garments, which rarely matched or fit him, nor in his morality, which was vigorous, impious, peculiar, and steadfast.

I told Will I had no family, that I'd gone to work as a canal boy for four months and run away from a master who not only beat me but refused to pay me for my work, that I'd met John the Brawn and liked him by contrast, since he never hit me, that I'd worked with him three months on the canal till his boat sank, and lately as a river rat, but was now a waterless orphan with a most uncertain future.

Will began instantly with his generous counsel, telling me of my need to keep working, fanning my already burning dread of orphanages, which were proliferating not only in the wake of the cholera but as havens for children, safe retreats from parents ready to murder them rather than feed another mouth. Will also decided I should know more about the world than I did (he was appalled that I thought the Mexican War had taken place over the border in Canada) and he counseled me on books to read—storytellers and poets, historians and playwrights of ancient days. I had learned to read from the nuns in school, and liked it well enough. These books from Will were much beyond my ken, but I plunged into them with a duty that in time became the most subtle of my pleasures in this world. Will also saw to it that his newspaper turned up at the Staats mansion every day so I might educate myself. The newspaper's arrival was anomalous in the home of Hillegond, who cared little for any world outside her own mystical province, even though her son, Dirck, was an editorial employee of Will's. I loved and devoured the paper, reading of murders and thievery, rapscallions and heroes. I read the commercial notices for pianofortes, ever-pointed pencils, and remedies for evil results arising from early abuse and unhappy contamination. The endless political bickering over issues that I could not follow bored me, but I grew fascinated with the wars between Spaniards and Arabs, between Britons and Kaffirs, between Ch'ing dynasty and the Taiping rebels. I cheered for fugitive slaves in the Carolinas and for the rebellious farmers of Ireland who, under the leadership of one William Smith O'Brien, were defying the English (my father's father had lost his land to the English). But my partisanship aroused no serious animosity toward the forces that opposed my favored side, I being smug and comfortable, far from such violence. But I did begin to see that violence was the norm of this bellicose world.

Will took me on my first visit in sunlight to the city of Albany several weeks after The Great Fire. The weeks of the new year had been deep with cold, snow, and ice that was at last giving way to a spring thaw, permitting a view of the cold ashes of disaster: the center of Albany's ancient commerce and density, its quays, its Great Pier, so many canalboats and sloops, all reduced to char and cinders save for an odd chimney fragment untoppled, or a lone house standing because of its owner's grit in bringing hundreds of buckets of water to wet down his walls and to douse the blankets on his roof, upon which flying embers would futilely spend their heat.

The good weather was also catalyzing the area's charred garbage, sending aromatic blossoms abroad to the citizenry, and this brought out packs of dogs and cats, and herds of roaming pigs, those enduring scavengers who joined the city workers in the ruins. The searchers sought three citizens still unaccounted for, and about whom I had read in Will's newspaper. Then, as Will and I picked our steps through the soft rubble, there before me rooted a pig, snuffling in the sludge. The animal brought forth with its jaws first the arm of an infant and then the attached torso, dragging it up from the dire muck and about to make off with it when I intervened, whacked the waddling ghoul with a charred board, distracting it, but insufficiently, for it would not open its jaws. I struck again and again at its back, but its jaws remained clenched, and then in desperation I kicked at its throat, whereupon it yielded up its booty and squealed off into deeper ashes, soon slowing to a lope and snuffling once again in the ruins.

Will and I stared down at the infant corpse, a black doll, rigid with ice, more rigid with death: hairless, faceless, sexless, yet a residual presence demanding attention. Will summoned a constable patrolling the erstwhile street and the dead child was taken by authority to a place of more secure rest.

"The child's father will thank you for what you did," Will said to me. "I know the man. His name is Bailey."

"How could anyone know whose child that was?"

"Only one child is missing. Would you object if I included a report of what you did in the newspaper?"

"It's what anyone would have done."

"Perhaps. But you did it, and there are people who loathe the pigs, and fear them, and would never do such a thing. Pigs can be nasty."

We walked to Will's newspaper office on lower Broadway, a street that sometimes flooded when the river overflowed its banks, but the newspaper was safe on the second floor. Three young printers were actually bouncing as they worked at the typecase

[50]

and stones, and among the tables that bore long metal galleys of copper-faced type. They all wore long white smocks and black derby hats, the smocks as protection against ink stains, the hats against the crumbling ceiling's falling plaster, which, as all know, rots the follicles in the scalp and, as some say, sends carbonic acid to the brain.

Will led me into his own work area, where his desk stood under a gas jet, next to a window, and beneath a vivid assemblage of chaos. Atop, beside, and on shelves adjacent to his desk lay a strew of magazines, clippings and letters, stacks of encyclopedias, dictionaries, new books, old books, boxed files, files not-so-boxed, with dust on some but not much of this clutter, and in the center of it all, an unopened copy of the morning *Chronicle:* the perfect centerpiece for the anarchy out of which it had come.

At an adjacent slanted desk, a model of neatness, sat a man writing in a ledger. Will introduced me and I made the acquaintance of Dirck Staats, the son of Hillegond. Will said to him, "Dirck, this young man is one of the guests in your house."

I extended my hand and said, "Daniel Quinn is my name, sir, and I am enjoying your house."

"I wish I could say the same," said Dirck, "but that she-devil of a mother of mine won't allow it."

"I recognize you from your portrait," I said to him.

"I was told she had my portraits turned to the wall."

"Oh, she has," I said, "but I turned one about to see the looks of a man who could rile a woman to such a point."

Dirck smiled at Will. "You speak directly," he said to me. "Are you a devotee of the word?"

"I can't be sure," I said, "since I don't know what 'devotee' means."

"It means you like something quite well and you pay close attention to it. Something such as words. I myself am such a devotee of words that I'm writing a book full of them."

"Words are useful," I said. "My dog might not have died if he'd been able to tell us what ailed him."

Dirck laughed at that and said, "Yes, yes, yes," and I was equally amused, for I'd never owned a dog.

Dirck Staats: if Will Canaday was a slender citizen, then Dirck was Will halved. He had a wild crop of dark hair around the back and sides of his head, his legs were long, his trousers not long enough, his waist no larger 'round than my own, and as a result of this design he looked as top-heavy as a hatstand. His face and high forehead were half as long as his chest, he wore unusually small spectacles across the top of his broad forehead when he was not reading, and, if such a thing were possible, his clothes fit him worse than did Will's. But I liked Dirck Staats during our meeting, and I liked even more the ambition with which he confronted the arcane elements of the life around him.

"What is your book about?" I asked.

"It reveals a mystery," he said, "but the people in it would like to keep it a mystery."

"Give the boy something to read while I write a piece about him," said Will. "He retrieved a child's corpse from the pigs awhile ago. A hero in the city's ashes."

"I am always glad to meet a hero," said Dirck, bowing profusely before me, offering me his chair at the desk. "By all means read what I am writing and give me your candid opinion. I confess I am at a loss for an intelligent response."

He went off then and I sat down in front of his two large red ledger books and looked at his writing. It is now, in memory, very like the mirror writing of da Vinci, the runes of the old Norsemen, the cuneiform writing of the Assyrians. It had about it a world of its own design, an impenetrable architecture that was a fascination by itself. What eventually I came to know was that this was his own language, invented for the purpose of composing this secret book about the secrecy that had come to obsess him. I studied his figures and letters-of-a-kind but could understand nothing. He came back at length and smiled at me.

"What have you discovered?"

"That I cannot read even one word."

"Excellent."

I stood up and offered him his chair, but he reached for his coat, which hung on a hook beside his desk. "We must to lunch," he said, and I knew not whether this included me and Will, whether he was speaking of another group entirely, or of himself as the collective.

"Is it all right that I can't read a word?" I asked.

"Of course it is."

"I do understand the print in Will's newspaper."

"Of course you do."

"Why do you draw pictures when you write?"

"So no one will understand what I say."

"If you don't mind my saying so, that is an odd reason to write things."

"I am as odd as ripe birdseed," said Dirck.

That was the last word Dirck spoke personally to me, for people were coming up the stairs and as Dirck made ready to leave he was confronted by a man I knew later to be the sheriff. Two other men were with him, one a deputy, the other a citizen of Utica named Babcock. The latter seemed to be the cause of this doing in that he claimed Dirck owed him four dollars, the value of a shirt and cravat Dirck had borrowed from him two years previous and not returned. Will Canaday heard the commotion and joined it, and I hung back and listened.

Questions flew: Could this good man Dirck really be a petty thief? Why was such a paltry event now the occasion for his arrest? Why was this happening now and not two years ago? Could Babcock be serious? Could the sheriff? Dirck offered to pay the four dollars, but the sheriff said that was no longer possible, that he must go to Utica to stand trial for petit larceny. Will offered double payment for the shirt and cravat, but the sheriff was negatively adamant and ordered Dirck taken down the stairs. We all followed to the street, where a carriage waited with two more men. One of the men wore a memorably drooping mustache and was sharpening a long knife on a small whetstone in the palm of his hand. Will pointed to the man and called out, "Aaron Plum," and he turned swiftly to the sheriff and told him Plum was one of the toughs who had stoned the newspaper's windows two days earlier and then fled when Will fired a pistol over the heads of the toughs. The sheriff said this was nonsense, that the man had showed him credentials and was a deputy sheriff from Utica. But I knew Will was right, for I had met Aaron Plum on John the Brawn's skiff when we carried four crates of harnesses for him from Troy to Albany. John told me the harnesses were stolen, and so we made the run at night to avoid spectators. I learned Aaron Plum's name because he had his brother with him as a helper, Eli Plum, a schoolmate of mine. We called Eli Peaches after they caught him filling a sack with peaches from the Corcorans' tree.

All this was coming back to me when Aaron Plum and the second man jumped from the carriage, grabbed roughly at both of Dirck's arms, and pushed him toward the carriage, whose door the sheriff opened.

"Murder!" screamed Dirck. "They will murder me!" Upon which remark he was thrown headlong into the carriage, the men climbing in behind him. Dirck screamed out to us before the carriage flew away behind the same matched pair I had seen in La Última's dead eyeball. "They want my book!" he yelled. "Save my book!"

And then poor Dirck was gone.

Will turned and ran back up the stairs to his office, I at his heels. After we entered the office a man rose from where he had been crouching behind Dirck's desk and ran down the stairs. Will yelled and ran after him and I did likewise. The man was clutching Dirck's ledgers, and as he ran headlong across the street to another waiting carriage, he fell. One ledger flew out of his grip and landed at my feet, and I immediately snatched it up. As the man arose and turned to me I had a full look at him. He had red hair, a poor crop of muttonchops, and the top of his left ear had been sliced or bitten off. He stared at me and I took that stare as a threat. But Will was closing fast on him, and so the one-eared burglar leaped onto the step of the waiting carriage, clutching Dirck's second ledger, and held on to the window as the carriage raced away. I looked at the ledger in my hands and saw it was the one in which I had studied Dirck's hieroglyphics.

"You did well, Daniel Quinn," Will said to me, and I handed him the ledger. "This is a terrible event and I must set it right. You'll go home now to the mansion, and I'll see you when I can." He signaled one of his printers in white smock and black derby who was standing (and bouncing) in the small crowd that had gathered. Will told the man to see that I got to Hillegond's house, and then he shook my hand.

"You are a friend of more things than you know, young man," Will said to me, and then he went to his office.

The printer found a cab for hire and took me to the Staats house. He said little as we rode, but I noticed he was bouncing even as he sat, and that I was not. I told him I had seen him bouncing at the newspaper and again in the crowd and that he was bouncing still. I asked him why.

"It is because of my hat," said the printer.

"I see," I said, and I said no more.

At the mansion I told my story to John the Brawn, but it made so little impression on him that he told me not to bother Hillegond with it, for she had no use for her son. I said I could hardly do such a thing after seeing Dirck kidnapped at knife point. John agreed I should tell her since there was a knife involved, which is a measure of the man's logic. We went to the music room, where Hillegond was sitting with Maud, listening to Magdalena playing the pianoforte and singing a love ballad:

[55]

"Hangman, hangman, hold the rope!
Hold it for a while.
I think I see my father coming,
Coming on the mile.
Father, did you bring me gold,
Or come to set me free?
Or did you come to see me hang
Upon that willow tree?"

"Daughter, I did not bring you gold,
Nor come to set you free,
But I have come to see you hang
Upon that willow tree."

I grew to love the song because of its message. All the daughter's relatives come to see her hang but it is her sweetheart alone who sets her free. Maud and I exchanged glances and then John the Brawn announced I had a story to tell. And I told it.

"Then Dirck is truly in trouble, the poor boy," said Hillegond when I had finished my tale. She arose and went to the east parlor and turned outward the two portraits of Dirck at ages twelve and nineteen. At twelve Dirck was fat as a dumpling; at nineteen he was emaciation incarnate—the pair of portraits telling the story of his improbable progress as an ascetic. "He will feel better knowing they're set right," said Hillegond.

"How will he know such a thing?" Maud asked. "Hasn't Daniel told us he was abducted?"

"He will get my message no matter where he is," said Hillegond.

"With trouble in the family," said Magdalena, "we must be on our way."

"You needn't leave," said Hillegond. "I do enjoy your company."

"We've overstayed already," said Magdalena. "This is such a

[56]

madcap time for you. And I must get back to my work in the theater."

"What will happen to Daniel?" asked Maud.

"Why, he'll come with us," said John the Brawn. "A group like this needs a slavey."

"I'll be lost for conversation," said Hillegond, who saw her new world of thumping, music, mysticism, and children about to vanish. "I will wither," she added.

"Nonsense," said Magdalena. "You'll blossom. And you'll find a purpose in life, working to help your son. Life must continue. We've loved being here, in spite of all the death."

I was bewildered. Nothing seemed to conclude. I was in the midst of a whirlwind panorama of violence and mystery, of tragedy and divine frenzy that mocked every effort at coherence. I now felt a physical sadness overtaking me, my body and brain losing their security and being thrust into hostile weather. I knew that apart from my family's being swept away by the cholera, what had happened to me in recent weeks was the most significant phase of my life thus far, the core of that significance being, and preeminently so, Maud. I longed only to watch her, talk with her, touch her hand, kiss her mouth. I had unholy longings to explore certain regions beneath her clothing, but I withheld such unschooled enterprise, for it seemed certain to generate trouble beyond my control. I had only one chance to talk alone with Maud in the next few days, an encounter in an upstairs hallway, outside the room filled with mirrors.

"You must not forget your promise to steal me," she said in an urgent whisper. "The chance will come very soon. I must take my life out of the hands of these people."

"But how will I ever do it?" I said to her. "I can't even find a way to get near you. Where would we go? And with what money? It's true what your aunt said. I'm penniless."

"You will have to figure it out," said Maud.

Then she was gone and we were busy with our goodbyes. In

the kitchen I embraced Capricorn and Matty, with whom I had spent a great deal of time. In the foyer Magdalena and Hillegond wept grand tears on each other, and as we left the great house John the Brawn surreptitiously (though I witnessed it) thrust his hand high under Hillegond's skirt to give her a farewell stroke. Into the carriage we lofted Magdalena's trunk, John's suitcase (which he'd retrieved from our old landlady), and the small traveling bags Hillegond had given Maud and me for our belongings.

I leaned out the carriage window for a final look at the mansion, which aroused pity and terror in my breast, but without Aristotle's cathartic effect. I pitied myself both for my inability to ever dream of living in such a place again, and also for my loss of its comforts as I reentered the world outside its doors. And its receding presence aroused in me the terror of John the Brawn, the terror of the unknown, the terror of once again being a penniless orphan.

Hillegond's driver took us to the pier at the Albany Basin, the mouth of the Erie Canal, which was opened because of the weeks of warm weather. Hillegond had suggested we save time by taking the train to the Schenectady highlands and boarding the packet boat there, as did everyone else. But Magdalena was against it, fearing for her safety behind a locomotive. Our final destination was Buffalo, but our first stopping point was to be Utica, where, said Magdalena, the opera house manager would welcome her, for on her last visit she had sold out the house for two weeks. Soon after we boarded the packet the boatmen hitched up the mules and we began our journey westward, scrunched in the salon with a half-dozen lumberjacks and drummers. I won no bed and John told me I could sleep on deck with the spare mule. I will refrain from reporting on the trivial details of the hours that followed, for they were hateful. I loathed being back on the canal, being looked upon as another higgler's boy, one of those shiftless and worthless rungates who deserve whatever their drunken masters mete out to them in whippings, kicks, and cuffings, and whose destiny is either the penitentiary, the Almshouse, or an early grave.

The mules moved us along as I schemed in silence on ways to steal Maud away from John the Brawn and La Última. I conceived of first stealing a horse and carriage, sweeping her into my grasp, fleeing down a gravel carriageway, leaping to the reins, and driving off into the cherished night of freedom, into the unchartable challenges of love. We would ride with the west wind and the flight of wild geese, imposing on each other the most exquisite splendors of which our adolescent imaginations were capable.

As I entered my world of romantic intention I fell into a sleep that, for reasons I judge escapist, proved narcotic. Unable to resolve the theft of Maud, I thrust it even out of my dreams and awoke from that comatose condition facing the rising sun, curled up on dry ground. I was at the edge of the towpath, and what I saw in my first glance was a meadow to one side, canal to the other, no canalboat anywhere, no people and no houses, only a lone cow beside a small shack in a far field. My small clothing bag was beside me and, atop that, wrapped in a greasy newspaper, a ragged chunk of stale bread, the crust John the Brawn had promised me. Slowly I realized I was desolate. But far worse was the intolerable dawning that while I'd been trying and failing to bring about the theft of Maud, scurrilous John the Brawn had stolen her from me.

I WEPT DESOLATED TEARS and felt the spiny urchins invading my soul. I shouldered my bag and walked eastward along the towpath, not knowing what town I was near, knowing only my position beneath the sky. Boats, mules, horses, and men passed, but I had commerce with none of them. I screamed, or thought I did, but wasn't certain. I began a new scream that I would surely hear, but the sound was inconsequential to the rising sun. I stifled it and picked up a green stick. I walked until I found the correct rock and then I beat the rock until the stick was limp sinews. This also was inconsequential and I began to believe then that no act, no thought of mine, could shape a response equal to the feeling the theft of Maud had generated in me.

I began to dwell on what it meant to find your love and then to have it taken from you, framing the question with a fifteen-year-old brain and a body in transition toward nefarious impulses. Even so, I could instantly see what a hollow game this was. If *my* condition was desolation, what, then, was Maud's? I was at least able-bodied, male, unsubjugated, and capable of self-sustenance, whereas she was this fragile and precocious visionary in a state of peril. Who would save her from the ritual bawdry that awaited her? What guardian quality in John the Brawn, that overmastering Priapus, would protect her from life-long invasion by the lust of strangers? The child was, to my mind, about to become a spangled womb, a witch of beauty wasted on the bloody and pecunious bed of ravaged hymen.

I yelled to a passing boatman, who told me I was twelve miles from Schenectady, and as I walked on I thought of telling Maud now all that had befallen me before I met her, those events that had brought me to the moment when I saved her from the bottom of the river. I thought the telling might even reach Maud in Utica, just as Hillegond had faith that her feelings would reach the kidnapped Dirck.

Coupling Dirck and Maud I realized I had witnessed the theft of two lives, and I brooded that Dirck, Maud, I, and all the others were parts of a great machine, generating immeasurable power in the universe. I drew little comfort from this thought for I seemed too minuscule a part to be of any significance. Men like John the Brawn with his strength, Will Canaday with his brain and his newspaper, and the captors of Dirck with their will to evil were the great turbines, were they not? Children like myself waited their turn at power.

But then I thought, no. Age alone does not determine whether one wields power, or even whether one remains a child. My own childhood had been terminated for me on a warm morning in April 1850, under the rising sun on the banks of the Erie Canal. There and then, Daniel Quinn, late a boy in possession of neither safety nor joy, a boy being shaped by fire, flood, ice, and the less comprehensible barbarities of men and women, was entering into a creaturehood of a more advanced order: young animal confounded—solitary, furious, eccentric, growing bold.

This is the message I sent through the sky to Maud about my new condition:

Maud, I begin on an event that took place a month before the raging of the plague. A stranger in old clothes walked crookedly up Van Woert Street and collapsed on Rhatigan's front stoop. Old Lydie Rhatigan came out in her apron, her broom in hand to shoo him away. But one look at him changed her mind.

"You're sick, is it?" said Lydie.

"My left leg is dead," the man said to her. "I couldn't walk another step. Feel the leg if you like."

"I'll do no such thing," said Lydie.

"Death is moving in me," said the man, and he shifted his position so that his back rested against the stoop's iron railing and his dead left leg dangled off the bottom step. The right leg he stretched along the width of the stoop.

"It's going into the right leg now," he said. "Two more minutes and the right'll be as dead as the left."

"What ails you?" asked Lydie.

"The death is what it is."

"What kind of death?"

"The only kind."

"Get on with ye. Is it a plate of food you're after?"

"Not anymore."

"Well, you can't clutter the stoop like this."

"It's in both arms now," said the man, and his left arm went limp. With his right hand he took off his hat, exposing a bald head, and put the hat on a step above him.

"At least get the last bit of sunshine on the pate," he said, and his right arm went as limp as his left.

Lydie dropped her broom. "God bless us and save us," she said.

"A prayer is a blessing," said the man, "but it doesn't bother death. Now it's in the stomach. And now the neck." He closed his eyes. "There it is in the chest," and he opened his eyes like two full moons. "Now I'm dead," he whispered, and dead he was, with his eyes as open as the sky.

Everyone thought of this as an isolated incident. Not until the others died was the man who had tracked the course of his own death seen as both carrier and emissary of the plague. It was a fiery hot summer, the worst time for it, the time when death grows fat. I was working for food with Emmett Daugherty, my father's great friend, helping him rebuild his shed and privy. Emmett lived two miles north of Van Woert Street, and because of the distance I stayed with him, and so I wasn't home the week death first walked up our street.

The McNierney family across from us had four die in two days that week, and the four others who lived on fled to no one still knows where. Two desperate stragglers from Vermont found the McNierney house empty and open (Pud McNierney didn't even close the front door when he ran out), and they went in and helped themselves to food, drink, and beds. Both were dead in those beds three days later.

Maud, I won't tell you all the horrid matter that comes out of the body when the cholera invades people; you probably know for yourself. But the sight of such things recurring so often put the fear into everybody in the city. A good many remembered the plague of '32 that killed four hundred in Albany, and so people locked their doors, wouldn't go out, wouldn't let anyone in. Prayer vigils were called and some brave souls came out to hear our preachers tell them their sins were causing people to die. One stranger stood up and called the preacher a madman for saying that and yelled out how it was pigs running loose in the city, not sin, that caused the cholera. But he didn't get far with that. They hit him with a plank and he stopped yelling.

My mother got sick while I was at Emmett's house, and when I came home she was in bed, smothered in blankets, shivering. She'd had the sickness for two days and the doctor gave her Veratrum to take on a piece of sugar. It didn't help at all, even with greater dosage, so Pa gave her Spirits of Camphor and she said she felt better. That same day Pa came home from work at the lumberyard (they wouldn't let him stay home) and found my sister Lizzie face down on the paving stones near the house. She was alive but very ill. Pa carried her to bed and gave her the Spirits of Camphor right off, along with the Veratrum. That was the day I came home from Emmett's house. I sat vigil with my mother and Lizzie both, and I never got sick, though I still don't know why I didn't.

We heard that looting was going on down the block, which was news, because after the first flurry of deaths nobody went near any of the death houses; for who could be sure which things were uncontaminated and safe to steal? But for some the lure of larceny is greater than the fear of death, and soon every empty house was a target for thieves in masks and gloves. When my mother heard this she told me to find our birdcage and bury it. I asked her why.

"Because I brought it from Ireland," she said, "and because a birdcage isn't all that it is, but you needn't mind about that. Just remember what I say. Study it well and mind you that there's value in it you can use someday. God knows the value. Now do it, boy, do what I say, and tell no one where you bury it."

The cage was empty. When my father lost his old job laying railroad ties he blamed our yellow bird, said it brought bad luck, and he let the creature loose in the trees, even though we'd had it for years. My mother cried and put the cage in a crawl space under the roof, up with the suitcases and blankets she and Pa carried for the months they spent on the boat coming over. When Pa saw me with the cage he asked what I was doing. I told him and he said, "Remember where you bury it and cover it with leaves or they'll see the fresh-dug dirt and go in after it." And then he said, "Take care of it, lad, and it'll take care of you."

When I came back from burying the cage Pa was sitting vigil with Ma and he said to me, "Go see Lizzie." I went down to our room and saw she was gone from us. Pa had put a rosary in her hand but it hadn't helped her. I looked at her awhile and went up to Pa's room and sat with him while Ma shivered and wailed. I heated the hot-water jars for her and rubbed her with Spirits of Camphor but that didn't do any good either.

After she died Pa never shed a tear, but his face went loose.

He couldn't control its blinking and twitching, or keep the white-
ness off it, or banish its shapeless grief. He went to get the priest
because Ma was close with the church. She used to go to Mass
three or four mornings a week, whenever the weather was good.
She loved the religion and was good friends with the pastor. But
Pa found out the pastor was sick himself from visiting so many
people with the plague, so he only brought back Jigger Kiley
and his wagon, which was the hearse on our street that month.
Pa said there wouldn't be any Mass or funeral for Ma just now.
Maybe later. Then he took himself to bed and let himself be sick
all the way. I sat vigil with him, doing the same useless things
I did for Ma, until he, too, shivered and died without a word.
I went and got Emmett Daugherty, and he came back with his
own wagon and helped me pack the things he said were valuable
and the things I wanted to keep. We locked up the house and
got in Jigger's wagon with Pa, and we dropped Pa off at the new
body depository near the arsenal, because that was the law. The
old Dead House out at the Almshouse couldn't handle so many
corpses. The rats were eating them before workers got them into
their graves.

I went to stay with Emmett at his house beside the canal and
live out the summer and winter there. I cried a good deal over
my sister and my lost parents and I stopped going to church. I
couldn't abide it anymore, all the talk about Christ. I liked Christ
fine, but who didn't? I felt like that stranger who didn't believe
the preacher's talk about sin. I didn't know what to make of
things, but I knew I had to do something for myself, that I had
no more time to be a child. And so in the spring of '48, when
Emmett heard that a canaler named Masterson needed a helper,
I asked for the job and got it, because I couldn't live off the
Daughertys forever. Emmett's niece was about to arrive from
Ireland, and Emmett himself was still ailing with the lung trouble
he'd picked up on a land-buying expedition with Lyman Fitzgibbon, the merchant-scientist.

I thanked Emmett for all his help, for saving me from God knows what, for being as close as blood. He said I was welcome anytime and he'd keep my things till I wanted them, and then I went off to work on the canal with Masterson for four of the worst months of my life. He beat me like a mutt and refused to pay me wages. I ran off when I saw how to get away clean, and I found work on John the Brawn's boat for three months till it sank. Then John bought the skiff and we worked the river out of Albany as ferrymen and haulers, water rats who'd go anywhere with anything between Albany, Troy, West Troy, and Greenbush.

One day on our river I saw you step into Carrick's boat and saw the boat hit by an ice floe. We put out to rescue you, I saved you from drowning, and that's how we met. My life was used to subtractions, not additions of beauty the likes of yours.

Maud, I send love.

When I reached Schenectady I asked a stagecoach driver for a ride, since I had no money to ride the train. The driver, for helping him load baggage, let me ride on the roof of the coach. I knotted myself in among the baggage tie-down ropes and we bounced away into the wind toward Albany. We came in on the Turnpike, which was rotten with mud, the wagon traffic moving so slowly outside the city that I leaped down and walked. I thought first of my old house, of which I had had no fear when the family took sick. But now the possibility of contamination waiting in it sent me into shivers and I decided to go instead to Emmett Daugherty's.

I cut across the city's western plateau and headed northeast in the direction the cattle drovers took when they moved the herds toward the river and swam them across to the Boston and New York trains. Emmett's house was a cabin, primitive and temporary. He planned to build a proper house once he married, but it was still a cabin in this year, and when I neared it I saw his niece, Josephine Daugherty, feeding chickens in the front yard.

She eyed me oddly until I told her my name, and then she said she was Josie and that she'd heard of me. She was a small redheaded girl of twenty-five with more freckles on her nose and chin than any woman ought to be burdened with. She was a greenhorn, in from Clonmel only a few months, and keeping house for Emmett, who had overcome his lung illness and was again working for old man Fitzgibbon at his Albany ironworks. Josie invited me in for tea, fed me cold chicken and potatoes, and I was glad for it. Her presence clearly meant there was no bed for me in the house, and so I would need money. What arose in memory was the birdcage, so valued by my parents. I remembered our broken spade I'd left with Emmett, and that would be tool enough to dig up the cage.

"Will you sit with us till Emmett comes home from work?" Josie asked me, and I said no, that I had to move along and pick up something I had left behind.

"I've got an old spade with a broken handle stored out in your shed with our other stuff," I said to her. "I have to do a little digging."

"Are you digging a garden?" she asked.

"No."

"Then you're shoveling ashes or some such."

"No."

"You won't say what it is."

"No."

"Then you'll hear no more foolish questions from me," she said, and abruptly left the room. I was sorry, but it wasn't any of her business. I went out the back door. I found the spade, took it back to the house and showed it to Josie, and she was all right again. She had a round face and a low forehead, both of which I have associated with nosy people ever since. There was nothing pretty about her and I made a wager with myself she would never marry. She was not smart, like Maud, and Maud was beautiful and the opposite of nosy.

"I'll be going now," I said to Josie. "I'll come back someday and wait for Emmett to come home."

"You're very young to be alone on the road," Josie said.

"There's younger than me on the road," I said.

"And the same in Ireland. It's a desperate time to be a child."

"I don't feel like a child anymore."

"Well, now, aren't we the grown-up?"

"We might be that," I said.

Josie made me two sandwiches and it was four in the afternoon when I left her, a day in mid-April, clear and sunny but growing chilly, with sundown an hour away. I would wait until dark to dig up the cage, but what I thought to do was approach our old house, imprint its image on memory, and say farewell to it forever.

I walked toward the city, down the West Troy Road, and when I neared Van Woert Street I gave myself a choice: to approach our house from the rear, over our hill and down through the trees, or walk directly up the street and perhaps meet old neighbors. Explain solitariness if you can: that I, more alone than I had ever been in life, did not want to encounter old neighbors, not even boys my age who'd been close friends. I was such an outcast from all that was home that I craved the intensification of exile. I believe I avoided friends from fear of what proximity to their comforts might arouse in me: anger, perhaps, or envy, or even the desire to steal from them. I saw their rooves and chimneys, their back doors and windows as I neared the street, saw Gallagher's spavined horse tethered in the back lot of Carney's grogshop, where my father used to drink. I saw the food store run by Joe Sullivan, who had only one arm. I veered from it all and came at the street from behind the house of the

widow Mulvaney, whose husband raised goats before he ran off
with a fancy woman and died of intense pleasure.

As I came onto the street proper I saw our house. The railing
was off the stoop on one side, the windows all broken in front.
Grass grew tall along the walls and in the cracks between the
paving slates of the sidewalk. I had heard our landlord died of
the cholera and that no one had cared for the house since we
left it. The inert quality of the place, the absence of life, gave
off a stark aura of isolation, and I now wonder whether I myself
was giving off the same aura as I neared the place.

I was no sooner on the path from the Mulvaneys' to our house
than I saw Peaches Plum. He was with one of his brothers and
they looked as alike as two peach pits: both blond and skinny,
both shoeless. They were prowling about our house, I suppose
scavenging, a late moment for that, though truly entrepreneurial
scavengers believe in the bottomlessness of others' dregs. They
saw me approaching and Peaches called me by name.

"Yeeouuu been diggin'," he said to me.

"No," I said.

"Then why you totin' that shovel?"

" 'Cause it's mine."

"Ain't nothin' in *your* house," Peaches said.

"We took most stuff out when the family died," I said. "What
we left wasn't *worth* nothin'."

"You a smarm," Peaches said. "Smart little poop."

"You think what you want, Peaches," I said, and I walked
around him toward the house.

"You gonna dig somepin' with that spade?" he said.

"No, I'm just totin' it," I said.

"What good's a broken spade? Lemme look at it."

"Leave it alone, Peaches," I said, and I picked up a rock the
size of a potato. "And you leave *me* alone, too. I ain't in none
of your way, so don't you go bein' in mine."

Peaches respected rocks. He and his brother (we called him Outa) stared me down and picked up rocks of their own. I kept my eye at a level with Peaches's and picked up a second potato, which made Peaches respect me twice as much. Peaches nodded at me and smiled. Then he wagged his head at Outa, and they went their way and left me alone with two fistfuls of rock. I stood where I was and knew they would look back, both of them, and they did, for the snake is the primal contortionist.

At last they were gone and I dropped the rocks and went to where I had buried the cage: the grove of trees behind the house, a stand of elms and cedar that had grown tall and interwoven their family virtues into a small but quite lovely haven of shade and intermittent sun that allowed for an almost tropical arousal of plant life. A fist-sized rising of water came from the ground halfway up the abrupt hill that sheltered us from northerly winds, and then it trickled down into the grove. This was a spring I had discovered at an early age and claimed as my own, and its water had the dark, sweet taste of the silent stones at the center of the earth.

I went to the spring and drank of that cold clarity to cleanse my mouth of the dust from the road, then sat in the fading light of the grove to await the safety of darkness. When the moon gave me light to work by, I dug up the cage that had been so indefinably valuable to my parents.

I looked at it in the moonlight but saw nothing beyond its basic shape. I could not tell whether it had rusted from being underground or was merely discolored from the soil. I yearned for light but yearned more to be indoors to evade the chill that was sinking into my bones. I looked steadily at the black shadow that was our derelict house and grew brave enough to argue with my fear. Had I not already survived in that house during the plague's heat? Would I not now survive its cold ashes?

I picked up my spade, pack, and birdcage, and at the back door I reentered the circus maximus, where my family had battled and died under my spectator's eye. I sealed all doors against the night, found the kitchen windows to be intact, and I closed off that room as my retreat. I lighted a candle from my pack and set the birdcage on the floor beside it. I made ready to eat some of the food Josie had given me but then in the window I perceived my image, illuminated by the reflected candlelight. What I saw was a body and a face I barely knew. I was too big for my clothes and I was urchin dirty, but urchin no more. My face had been wrenched out of the puffy adolescence of reasonable expectation. That condition, said my mouth and eyes, is a luxury that is part of your past.

I sat beside the birdcage and studied it. Its slender bars had rusted, as had the round, heavy plate that was its bottom. I let the candlelight search out its secret, but I could find no secret. As I handled it, two of its bars snapped from the rusting.

What was I to do with such a worthless object? What was its meaning? I stared at it while I ate a sandwich. I wondered whether my mother and father had made a talisman of the cage, imposing upon it the values of the people of Clonmel, Cashel, and the towns in Mayo and Tyrone where the family had flourished. My father's life was troubled from the time he was two, his father running off then to America. When Pa came here himself he never tried to find his father, nor did I, nor will I. Maybe Pa came with a birdcage instead of memories, but if he did, that was years behind us, all value long gone certainly from this rusty relic on the floor in front of me. My parents were gone themselves, along with their unknowns, all now remaining of what they deemed valuable embodied in me, this urchin particle floating in time, waiting for the next blow to fall.

My candle died with a guttering hiss; I lay my head on my pack of rags, and I fell asleep thinking of the cool and soothing quality of water. I awoke to a noise and opened my eyes in daylight to see a form moving away from the kitchen window. I sat up and immediately gathered my belongings to move out, and as I did, the kitchen door opened and Peaches and his brother walked through it, carrying clubs.

"I seen where you dug," said Peaches, looking around the room. "You dug up that cage," and he picked it up and looked at it. It looked even more worthless now than it had by candlelight.

"It belonged to my mother. I wanted to see it again."

"I think I'll jes take it with me."

"Take it," I said. "It ain't worth a penny. I was just gonna leave it where it sits."

Peaches opened the cage door and one hinge broke. He grunted and dropped it and the bottom came loose.

"I remember when my father buried it," I said. "I thought he might've put a bag of money in it."

"Bag of money? I'd like to have some o' that."

"Wasn't no money in it. You find any money in this house I'll cut it up halvies with you."

Outa Plum tipped the contents of my sack onto the kitchen floor: clothes, candles, matches, a sandwich, and a glove that belonged to Maud.

"You got no money at all," Peaches said.

"None." I pulled my pockets out to prove it.

"Then I'll just take this birdcage," Peaches said, picking it up.

"Take it. Only thing you can't take's my spade. Worth a lot of money, that spade. My daddy used it when he dug the grave of Andy Jackson. People'll pay me a lot of money for it when they know it buried a President of the United States."

Peaches dropped the cage and picked up the spade.

"I just better take this ol' spade," he said.

"Hey, you can't take that," I said and I moved toward him. He threatened me with the spade and Outa raised his club at me.

"I'm gonna tell somebody," I said. "I'm gonna tell your folks."

Peaches and Outa smiled. "You tell 'em," said Peaches. "You jes tell 'em."

They backed out the door and ran with the heirloom. I smiled myself and put my things back in my sack. I looked at the cage. I could not abandon it, despite its being worthless. As I picked it up, the ruptured base separated further and I saw the cage had a false bottom. I pulled the covering off and found beneath it a circular metal disk bearing an odd trompe l'oeil design. Now it was a screaming mouth with vicious eyes, now a comic puppy with bulbous nose and tiny mouth. Depending on where the light hit the eyes they were glassy, or sad, or hypnotic. I had no time to dwell on the disk for I feared Peaches would change his mind about the spade. But I believed the disk was valuable in some way yet to be understood. It was like nothing I'd ever seen. It might be a platter. It might be gold, or silver, for it had not rusted. But even if it wasn't precious metal it had value as a thing to look at. I stuffed it into my sack and left the house, brimming with a brand-new faith in the unknown that I had found at the bottom of a birdcage.

THAT MYSTERY REVEALS ITSELF quickly only to those without the imagination to perpetuate it is a fact that came clear to me when I decided my newfound disk might have been a serving platter for potatoes.

"Potatoes?" exclaimed Will Canaday. "Why, it's too small for potatoes. And what's more, it's flat as a coin. They'd roll off."

I saw Will had a point and the mystery of the disk continued. That mystery, along with my desolation and my desire to abdicate forever the river and the canal, had an hour earlier led me into a reverie as I left Van Woert Street. You know nothing, the reverie began. You are a penniless, ignorant orphan who thought the Mexican War was fought in Canada, and you let John the Brawn steal your most valuable possession. You are inferior to everybody in something, even to Peaches Plum, who knows stealth and violence better than you. Quinn, when will you become wise, or even smart?

This question brought back Will's words to me when we were leaving Hillegond's mansion: "If you find yourself interested in an education, or in the life of the mind, come and see me." And so in my reverie on ignorance I thought of the *Albany Chronicle* as a source of enlightenment about both the disk and my future.

Will was at work in his office, coatless with shirtsleeves rolled, writing one of the editorials about the abduction of Dirck Staats that would bring him national attention. He finished writing on a page of foolscap, tossed it into a box marked "copy," and then he saw me, his face registering genuine surprise.

"Back so soon?" he said.

I told him straightaway of being put off the canalboat.

"Who would do such a thing?"

"It must have been John the Brawn."

"The man's a villain."

"I think I will have trouble forgiving him."

"And I as well," said Will. "But more important than that is what do we do with you? If you want to peddle the *Chronicle* you're welcome to live with our other orphan newsboys on the third floor," and his finger pointed to the ceiling.

"That would be good," I said, and already I felt rescued. "But I think I am interested in a life of the mind. Would I get that as a newsboy?"

"A life of the mind?" said Will, much amused. "In that case we'd better make a reporter of you."

"On what would I report?"

"On the nature of things," said Will. "Does that seem a fit subject?"

"On the nature of what things?"

"All things."

"It sounds a bit more than I can handle."

"Nonsense. Before you know it you'll be as expert on everything under the sun as all the other reporters in this world."

"When shall I begin?"

"Now is as good a time as any. Do you have something in mind to report on?"

"I could report on my platter," I said, and I fished in my sack for it and told Will my story. I've recounted his response about the potatoes, but I was thinking of my parents' stories about bad times in Ireland, and of the presence on their table of very small potatoes, when there were any potatoes at all, while Will, I

[75]

suspect, had the superabundance of the American potato in mind. Will stroked the platter with his fingertips. "It seems to be bronze," he said. "Very old, and very handsome at that. Did your parents get it in Ireland?"

"I suppose so," I said. "Except for Albany that's the only place they ever lived."

"It's possible this is the work of the Vikings, or even the Romans. In any case I suspect it's worth considerable money."

"Is bronze worth money?"

"When it's shaped this way it is."

"Who would buy an old platter?"

"A museum curator, or someone who values relics from another age."

"My parents wouldn't want me to sell it. They said it would take care of me."

"Yes," said Will, smiling one of his patient smiles of forbearance in the face of idiocy. "But I suggest that money may be a way in which one is taken care of."

"Then why didn't my parents sell it themselves? They never had any money."

"A good question," said Will, a bit vexed, "and one you must answer for yourself. Rest easy, Daniel. We'll not sell your relic against your will. But you must protect it. You can't carry it around in that sack."

"I could bury it again."

"There are tidier ways to protect things," said Will. "For the moment you may put it in our safe, if you find that agreeable."

"Very agreeable," I said. "But I think I would not want to live upstairs. I've lived with orphans on the canal, and they stole from me and fought over everything. I'd rather live with Mrs. Staats, if it's all the same to you."

"It's all the same to me," said Will, amused again, "but I can't say how it will sit with Mrs. Staats."

"I'd work for my keep," I said.

"Work for me and work for your keep both?" said Will.

"I don't need much sleep," I said.

Will forbore, then said he'd take me to see Hillegond. He put my platter in his safe, told me to stop calling it a platter, then gave me a file of *Chronicles* to read while he finished his work. He pointed out what he and others had written about Dirck. "If you are going to live with Mrs. Staats," he said, "you had better understand what is happening to her son."

Dirck's abduction appeared under Local Events at first mention in Will's newspaper, written straightforwardly, not unlike the way I have already recounted it. But Will also took the liberty of charging the sheriff with provocative behavior, said he intended to follow the case with intensive fidelity to the facts and would pursue "the deeper darkness that lies beyond this black deed." He also said Dirck never reached Utica, that his arrest was a fraud, and that Aaron Plum was a felon thrice-accused (always for grievous assault with a weapon), after which Plum became a wanted man. The sheriff was relieved of his duties but charged with no crimes, and vanished from his home. In all, the case of Dirck Staats overnight became synonymous with violence, collusion, and mystery.

Will did not, at first, write of Dirck's secret ledgers, though they loomed large; and I began to understand the power of the word to transform this simple abduction of a man into an event that alters the trajectory of history's arrow. I asked Will about Dirck's book and when he would publish it.

"I would publish it tomorrow," he said, "but no one can read it without the key to Dirck's code, and we haven't yet found that."

The search for the code had been ongoing at the newspaper, also among Dirck's friends, in the places he frequented, in the rooms he kept, and at the mansion. Nothing had turned up.

I ended my reading when Will appeared in coat and hat, saying it was time to visit Hillegond, and on the street he hailed a passing carriage. I anticipated the mansion with excitement and affection, as if I were going home, the complacent impoverishment of my former self now thoroughly transformed by the vision of luxury.

As we rode up the gravel driveway I thought that the house's splendor was probably unmatched in this world, and though I have since seen greater monuments, such as Versailles and the Alhambra, I have not changed my mind about the Staats house's singular beauty, or its wondrously eclectic sprawl.

Capricorn answered our knock, told us Hillegond was with a visitor in the east parlor, then announced us to her. Out she came, devoid of the bright colors that were her style, and wrapped instead in a slate-colored dress and black lace shawl, her uniform of mourning for lost kin. Her face was a mask of gravity, but she brightened when she saw me, and she hugged me.

"Master Daniel," she said, and smothered me in her abundantly dark bosom. "Why are you here, and where are the others?"

"Gone," I said. "John the Brawn put me off the canalboat while I slept, and I walked back to Albany."

"A dreadful deed," said Hillegond, but I knew she was of two minds about John and his deeds.

"The boy wants to stay here with you," Will said.

"Well, he surely can," said Hillegond, and my future exploded with rainbows. Only hours out of my family's tumbledown house of death, now I was to become a dweller in this grand villa of life.

"You're both just in time to see me magnetized," Hillegond said with a verve that reversed her bleak mood. "It's a very daring thing to do."

She led us into the parlor and I saw that Dirck's two portraits, face out, were draped with bright red ribbon—red the color of protection in Hillegond's spiritual spectrum. A man in his thirties, wearing a hemisphere of whiskers along his total jawline, the rest of his face clean-shaven, rose to greet us.

"And this is Maximilian Schiffer," said Hillegond. "He's a wonderful animal magnetist. He's helping me to find Dirck."

Maximilian shook hands stiffly with both of us, then inquired grimly of Hillegond, "Are these visitors to be present during experiment? Witnesses can be distraction."

"They won't be a distraction," said Hillegond. "My son worked for this man, and this boy was one of the last to see him before his abduction."

Max nodded at that, which ended the sociable aspect of our visit. He then picked up a single piece of paper from the table in front of Hillegond and handed it to her.

"Put this alongside head. You will read it with ear when I tell you."

"With her ear?" said Will.

"Correct," said Max testily.

"Maximilian is a world-renowned phrenomagnetist," said Hillegond. "He's examined the bumps on my skull and he says the one behind my ear gives me the gift of vision. He's certain I'll be able to see Dirck by reading his scrawlings through my ear bump."

"Do you really think your bumps are so special?" asked Will with a small smile.

"I have always thought so," said Hillegond.

"Please, no talking," said Max, and he guided Hillegond's hand with the paper, on which I was able to see some marks. Max positioned it behind Hillegond's left ear, then moved both his hands over her head, arms, and lap, humming like the lowest note on an organ. In time I recognized the word "sleep," by which moment Hillegond was deep in her magnetic trance.

"Now tell about son Dirck," said Max.

"He's a nuisance and a most foolish child," said Hillegond, her eyes closed. "He won't go to church, and he talks back to

[79]

his mother. He won't play with other children, for all he wants to do is draw pictures and read books, which isn't healthy in a young boy. I tell him he'll turn into an idiot from being alone so much, and I only allow him to wear clothing that doesn't fit him so he'll look even more foolish than he is. 'When you behave properly you shall have proper clothing,' I tell him, but he doesn't change. I would have my husband whip him if I had a husband. I had such hopes for the boy. I thought he would grow up to make us proud of the Staats name again. I thought he would make new money for us and preserve our mansion, but he can't button his own shoes."

"Please tell of Dirck, and where is," said Max.

Hillegond pressed the paper closer to her ear, opened her eyes in a gaze at nothing in particular, and then in a voice several tones higher than her previous pronouncements, spoke with the articulation of a masterful actress.

"My son is a splendid man. He is tied to a chair and watched by a man with a mustache and an old woman in a plaid dress. My son is unhappy to an immoderate degree. People are cruel to him but he is strong and healthy. My son worries about his work and his books, and they are not feeding him. My son will not let these inferior people destroy his will to persevere on behalf of rectitude. My son is a grand citizen of the republic and serves his country with the same nobility that marked the careers of his ancestors. My son is in a black state of mind. My son is vomiting. My son—"

"Where is son?" asked Max.

"I don't know the place."

"Talk about place."

"The place is . . . on a road. I can't see the place. The place is in the country? I don't know. By a hill? I can't see the place. I can't, I can't—" and Hillegond swooned in her chair, the paper fluttering to the floor at my feet. I picked it up and saw it to be two very short lines of runic writing comparable to the script in

Dirck's ledger. I handed the paper to Will as Max spoke urgently into Hillegond's ear and brought her out of her swoon. She awoke from the trance complaining of a severe headache, and Max immediately lowered her head between her knees, passed his hands over the back of her neck, raised her up, and poof, her headache was gone.

"That was quite fascinating what you said," Will told her.

"What did I say?"

"You were talking about Dirck. You said he might be on a country road. Which road?"

"I have no idea," said Hillegond. "I don't even remember saying it."

"She will remember if I tell her remember," said Max.

"Then you should tell her."

"In time."

"Where'd you get this paper?" Will asked her.

"Dirck's room," she said. "I found it in an old envelope. It's those crazy drawings he's been doing all his life."

"Do you know what they mean?" asked Will.

"Of course not. They don't mean anything."

Will nodded and stuffed the paper into his pocket.

"You mentioned a man with a mustache," Will said. "Do you remember him?"

"Nothing," said Hillegond.

"Make her remember," Will said to Max.

"Is too soon," said Max with a defiant lip.

"Can't be soon enough if there's anything genuine in all this hocus-pocus," said Will. "You make her remember right now or I might forget I'm a gentleman."

Max paused long enough to suggest his imperviousness to threat, then turned to Hillegond. "You will remember everything you tell about son," he said.

"I remember the man had a long, drooping mustache and a bald head and very shifty eyes," said Hillegond immediately.

[81]

"Was it Aaron Plum?" said Will.

"Yes, I think it was. How could you know that, Will?"

"I have special bumps of my own," said Will.

Hillegond continued recalling all she'd told us and Will quizzed her further on the Plum family. She knew them, but not well. I told Will then for the first time about how John the Brawn and I had carried what were probably stolen harnesses for Aaron Plum and his brother Peaches, and I also added the story of Peaches's theft of my broken spade.

"I think we should pay another visit to the Plums," Will said. He had gone to the Plum farm immediately after the kidnapping but found only a handyman, and no family.

"You must be careful," Hillegond said. "They're dangerous people."

"It will only be a social call," said Will. "We'll inquire about Daniel's spade."

"It's worthless," I said.

"Maybe so, but that worthlessness is yours, not theirs."

We excused ourselves from Hillegond and she said she would have Matty get my old room ready for when I returned. I thought of Maud and how we had lived under this same roof for months, and I grew sad and vowed we would live together again one day. But of course that was an empty wish and Maud was God knows where.

Will and I walked to Will's house through the open fields, the sky cloudy bright. In his barn he hitched one of his three horses to a wagon and gave me my first lesson in Plum history, about which he had written much.

The first Plum in the New World was Ezra, who came to Albany from England in 1759 at age eighteen and hired on as the city's official whipper. In 1786 he was promoted to city hangman, expediting into the beyond numerous robbers, counterfeiters, and forgers until 1796, when whipping posts and execution, except for murder, were abolished. In 1801, when Ezra was sixty, an unknown assailant cut off his head with an ax—the assailant widely believed to be his grandson, Jeremiah.

Jeremiah was the son of Ezra's only child, Bliss, who first proved that murder ran in the family. At age twenty, married only three weeks, Bliss informally executed two of his young cousins, newly arrived from England, clubbing one, hanging the other, thus removing them as competition for an inheritance Bliss coveted. Bliss feigned innocence but in time confessed and was hanged before he turned twenty-one.

Bliss's son, Jeremiah, was conceived during Bliss's three-week marriage to a woman named Blessed Benson. Jeremiah, born the year his father swung, inherited all Plum property and became family patriarch in our time-present, 1850.

Jeremiah married Priscilla Swett of Vermont, who, at a later moment, was convicted of almost eviscerating a woman neighbor with a carving knife in an argument over the neighbor's fur hat, which Priscilla, called Priss, had stolen. Priss was sentenced to twenty years in jail but that was reversed in higher court through the influence of her son, Mason Plum, a lawyer who earned fame for keeping his family out of jail.

Other Plums: Aaron, a blond hunter thrice charged with near murders; Hanna, a beauty; and Eli (Peaches), whom Priscilla claimed as her own in order to cap a scandal, for Peaches was actually the offspring of his own sister, Hanna, when Hanna was fifteen. And the sire was Hanna's father, Jeremiah. There was also Fletcher Plum, a cousin, whose talent for stealing horses and altering their color and markings with charcoal and dye was so well developed that even the owners of the horses were deceived. There were other Plums, but enough.

Will put a pistol in his belt, and another under a blanket on the seat between us as we drove toward the Plum farm. Will assured me there would be no violence, that the pistols were only to fend off highwaymen, but I didn't quite believe that.

"All I want you to do when we get to the Plums'," Will said to me, "is to identify that spade if we come across it. Otherwise let me do the talking."

The Plum estate—house, barns, and outbuildings—sat on a knoll about two miles from Will's house, back in the woods on a road that was all but uninhabited except by the Plum family and their poor cousins, who lived in shacks and worked the land for the Plums. Cows grazed in a low meadow, goats on a hillside, and in the corral you could count two dozen horses.

Will pulled up in front of the house and handed me the reins. He mounted the steps but before he could knock, Priss Plum came to the door in what some people might have taken for a plaid housedress. Her hair was a flaming, unnatural red, and she was a bit of a looker, even at sixty.

"Who are you? Whataya want?" she asked Will.

"Canaday is my name," said Will. "I'd like to speak with Jeremiah."

"He ain't here."

"Is Peaches here?"

"What's anybody wanna see *him* for?"

"It's about a piece of personal property," said Will.

"You claimin' he stole somethin'?"

"Not at all. Is Aaron here?"

"He don't live here no more."

"When did he move out?" Will asked.

"That ain't none of your business."

"You wouldn't know the whereabouts by any chance of a man named Dirck Staats? Last time I saw him he was with Aaron."

"Never heard of no Dirck Staats."

In the doorway of the barn I could see a man with a heavily waxed black handlebar mustache, and with slick, ridiculously black hair, watching us. This was Jeremiah Plum, his hair dyed the way the Plums dyed spots on horseflesh. I also saw my spade leaning against the barn door. Then from around behind Jeremiah came Peaches, and I called out, "Hey, Peaches, I want my spade back. That's my spade." I wanted all my worthlessness in my possession, now that Will had told me that's how it should be.

Will turned and walked off the porch. I saw Jeremiah reach to his right and come up with a shotgun, which he almost pointed until he saw the pistol in Will's hand.

"Howdy, Jeremiah," Will said as he walked toward the barn.

"Didn't know you carried a pistol, Will."

"Only when I go into the forest," Will said. "Like to protect myself from the wild animals."

"What brings you all the way out here?" said Jeremiah. Peaches wrapped his arms around Jeremiah's midsection and peered out at Will.

"Just lookin' for my good friend Dirck Staats."

Jeremiah said nothing.

"Also came by to pick up that spade your boy Peaches borrowed from my young friend here. You know this boy, don't you, Peaches?" Will said, pointing to me. Peaches didn't answer.

"You're right talky today, Will," said Jeremiah. "Carryin' a pistol, yappin' like a magpie, lookin' for shovels."

"A spade, Jeremiah, a spade is what I'm looking for."

Will half turned to glance at the spade, then turned back to Jeremiah. Without looking at the spade Will fired a shot from belt level that put a hole in the center of its blade.

"That your spade, Daniel?" Will asked, his back to me.

"That's it," I said.

"That spade ain't worth a whole lot," Will said. "It's got a hole in it. But I guess we'll take it along just for old times' sake. You know there's folks in this world'll do anything to get back an old spade they feel sentimental about. Sentiment's a powerful thing, Jeremiah, and you ought to take stock of what I'm sayin' because, well, you take this barn here. I know you love barns and I know how many you've burned. I raise this issue because I want you to know how anxious I am for news of Dirck Staats, and how if I don't hear about him by tomorrow, I'll be comin' back out here with more than a boy and a horse. And Jeremiah, if I find somebody's hurt Dirck, then I'll start doing things to people the way I did when I was ridin' with Big Thunder in the Rent War, and I know you remember those days, and how I was one barn-burnin', tar-and-featherin' son of a bitch, and not a bad shot either, Jeremiah," and Will let go another shot from the hip that went into that spade no more than a cat's whisker distant from the previous bullet hole, the sweetest shooting I ever saw. Then Will said to me without turning, "Daniel, come and get your spade."

I didn't want to move. Against all logic I felt protected in the wagon. But I climbed down and walked across the yard toward the spade, which was no longer worthless now that it had those two bullet holes of Will's in it. I saved that spade for years to remind myself that courage is a worthy commodity, but that courage alone wouldn't have gotten me back what was mine. I looked in at Peaches when I picked up the spade.

"Hey, Peaches," I said. "I ain't gonna let nobody take this spade no more, so don't come askin'."

Peaches stuck his tongue out at me and then ducked back behind Jeremiah. I went back to the wagon and Will backed toward it also.

"We'll be moseyin' now, Jeremiah," said Will. "Can't socialize like this or I'll never get my newspaper out," and he climbed up onto the wagon, still holding his pistol. He turned to Priss in the doorway and said, "I'll say so long to you, too, Mrs. Plum, so long for now anyway." He took the reins from me with his free hand and whacked the horse, and then we moved slowly, much too slowly for my internal fluids, down the wagon path to the road.

DIRCK'S BOOK WAS PUBLISHED in an extraordinary edition of Will Canaday's *Chronicle* two weeks after our visit to the Plums'. Will did not publish a paper for three days running, offering no public explanation for the uncommon lapse, then came forth with a twenty-page issue carrying all he possessed of Dirck's manuscript. I am pleased to report that it was my adroitness in snatching up the paper that fell from behind Hillegond's ear during her talk with the phrenomagnetist that led to the breaking of Dirck's code.

The paper had on it two carefully inked lines of Dirck's runic designs. Will's unavailing scrutiny of them led him to think of the lines as a code and he took the paper to a scholar at Columbia College in Manhattan. The scholar saw instantly that the designs came from more than one language: ancient Teutonic runes and Hebrew and Arabic characters forming most of the consonants, and signs of the zodiac serving as vowels. Dirck wrote words in normal sequence but also spelled them backward. Knowing this, a translation became possible; and the opening sentences had this to say:

Maleficence flowers, malevolence reigns in the ranks of The Society, a secret organization that dominates many thousands of American lives. Evidence has accrued that leaders of The Society are often the same men who hold leadership positions in this community, this state, this nation, in commerce, finance, politics, industry, and invention, and that as a way of preserving power over what they consider lesser beings, they are, in seriate accumulation, as guilty of fratricide as was Cain, as guilty of ritual murder as are the disciples of Kali, as devout in their myriad hatreds as any demon from the caverns of hell.

> Whom do they hate?
> Thee and me.
> Which brothers do they kill?
> Thine and mine.

Dirck carried on throughout with such shameless rhetorical flourishes, also interposing an appalling study of clandestine conspiracy to defraud, destroy, debase, and eliminate not only men but families and entire organizations that obstructed the aims of The Society, and to ostracize foreigners from public office, power, and lofty social position. Sudden death on a dark pier, legal theft of an iron foundry's ownership, burning of barns, poisoning of livestock, terrorizing of immigrant and religious gatherings—all such events had been reported in the newspapers, and Dirck cited dates and places. Taken discretely, the events reflected a randomly base quality to much of human behavior. But linked by Dirck's genius for correlation, they coalesced as the scheme of a ruthless and invisible oligarchy.

Dirck's writing went well beyond summary of the plotted web. It also named beneficiaries and heretofore untouchable agents of the vile deeds. Even when his proof was firm but unsubstantiable, he described his targets with a partial fidelity that ensured identification; for instance: "The corrupt magistrate D____ van E____ of the nearby village of C____."

The recklessness of this attack (Will was sued numerous times for libel) was a calculation that placed Will's and Dirck's moral positions above anything purporting to be a fair-minded rendering of reality. Damn fair-mindedness! We are in possession of dastardly truth!

The community response was swift. Committees assembled to confront The Society's suddenly visible leaders with a cascade of shame and alarm that such secrecy had been so powerfully loosed upon the land. A spate of resignations from the order also followed in protest against the criminal revelation. Many of the accused denied The Society even existed, but sudden departures from the city by certain bankers, politicians, artisans became known, and a few notorious members of the lower classes also vanished, men known to have been available for hired thuggery. Dirck's book was widely reprinted, or paraphrased by cautious editors, elsewhere in the nation, and Dirck, in absentia, became a hero, as did Will for publishing him.

Two known deaths ensued from what Dirck wrote. A magistrate renowned as a temperance advocate shot himself through the right eye after Dirck revealed him as the actual owner of a brothel and four grogshops; and an actors' dresser, one Abner Green, was found hanging from a crossbeam backstage at The Museum. The City Physician rendered a report of suicide on Green, but Will believed it to be murder, for he knew Green had been one of Dirck's informants. Green's death convinced Will that Dirck also had been killed, for Abner Green had given Dirck certain data on the oath that members took to gain entry to The Order of the Cross, the elite group responsible for discipline within The Society. Dirck wrote:

Deprived of clothing, food, light, and the right to speak, naked in the darkness for as much as twenty-four hours, the candidates for this Order are at last given food to eat, then are told it has been befouled by human waste. The food has not been befouled, only tainted with certain odors. Yet believing it excrementalized, the candidates dutifully devour it. If they retch they must devour a new portion.

Of the oath, Dirck quoted this cautionary segment:

I will defend The Society with my life, not only its known aims, but those yet to be defined. I will punish its enemies without fear of reprisal by any man, any law. If ever I betray this oath, I agree that my stomach should be opened by a blade, and my organs and entrails exposed to the tooth and fang of ravenous rats.

Since Abner Green had not died in this manner, Will was not sure it had been a ritual murder. He distrusted all official information from the city, and so called me into his office.

"How would you like to become an actor?" he asked me.

"I would not like it at all," I said. "I've never set foot in a theater. Just thinking about being onstage gives me chilblains."

"Nonsense," said Will. "All actors are terrified. But they overcome that and find something of themselves worth presenting to public view."

"Not me," said I.

"Frankly," said Will in his forbearing tone, "I'm not interested in your lack of dramatic ambition. I only want you to go to The Museum to audition for the new show, and to keep alert for talk of Abner Green and Dirck. They won't suspect anything of a boy your age. Tell them you can act. Tell them you can sing."

"You want me to do this all by myself?"

"I do."

"But I'm afraid," I said.

"You are not afraid," said Will.

"Oh yes I am."

"Oh no you are not."

"Then why do I think I am?"

"Because you are a boy who still believes in fear, and it's time you grew out of that."

And so, browbeaten by my elder, I took myself to The Museum, which had begun its existence more than twenty years earlier as a showplace of curiosities—a rhinoceros purportedly shot by Benjamin Franklin, a living Chinese torso without arms or legs, a wax effigy of the last man legally hanged in Albany, the unique one-hundred-and-forty-pound Amazonian rat (stuffed). The Museum, in the '40s, had turned to melodrama, but also had seen Edwin Forrest incarnate Hamlet, Lear, and Othello on its boards. Several live-horse dramas gained popularity on its huge stage, but all were eclipsed by the success of Magdalena Colón's sensational dancing. Since Magdalena, the audiences had been a thin gruel, and theater manager Waldorf (Dorf) Miller now hoped to woo people back with a production bridging two genres: the minstrel show and the Irish frolic. Its title: *Tambo and Paddy Go to Town.*

A dozen workers were in assorted forms of frenzy—sweeping, painting, doing carpentry work—as I entered. One man was sawing a huge, decrepit rhinoceros into thirds to get it out the door (its skin had been stuffed years earlier inside the theater), and onstage a cadaverous white man was shuffling to the music of two banjos and singing:

> *Dere's music in de wells,*
> *Dere's music in de air*
> *Dere's music in a nigger's knee*
> *When de banjo's dere.*

When the singer finished, Dorf Miller, a somewhat round man in a silver leather vest, with sprouts of hair behind his ears but nowhere else on his head, told him he was hired and asked did he have a costume for the show. The man said he did not, and so Dorf nodded and pulled aside a curtain onstage, revealing people fitting costumes on performers. I went to the manager and gave my name and said I would like a role in his new show.

"A role, you say, Master Quinn?"

"Yes, sir, a role."

"Are you an actor, Master Quinn?"

"I hope to be," I said, a great lie that slid so easily off my tongue that I realized I must be very close to damnation. "And I sing. My mother said I had quite a good voice," another lie that amused Dorf Miller, and he announced to all present, "Hear, hear. This boy says his mother likes his singing," and all laughed. "What brought you to *our* door?" he asked me.

"My mother was a close friend of Mrs. Hillegond Staats and my father knew Abner Green. Both of them spoke often of The Museum, and Mr. Green told my father to send me here if I needed work. Are you Mr. Green?"

"No," said the manager, "my name is Miller. Who is your father and how did he know Abner Green?"

"Davey Quinn was his name, and he's dead and buried, God rest his soul. He and Mr. Green were members of the same organization."

"Organization," said Dorf, growing somber, and I noted two carpenters within earshot looked at me and then at each other. They nodded their heads knowingly and then kept nodding long after any meaning had been conveyed.

"The Society, I think they called it," I said.

"Your father was in The Society? I didn't think they allowed the Irish in."

"I'm sure I don't know what they allowed," I said. "All I know is what was said."

One carpenter whispered to the other, both of them nodding furiously. Then one of them went out of the theater.

"Abner Green," said Dorf reflectively.

"My father said he was a good man."

"Yes, he was all of that. It's a shame what they—" and he caught himself. "It's a shame he died."

[93]

"Oh, is he dead?"

"He is. But I'll attend to you myself in his absence, young sir, and if you've a mind to, let us hear this voice that your mother loves so well."

"Oh indeed, sir. But my mother is dead and buried too, God rest her soul. And sir, if my voice fails to please you, is there another sort of job here for me?"

"Let us have first things first. What song will you sing?"

" 'Kathleen Mavourneen.' It was my father's favorite."

"A lovely song, but very difficult," said Dorf, and he sat on a chair while I faced the banjo players and others. I then sang, a capella, and very badly indeed, the only song whose words I knew to the end, pounded into my memorious brain by my relentlessly lyrical father. I could see from Dorf's face that my talent lay in a direction other than music. He was about to tell me as much when a young man in a plug hat and galluses, and only slightly older than myself, joined me in my progress toward a high note I knew I would never hit. His voice overpowered mine with such mellifluity that all in the theater were thrown into a fit of awe. It was the purest voice I could imagine, and what's more he also knew the words.

> *Oh hast thou forgotten*
> *How soon we must sever,*
> *Oh hast thou forgotten*
> *This day we must part.*
> *It may be for years,*
> *And it may be forever,*
> *Oh why art thou silent,*
> *Thou voice of my heart . . .*

I desisted from singing when he began, but continued humming along somewhat unobtrusively, reluctant to abandon my own song entirely. When the song ended, all in the theater (myself included) burst into applause, so obviously grand and crystalline was the fellow's talent. He had not been in the theater when I arrived, but must have come in behind me to unite with my song like a usurper. But his usurpation was justified: he talented, I without a shred. He extended his hand to me.

"I apologize for interfering with your song," he said. "But I saw you were in difficulties. Perhaps if you did a different song . . ."

"I don't know a different song," I said, shaking his hand.

"That is a pity, then. I've ruined it for you."

"You've ruined nothing," said Dorf, coming between us. "I believe it's a wonderful act. This lad here with a very small voice, terrified of performing and quite sympathetic for all that, and then you, rising from the audience like the deus ex machina himself and booming out your splendid tenor's gift. And then, yes . . . yes, yes, you climb onto the stage, singing all the while, and the two of you finish together in grand elevation. The lad is rescued, the tenor triumphant. Oh, I'm fond of it, very fond. How do you call yourself, young sir?"

"Joseph K. Moran," said the usurper.

We all exchanged names and Dorf told us to come for rehearsal tomorrow at ten. He then busied himself with the next aspirants, a pair of twins who had been dancing in the wings to the jangle of their own tambourines when I came in. I discovered that Joseph Moran had just arrived from Utica after visiting his ailing mother. I quizzed him on La Última and he said she'd sold out the theater there for two weeks, as she had here. I inquired after Maud and he vaguely recalled hearing of a young girl who appeared on stage with La Última, but doing precisely what, he could not say. I liked Joseph Moran in spite of his usurping ways. He was only a year older than I, though he looked to be near the age of twenty, and carried himself with a sophisticated swagger I mistrusted without knowing why.

A man entered as we talked and said to Dorf, "I'm looking for a young fellow called Daniel Quinn." Dorf pointed me out and the man came over to me.

"I've a message," he said in a whisper. "Mr. Staats awaits your visit."

"Mr. Staats?" I said. "Mr. Dirck Staats?"

"I wouldn't know that," said the man. "Staats is all they told me."

"Who is they?"

"Mr. Staats. He was with others."

"Where is he?"

"Out the road north. I'm to take you. You're not likely to find it alone."

"Is he all right?"

"All right? What constitutes all right in this life?"

"Is he well?"

"He's among the living, if that's what you're asking."

"Then I think I must go." I said this more to convince myself than anyone else, but I don't think I succeeded, for Joseph Moran spoke up.

"Is there trouble? You look worried."

"Not at all," I said. "Nothing to be afraid of."

"Then we'll meet here in the morning."

"Ten o'clock," I said, and went out with the man.

He was the driver of an open carriage drawn by two horses, and I rode alone beside him, staring out at the dismally gray afternoon, seeing the houses move farther and farther apart as we left the city. The trees were in early leaf and the grass was as green as April can make it. We'd had a week of heavy rain and the overcast sky threatened us today as well. We turned off the main highway and onto a narrow dirt road, rutted with mud but navigable with the help of the two animals. Certain wooded landscapes in the distance seemed familiar to me, and then I realized we were nearing the Plum spread. I asked the driver, "Are we going to the Plums'?"

He did not answer. I asked a second time, and a second time won no response. At the road leading into the Plum place the driver stopped. I chose not to move. He was a stringy man of anxious mien, a jittery presence inside his scruffy clothing.

"Up there you go," he said impatiently, pointing over his shoulder with his right thumb. "In the barn, they said."

"What's in the barn?"

"Your friend Staats."

"Then why don't we drive to the barn?"

"I go no farther than this," he said, brushing his lapels with the backs of his fingers. I saw no alternative but to climb down. I stood beside the carriage and looked to the barn, then again to him.

"You'll wait here for me," I said.

"I go no farther than this," he said, and he again brushed his lapels.

I walked toward the barn, looking for signs of Plum people, but saw no one; nor did I see any Plum animals. The horses were gone from the corral, and no cows grazed on the hillside. The barn door stood open, as it had when Will and I last visited. I looked back at the carriage and saw the driver still on his perch, holding the reins, looking straight ahead. I entered the barn cautiously, hearing no sound. I surveyed the interior from one step inside the door, discovering an open area for carriages and wagons, a hayloft, and two dozen animal stalls. I saw no sign of Dirck, and so stepped forward, making silent inquiry to the Deity whether in the next instant I would be exploded by a shotgun blast or impaled on the prongs of a rusty pitchfork.

I found Dirck in the farthermost stall, face down in soiled hay, wearing the same ill-fitting clothes he'd been wearing when abducted. On close look it was not animal droppings but his own

blood that had soiled the hay. I rolled him over to see his face
and found it a total wound, a horrifying smear of blood, gash,
and swelling. His eyes told me he was still alive, but not for
long, I judged. I did not know how to help him, but my instinct
was to clean his face, find his bleeding and stop it, just as I had
aided John the Brawn in conserving what remained of his blood
after a street fight.

Dirck gave me recognition with his eyes, then closed them. I
thought he'd died but he hadn't; and on he breathed. I lifted
him, found he had no power to stand alone and that I was of
insufficient strength to carry him. I ran to the door to call the
carriage driver and found the low buzzard had driven off. I felt
sure now that no one remained on the Plum place except myself
and the bleeding Dirck. I spied a pump near the house, a bucket
beside it. I filled the bucket, which leaked, and so ran with it
to Dirck. I soaked my shirttail to wash the blood from his face,
saw his lower lip was split open at the left corner, and his mouth
full of partly clotted blood. I blotted and cleaned what I could,
fearful of disturbing any clot, and Dirck made no move except
to breathe. It appeared he'd been smashed in the face, so swollen
was he. After the cleansing I could see his blood flow was mostly
stanched, perhaps by time, or by the downward pressure of his
wound onto the straw; and that gave rise to small hope in me.
He was, nevertheless, all but dead, and would surely die with
thoroughness if I did not find help. What I needed was a horse
and wagon, and the Plum barn offered neither. I ran to the
house, went 'round it to see what was behind, but found nothing.
I peered in a window and saw the house had been emptied of
furniture, and I began to understand not only how deeply the
Plums had been involved in, but also how radically their lives
had been changed by, the events set into motion by Dirck.

Beyond the outhouse I saw a shed that probably once held
pigs, or possibly chickens, or both, and I went toward it with
renewed trepidation, but also thinking I should run for help,

find someone with a wagon. But run where? Find whom? The Plum house was near nothing and no one. Will Canaday's house was miles away. Emmett Daugherty was perhaps a bit closer, but of that I was uncertain. Would either of them be home? How long would it take to run those miles? And what if . . . ?

The chicken-pig house door was open and I entered through it into a black dream, finding a man lying spread-eagled on the floor, a railroad spike driven into each of his hands, each of his feet. He was long dead and much of him was absent, but his red hair, his muttonchops, and his ear partially sliced or bitten away identified him to me as the man who had stolen Dirck's ledgers from Will's office. He had been stripped to below the waist, slit up the middle, and now a globular rat was eating his liver. When I came in, the rat scurried off, then paused near an exit hole to observe me, waiting for me to decide whether he should, or should not, be allowed to resume his gluttony.

I am impressed by the practicality of the human mind, even in times of terror. I do not join with those who see terror superseding all other emotions, for what I did at this moment was to cast my glance dutifully about the henhouse and discover a four-sided barrow with wheel and handles: a vehicle. Sent. I glanced anew at the sliced man to reassure myself it was he, to convince myself that he had indeed been crucified and split and was now rat-ridden, proving it to my incredulous eye so I would not later think I had merely imagined it. Then I lunged toward the barrow with sufficiently broad gesture to scare the rat into his exit hole, and I wheeled my vehicle out the door and toward the livid lump that Dirck Staats had become.

Dirck had not moved, but his eyes were open when I arrived.

"Can you move at all? Can you stand?"

He tried valiantly to sit up, but his pain had stupefied him, and he fell back. I heaped straw into the barrow as a cushion for him, then lifted him so he was sitting in the barrow's center.

His legs dangled and touched the ground, making it impossible to wheel him. I found a filthy tethering rope in one stall, wrapped it 'round Dirck's ankles, and then pulled it taut and fastened it to the barrow's handles, thus lifting his legs and pointing them straight ahead. I wrapped the rest of the rope around his arms and torso and secured that also to the handles, making him my somewhat upright prisoner. His head was bouncing up, down, and sideward, but that seemed to me irrelevant to his safe passage.

I wheeled him out of the barn and off Plum land, then went a mile at least before I saw another dwelling, high on a hillside. I left Dirck on the road, climbed the hill and knocked at the door. A bearded old man leaning on half a crutch answered.

"What is it, boy?"

"An injured man," I said, "very badly hurt and bleeding. I have him tied up in that barrow down there. Could I borrow a horse or wagon, or could you take me to get help?"

"What kind of thing is that, tying up a sick man in a barrow?"

"It's all there was, and I couldn't carry him, or even lift him. Is there a doctor near here?"

"No doctor'd put a sick man in a barrow."

"You don't understand. I'm trying to help him. He'll die if he doesn't get help."

"Whatever ails him, that barrow'll make him worse. Who is he?"

"His name is Dirck Staats."

"Never heard of him."

"That doesn't matter," I said with maximum exasperation. "Can you help him?"

"Where'd you get him?"

"About a mile up the road. In a barn."

"The Plums'?"

"It used to be their place but they're all gone now."

"Plums are gone? Where'd they go?"

"I don't know. Can you *please, please,* help us?"

"I wouldn't help a Plum if he was dyin' on my doorstep."

"He's *not a Plum!*" I yelled. "His name is Dirck Staats! The Plums are the ones who *hurt* him!"

"Why'd they hurt him?"

"I don't know! *I don't know!*"

"I wouldn't help a Plum if he was dyin' in my barn. If a Plum got kicked by a horse right in front of me I'd let him lay. If a Plum was being pecked to death by woodpeckers I'd buy a ticket and watch."

Then he closed the door on me.

I wheeled Dirck toward the main road, another half mile at least, some of it uphill and much of it through mud. I often had to go off the road into a field to get past the mud, and climbing crisscross on a hill, I almost lost Dirck overboard twice, his head bobbing like a dead chicken's.

When I got to the highway I waved down two carriages, but they both kept on. A man carrying a sack of flour on his shoulder stopped to look at Dirck, then went on his way without a word. I sensed Dirck was giving forth an efflux of dread to all who came near him, and felt also that the Christian virtues of charity and compassion were little heeded by my neighbors.

At the next house I roused only a barking dog. At the next I found a feeble woman, useless to my cause except for her remark that I was near the West Troy Road, and so I knew I could find my way to Emmett Daugherty's. Fixing on Emmett as my destination seemed superior to the futile beseeching of strangers, and so I pushed our barrow with renewed vigor, trying not to dwell on Dirck's painful descent into hell. I grew impermeable to all glances, certain that any imagined court of mercy along the way would turn into a waste of Dirck's diminishing time.

I was not even sure Dirck could still hear me. But if he *was* alive I knew he'd welcome distraction from his pain and discomfort, and so I talked to him aloud of my meeting with Joseph

Moran and of our duet on "Kathleen Mavourneen." I involved Dirck in my future plans at the newspaper and said I hoped he would tutor me in the writing arts. I told him I was grateful beyond measure for this chance to help him, especially after being allowed to live in his own house with his mother, to whom I was growing very close, and as well to Will Canaday, who, through his newspaper and his tutelage, was opening my eyes to the world in ways not accessible to the being I used to be. I gave thanks to Dirck himself for his revelation to me of the significance of the word, which, I could now see, releases boundless emotion and mystery, even into the lives of such folk as the Plums. I did not mention the fate of the sliced man. I focused on Dirck as someone who could change the world with his writing: a maestro of language, a champion of the heroic sentence. Of course I said these things in my limited way, and Dirck had no choice but to accept them in that form.

I ended my monologue wondering silently whether I should tell Dirck about my love for Maud, and my loss of her, but then we were at Main Street, entering into the most easeful steps of my life: that short walk down the sloping grade to Emmett's house. I saw Emmett sitting on his front step as I turned the corner. He was smoking his pipe, and when I saw smoke rise from it, I knew salvation.

"We're here, Dirck," I said, and I almost broke into laughter, for he raised his head and blinked vitally at me.

Quickly now I sharpen my point. We put Dirck to bed in fresh nightclothes, washed him, made him warm. When Josie saw Dirck's condition she blessed herself, said a silent prayer, and went to a cupboard for a ball of string. With a length of it she took Dirck's measure from scalp to toe, cut the string, then went to the yard, dug a hole, and buried it.

"They'll not now take his soul," she told us.

Emmett sent Josie for the doctor and gave Dirck a warm spoonful of the chicken soup Josie had made. Dirck ejected it violently, at the same time loosening a ball of coagulated blood and straw that had settled in the front of his mouth. Emmett moved the oil lamp close to Dirck's face to study his wound, and when he turned to me, his eyes were afloat in tears.

"The cruel, cruel bastards," he said. "They took his one and only tongue."

THE *Albany Chronicle*, as we had known it, failed of business one month after Dirck's return to the human race. Four attempts to set the premises ablaze were foiled, but nighttime vandals finally overpowered our sentinels and destroyed Will's press with aggravated sledgings. Within one week Will was printing at the shop that published *The Paddle*, a penny-awful sheet of scandal and mayhem from around the globe (the terrible fate of eunuchs in a Persian harem, the Mouth Murders by the mad dentist of Baltimore); but by then The Society's many members had withdrawn their paid notices. Even advertisers loyal to Will, finding themselves threatened, withdrew also. Will pressed on with his waning capital, being but a week from closing when Hillegond bought out *The Paddle* and installed Will as editor. Will merged the publications, fusing the inherited mayhem with his own politics, and naming the new publication the *Chronicle-Paddle*, a grotesque and short-lived fusion. Will kept it long enough to ensure an orderly transition of readers, but then diminished the word *Paddle* to minuscularity and, after a year, banished it altogether.

Dirck recovered his health but found his tongueless words no more than idiot grunts; and so he went silent. Because he believed I had saved his life (actually, he might have survived alone, even in the filthy hay—unlike Maud, who required my intercession to remain among the quick), Dirck made me his intermediary. He would scrawl swift messages with his everpointed pencil, then thrust the scrawls at me to read aloud. He wrote of his ordeals in fragments that belied their own truth: "Held me in wonderful chicken coop . . . The gentle Jeremiah Plum took orders from kindly bass-voiced stranger who visited me wearing black veil on his face . . . Unfortunate man with partial ear guarded me with kindness . . . I nevertheless felt selfish need to loosen ropes to escape and return to work at *Chronicle* . . . Hid in barn, too weak to run . . . Surely against his wishes, Aaron Plum smashed my face with plank and severed my tongue while holding it with pincers . . . Man with veil cautioned Aaron not to kill me while severing tongue . . . My father, wondrous man, saved my life."

This euphoric response to Plum captivity and torture was peculiar indeed. Will viewed Dirck's behavior as akin to that of the Christian martyrs who found in all horrors the glorification of that which was greater than themselves: vileness is beauty, punishment is reward, death is life. I saw this equation then, and I see it still, as crackbrained. Dirck's remark about his father was the most peculiar of all, for Petrus Staats had died in 1835, fifteen years before these events took place.

Petrus entered my life indirectly upon the arrival at the mansion of Lyman Fitzgibbon, the merchant-scientist. He was the godfather of Dirck, the former business partner of Petrus, and an inventor of infinite and ingenious improvements on metalworking machines. He was also the father of Gordon Hamilton Fitzgibbon, who would become one of the most confounding figures in my life, an ambivalent man of prodigious energy and erudition, also a writer of sorts, who on this night was away at law school in Yale College.

I was in the foyer when Lyman rapped with the knocker. I opened the door to see this tall and muscular man with a full white beard, full head of white hair, and beside him his handsome wife, Emily, in a long gown of black satin.

"Who are we here?" the man inquired of me.

[105]

"We are Daniel Quinn, sir, and we live here through the kindness of Mrs. Staats. May I announce you to her?"

"A quick tongue on you, boy. I like that. Tell Hillegond Lyman has come back."

He had returned from Washington, where in recent years he had been serving in an English diplomatic post. London-born, Oxford-educated, Lyman Fitzgibbon had come to America at the age of twenty-six, met and married the wealthy Emily Taylor (her wealth came from shipping), and swiftly joined his wife's wealth with Petrus in the nailworks that would become an ironworks and then the largest stove-making foundry in the city. Lyman became an investor in banks, insurance, railroads, and assorted commerce as far west as Buffalo and, not least, a land speculator of grand proportion, the speculation generally in service of a commercial enterprise higher than itself. He would, by the mature decades of his life, be Albany's richest man, his vaunted power, when coupled to nothing more than resolute silence, capable of turning men of perfectly sound ego into cringing and snivelous whelps.

I led the Fitzgibbons to the east parlor to await Hillegond's appearance. Lyman stopped before Dirck's portrait on the east wall and spoke toward it.

"How is the boy?"

"He's recovering, but cannot speak," I said.

"You were his rescuer," he said, turning to me.

"I helped him in his trouble," I said.

"You're quick, and you're modest. You will go far in this world, young man."

"I thank you, sir."

"Don't thank me. Thank whoever it was taught you to be quick and modest. You'll shed that modesty in time."

I nodded, perceiving in myself not modesty but inadequacy, and wondering with what one replaced modesty, once shed. I

found Dirck and told him of Lyman's arrival, and went with
him to the east parlor. Lyman embraced Dirck, saying, "You
shouldn't have written that book, son. You know it was
wrong."

Dirck stared at Lyman, neither contradicting nor agreeing.
The knocker sounded again, and Capricorn this time admitted
Will Canaday and his ladylove, the handsome widow woman
Felicity Baker, a teacher of needlework and deportment at the
Albany Female Academy. Our spate of visitors on this evening
had been summoned to a musical soiree through which Hillegond
hoped to buoy the warped and muted spirit of Dirck. Long a
benefactress of The Museum, Hillegond had asked Dorf Miller
to choose among his current talent and provide us with an hour's
entertainment. Dorf arrived with pianoforte, violin, tambourine,
and banjo virtuosi; also with Joseph K. Moran and a young
woman I'd not seen before. Dorf introduced her as Heidi Grahn,
a songstress late of Sweden, and at the first sight of her, Dirck's
dark mood faded. He separated himself from his godfather and
entered into a fury of note writing: "Be sure she stays after
performance," said the first note he thrust at me. "Tell her I am
taken with her voice" (she had not yet uttered a note) . . . "Is
she married, betrothed? . . . Ask whether she enjoys poetry . . ."

I had no chance to do this, for by then our guests had filed
into the music room, a polygonal extension from an eastern wall
of the mansion, a semicircular room with mullioned windows
and an intricately carved oak ceiling that gave one the sense of
being in the apse of a cathedral. The guests besat themselves on
plush mahogany benches beneath a pair of murals painted by
Ruggiero and depicting the contemporary Staatses: Petrus and
Hillegond, whose peripatetic excursions in Europe (in company
with the Fitzgibbons) had been the source of many of the works
of art, and not-art, that abounded in the mansion. In his portrait

Petrus played a great gilded harp (which remained in the far corner of the salon, as Petrus did not), and the image of Hillegond ebulliently fingered the pianoforte, from which she was, in life, incapable of extracting even minimal musical coherence.

Joseph K. Moran saw me and waved from the front of the room. Our plans to do the tenor-to-the-rescue act for Dorf had collapsed when I became linked to Dirck in his infirm time, and well enough so, for Joseph needed no collaborators. His two songs on the opening night of *Tambo and Paddy* had engendered two encores, so Dorf gave him four songs the second night, engendering four encores; and even that left the audience unsated. The talk abroad in the city was that Joseph Moran would be a performer of great magnitude ere long.

"We meet again," Joseph said, coming over to me. "I have something for you," and he handed me a letter, the first article of mail I had received in my fifteen years of life. "It came from Rochester," he said. "I mentioned to a traveling actor your interest in La Última, and when he met her he spoke of you."

I took the letter in hand and at the sight of the handwriting the life within me gathered great potency. I knew the letter was from Maud, for in my possession since before she left were four words she had written on a piece of stationery in a near-perfect hand: "The sadness of bumblebees"—this meaning I knew not what. When I saw her throw it away, I salvaged and kept it.

"I'm very grateful to you," I said.

"We must keep track of our friends," Joseph said.

He spoke of my rescue of Dirck, said he adjudged me a hero and was proud to know me. He carried on in that vein, asking me questions as Dirck thrust more messages into my fist ("Ask her age . . . where she lives . . . what her religion . . . her favorite flower . . ."), and so, with my head full of questions and my hand full of scraps of paper, I had to relegate Maud's communiqué to my trouser pocket.

"What a grand house this is," said Joseph Moran. "I would like to live in it one day."

"Yes," I said, feeling possessive, "I live in it now."

Dorf set his tambourinist and banjoist to playing and followed their medley with an introduction of Heidi Grahn singing an air from *The Marriage of Figaro* that Jenny Lind had often sung, and in truth I know not how the Swedish Nightingale could have sung it more melodiously. Dirck's pencil fell silent at last, he in rapture at the sound of the young woman's voice, and I, at last, was able to open Maud's letter and read her salutation, "Dearest Daniel," at which my heart began a percussive thumping. My eye followed down the page, running ahead of itself too quickly to allow me to make sense of anything. But then I read these words: "am awaiting the fulfillment of your promise to steal me," and I could read no further, so rich was my excitement. Then the ecstasy was violated by a loud knocking that intruded as well on Heidi's melody.

We turned to the foyer to see Capricorn admitting, to my great surprise, a most serious-visaged Emmett Daugherty, and with him a weeping girl of perhaps eight years, a boy somewhat younger than myself who was tilting his head back and blotting his nose with a filthy and bloody rag, and a woman, the children's mother, in a state as wretched as womanhood can inhabit. The music trailed off as we stared at these representatives of a gravely negative unknown.

Emmett led the woman and children to a sofa in the foyer, then asked to speak with Lyman, who heard Emmett's request and rose from his seat in the music room. I followed but kept my distance, seeing Matty run to the kitchen and return with a wet towel to clean the boy's bloody face, take the old rag from him, and lay him full-length on a bench with his head back.

"It's a tragic thing," Emmett said. "Alfie Palmer, one of the moulders let go in the layoff, he did this to them."

"Why do you bring them here?" Lyman asked.

"It's a foundry matter, Lyman," said Emmett. "And it's your foundry."

"Does Harris know about this?" Lyman asked, Harris being the Yankee engineer who ran the foundry in Lyman's absence.

"I've no use for that man, Lyman. It's his layoffs began this trouble. Your good self is what's needed. None other. Alfie was always a hard-luck man, and with the layoff he had no doctor money when his son got sick, and he could only watch the boy die. It maddened him, as it would any man, and he took to the drink, though I don't know where he got money for that. And there's been fights—dozens—between the new hired men and the old let go, and Alfie in more than his share of those. But he went beyond a punch-up tonight. He followed Toddy Ryan home when Toddy left the foundry, giving him heat, don't you know. But Toddy's only the half-pint, with no health to him at all, and he knew if he fought Alfie he'd be killed sure as sure is, and so he ran to his shack and barred the door, but Alfie broke it in and split Toddy's skull with an ax handle. Then he went after young Joey here, and it looks like he broke the lad's nose. Toddy's wife throws the boilin' tea in Alfie's face, gets the children out, and brings them to the foundry to find me. But her Toddy's dead on the floor and there's no peace for it now, Lyman, no peace. Alfie's on the run and the men are in camps, the old and the new. They'll fight in bunches, and they're forming already. There'll be blood in the streets by morning."

Emmett, his craggy face overgrown with two days' stubble of beard, was a scolding presence. He was foreman at Lyman's North End foundry, and had risen in eleven years, despite his lung ailment, from apprentice to moulder to chief grievance spokesman, a voice of righteous reason from below. His rise in status began when he hired on as coachman for Lyman on an expedition to buy land in the Adirondack region for a new railroad line. Animosity toward the venture was strong, the natives convinced the railroad would before long destroy their pristine world (and so it would), and the animus peaked when half a dozen mountain men set upon Lyman and his lawyer with plans to tar and feather both.

While Lyman contemplated probable death by absurdity, Emmett garroted one of the attackers and bargained the man's breath for the two captives, an act of bravery that ensured not only his own security ever after through Lyman's gratitude, but also the education of any Daugherty heir not yet born, or even conceived, on this night of tribulation in the foyer of Hillegond's mansion.

Maud, I speak to you now of the Irish, knowing you are in my pocket, to tell you of the Ryans and their misery and how it distracts me, for it is part of me: Joey Ryan—with broken nose, dead father, sickly mother—is surely myself in another guise, just as Molly Ryan, that tiny waif, could be you. They are the famine Irish, Maud, and they are villains in this city. It wasn't this way for the Irish when I was little, but now they are viewed not only as carriers of the cholera plague but as a plague themselves, such is their number: several thousand setting up life here in only a few years, living in hovels, in shanties, ten families to a small house, some unable to speak anything but the Irish tongue, their wretchedness so fierce and relentless that not only does the city shun them but the constabulary and the posses meet them at the docks and on the turnpikes to herd them together in encampments on the city's great western plain. Keep them moving is the edict of the city's leaders, and with obscene pleasure the

Albany wharf rats and river scum (some Irish among these, preying on their own) carry out this edict by stoning the canalboats that try to unload newcomers here. It is no wonder the greenhorns grow feral in response, finding in this new land a hatred as great as that which drove them out of Ireland, that suppurating, dying sow of a nation.

Looking at the Ryans one could believe them carriers of any perniciousness: defeated, low in spirit, clad in rags, their skin flaked, pale, and dirty, their hair matted, their eyes raw with the disease of all victims. Who would invite their like? Who would give them bread or bed? None in this city today, and yet not quite none, for Hillegond is doing for them what she did for us: telling Capricorn to find them street and bed clothes; telling Matty to cook for, cleanse, and accept them on their night of trouble here in this haven for ravaged souls.

People are breaking into groups in the mansion, Maud. In the east parlor Emmett, Will, and Lyman are in dark communion. In the music room Dirck is boldly handing notes to Heidi Grahn. In the foyer Joseph Moran is extolling to Hillegond the virtues of her home. "It's more splendid than any house in Utica," he coos, and she receives his word as if he mattered. I want with desperation of heart to read the rest of your letter and yet I cannot. I am beginning to sense what it will say and I choose postponement until I have intuited your full message, believing if I am right in my intuition we will be closer than ever and this communion across the miles will be with us for the rest of our lives.

And so I have sought out the person with whom I have most in common: Joey Ryan of the bleeding nose—but bleeding no more—seated now at the kitchen table eating Matty's chicken soup and corn bread. I told him I was sorry for his trouble and that my father was dead also, and at least he had his mother with him, but that my mother was dead and so was my sister.

"You're an orphan, then," he said.

"I am."

"What do they do to orphans? Do they kill them?"

"I've never heard of that," I said, "and they haven't killed me yet. But sometimes they put them in orphan homes, and sometimes they let them run loose."

"I'd fancy to run loose," he said.

"I would too," I said.

"Run loose till I grow up enough to solve the man who killed me father."

"How will you solve him?"

"I'll break his skull."

"You aren't big enough for that."

"I'll get bigger and find him and break his skull like he broke me father's."

"They'll hang you."

"Do they hang orphans?"

"They hang you for breaking a man's skull."

"Will they hang the man that killed me father?"

"If they catch him they might."

"I'll hang him meself, and then I'll cut off his head."

Maud, the boy is a little fellow, no bigger than yourself. But vengeance burns in his eyes, and if he doesn't break one man's skull before long, he'll break another's. Anger took seed in him farther back than the clubbing of his father, as I learned when I asked where he came from in Ireland.

"From a ditch near Cashel," he said. "The landlord tumbled our house and put us off our land, and me father piled all we owned in a cart and we pushed it till we couldn't climb the hill. Then we lived in the ditch and used the wagon as a roof. We could see the Galty Mountains from the ditch. They tumbled our house to make room for the landlord's cows. 'They're in grave need of pasture,' the landlord told me pa. Then we left

the ditch, threw things away to lighten our load, and the three
of us hauled the cart up the mountain, a terrible high mountain
of four hundred feet it was, and me sister settin' the block at the
wheel. We done it at last and got over the mountain, but goin'
down the back side was near as troublesome as goin' up the
front, and we almost lost the cart two or three assorted times.
We begged food, and when we couldn't get any we stole it, or
we ate grass. Then we went to me uncle's place on the road to
Tipperary, and he took us in and paid for Pa to go to America.
Pa himself is all of us that went over. The night before he left
we had a wake for his leavin', with me ma keenin' for hours
over his goin'. 'Ye won't come back for us,' she kept saying. It
was near to bury him, is what it was. But he sent remittances
and got us all over here, me and me sister and me mother. And
didn't we all come to this town of Albany, because we couldn't
fit in New York in the wee room Pa lived in. We was here just
a few weeks and no money left when he got the foundry job,
and then, a little after that, they broke his skull, the man did,
the bastard man."

I talked more with him, Maud, but it was so painful I soon
left him and thought of going to bed, for I could find no one else
to talk to. People were all over the house talking of the coming
fight and how awful it would be, and I knew I would watch it
when it came. More death is what I thought, and that put me
in mind of the *Dood Kamer*, where you and I watched John and
Magdalena and Hillegond love each other, after a fashion, and
that was where I sat and read your letter.

Dearest Daniel [you began],

I write to you because a person named Joseph K. Moran has
said he met you and that you asked for my well-being, for
which I send gratitude. I worry, too, about *your* well-being,
for you know I consider you my true love for all time and ever
after, and am awaiting the fulfillment of your promise to steal

me away from my loving but inconstant aunt and her companion, the ridiculous John McGee. That man had the boldness to tell me you stole money from us, then jumped off the canalboat and ran away. I told him he was a poor liar and a worse scoundrel, and when I received the full impact of your absence I went into a swoon and as in the past I refused to eat, coming so near to death I terrified everyone. I think you would have been quite proud of me. A most peculiar thing happened in my starving condition. I could see what people around me were thinking, not an uplifting thing to be able to do. I also was able to communicate with spirits of the dead, or at least I think they are dead. They certainly seem to be spirits, for no one can see them, not even I. Yet they make violent sounds, of which everyone save myself is terribly frightened. I rather like their rhythms.

Please note that we will soon be in Saratoga Springs, where my aunt is to perform her dancing. I have assisted in some of her performances and may again, but will not now say how, as I wish to surprise you. We arrive in Saratoga May 30th, and I expect to see you soon thereafter, at which time we shall make plans for you to steal me. You have my love forever and a day, and another forever and another day.

Maud

P.S. I saw Joseph K. Moran perform in Utica and thought him an affecting person. Please thank him for putting me in touch with you. I await you, Daniel Quinn.

Maud, nothing in my life has been equivalent to the thrill of reading this letter. I confess I had hoped for a hint of your affection, but am overwhelmed by what you have said. I must add that your meetings with spirits and your plans involving me give me great unrest that I cannot solve of the instant. You consider me more powerful than I am. However, I will do what I am capable of doing.

Maud, I send you love.

Capricorn brought the news that the warring factions from the foundry were assuming positions. Lyman said he feared that if word of the presence of the Ryans in the mansion reached Alfie, he and his cronies might seek satisfaction of the bloodlust that was upon them. Before sunrise the call went out for all in the mansion to be ready, and so Hillegond took Petrus's pistol from its case, loaded it, and sat with it in the lap of her night robe; and Capricorn laid four rifles and two more pistols on the dining table. I could not believe we were anticipating that men from the foundry would invade this grand home to kill children.

As for Joey, he kept himself busy through the night creating a slungshot, a bludgeon fashioned from a rock wrapped in oil-cloth and wound tight with string. I saw him in an upstairs hallway flexing his creation cleverly: slapping it with thuds against his left palm. When I saw his mother, Margaret Ryan, and his sister, Molly, at morning, they looked no less affrighted than they had the previous evening, but immeasurably more comely with clean skin and hair and fresh clothing.

Dorf Miller and his company, as well as Emmett and Will, had left the mansion during the night. Lyman stayed in the room long reserved for him on the fourth floor—his aerie, he called it—which gave him his preferred morning view of the Staats woodland and creek, and of the pond Petrus built when Hillegond first became enamored of the wild ducks that inhabited the swamp.

By the first rays of the morning sun the tea was steeping in the kitchen, Matty was taking bread from the oven, and our cluster of souls was gathering near the warmth of the fire. The good feeling among us all seemed inappropriate with a death struggle in the offing, but I attest that thirteen years hence the same feelings would prevail in me when, as a correspondent in the war, I'd speak with soldiers and other journalists around a fire. We would drink coffee of the rankest order and convince each other it was fitting nectar for those about to conquer, or die, or both, or neither.

I must convey now that the fated stroke that aligned Alfie Palmer against the Ryans was an event of historical moment in Albany, for it defined boundaries, escalated hatreds, and set laboring men of near-equal dimension and common goal against each other. In years to come, periodic battles would be waged anew as a consequence of what was about to happen this day. These battles, which invariably took place on Sundays, when men were off work and free to maim one another, raged for hours without interference from the constabulary. The battles (the first was called the Ryans against the Palmers) were in time called the Hills against the Creeks, the Hills being the neighborhood to which Alfie Palmer, and others like him, had risen: high ground that represented a social ascendancy from where the Creeks lived—the low-lying slums, the mean and fetid nest of hovels on the shores of the Foxenkill, that foul creek where the shacks of the Irish erupted overnight like anarchic mushrooms and where the killing of Toddy Ryan took place.

Will Canaday returned after breakfast, and he, Lyman, and Dirck made ready to leave the mansion. I followed behind, and Joey Ryan behind me.

"No, no," Will said to us. "You stay here. Down there is no place for children. Take care of the boy here," and he pointed to Joey.

"It would be good for my education to see such a thing," I said.

"I want you alive to get an education," said Will as he and the others climbed into the carriage. Hillegond stood in the doorway as the carriage pulled away, and then called Joey and me inside.

"Come in where it's safe," she called.

"No," said Joey, and he broke into a run, following in the wake of the carriage.

"I'll get him," I said, and then I, too, was running, with Hillegond's screams fading behind me.

I COULDN'T CATCH JOEY. He was fleet as a wild animal, and more fit than I for such a run, which was two miles or more across open fields, down the gully, and over the footbridge that spanned the Patroon creek, then up the hill on the far side, where I lost sight of him amid distant houses. It was my assumption he would head for Canal Street, where he lived, and it was toward that notorious thoroughfare that I headed.

Bells welcomed me to the populated city, and I saw women and children walking—toward church, I presumed. People were also moving into a vacant field that began the long slope eastward toward the canal and the river. At the crest of the field I saw forty or more men below me, standing, talking, many with clubs in hand. I sensed what they were about and that they would not be likely to give allegiance to Toddy Ryan.

I kept walking south and approached Canal Street, with its creek coursing beside it. This was the neighborhood called Gander Bay, named after the sassy fowl the Irish kept in the Foxenkill. It was a place of dread and danger, of woe and truculence. Its dirt pathways, which became deep and pervasive mud when it rained, were narrow, crooked, and violable by the sudden erection of hovels that would force a detour. Many of these hovels looked as if they'd been thrown together in a day, an upthrust of uneven boards with no windows, buttressed by sod or raw earth. Looming up among them was the occasional giant of an ordinary house, half a century old, built when this was open space and the crowd had not yet arrived.

I'd been in the area before, but not often. It gave no welcome to strangers. In one of the big houses near the creek lived two old brothers, Dinny Reilly, who collected grease from neighbors to make soap (for a certain amount of grease he'd give you a bar of soap), and Johnny Reilly, called Johnny the Cats, who went to jail at cholera time for throwing dead cats into the Foxenkill. Johnny won his name by living with four dozen cats, and the neighborhood rhyme about the men was known to many:

> *Pitty-pat, sugar and fat,*
> *Old Dinny Reilly*
> *And Johnny the Cats.*

Children were running free, and women were doing their washing in the creek, clothes already drying on tree limbs in Gander Bay's early sunlight. A man sat astride a backless chair in the doorway of one shanty, arms folded, pipe in teeth, back stiff and straight: prepared for events. Around him lay half a dozen cats and I took him to be Johnny of the rhyme.

"Good morning, sir," I said.

"It's a good morning if ye think it is," he said.

"Do you know where the Ryans live?"

"There's Ryans the world over."

"A boy. Joey Ryan. His father was Toddy."

"Aaah, those Ryans. Ye'd best stay away from *that* house."

"I know Joey. I want to help him."

"Then folly your nose that way and ye won't miss it."

My nose led me along a dirt lane, soft from the previous day's moderate rains, to a turning where I saw a crowd of people, and above them the head and shoulders of a young man in sweater and cap, standing in a wagon, haranguing the crowd in vibrant oratory: "This what is comes of bein' an Irish workin'man," and he turned his gaze downward, then up again to the crowd. "A good man . . . alive with the family last night . . . then murdered in front of his children . . . Toddy Ryan gone today . . . who'll go tomorrow?"

The silent crowd was with the man, nodding its reverence. Children on the edge moved away when his pause broke their attention. A gray-haired woman in a threadbare shawl pushed forward, her hair tight in a bun, her jaw jutting out with anger.

"I knew Toddy Ryan," she said. "He was a good man and he deserves better than you're givin' him. Look at him there, shameful." (We all looked toward the wagon, but I could see nothing because of intervening bodies.) "Bring the man indoors and wake him properly. It's sacrilegious, this is."

"Ah, close your mutt, woman," said the man in the wagon. "They'll be after you next, and then after your children."

"Where's this fight you're talkin' about?" a man in the crowd asked.

"We start at the foot of Lumber Street," came the answer. "There'll be clubs there for all. We'll move in a body and meet the divvil himself if he's a mind to fight us."

Satisfied with the answer, the questioner nodded and moved away. Others followed him, leaving an opening that let me see the wagon. Toddy Ryan lay on three boards nailed together, tied down with a rope around his waist so he wouldn't slide off, the boards slanted to allow us full view of his final image: hands folded on his chest, toes of his shoes too long and turned up, ill-fitting clothes full of stains and holes—a runt of a man who, in addition to being horridly dead, had died in terrible health. His cranial cleft and the caked blood of his wound were the unforgettable focus of the cautionary tableau he offered us: here lies a dead Irishman.

The speaker resumed his harangue and some in the crowd fell away. But newcomers kept arriving in a steady stream, and I learned that Toddy, since daybreak, had been on tour of all Irish

WILLIAM KENNEDY

neighborhoods in the city's north and west ends, a traveling
theater piece: drama in the flesh. I asked a woman beside me
where the dead man had lived.

"Over there, isn't it?" she said, pointing to a board shanty. I
went to it and saw the door and wooden latch Alfie Palmer had
kicked in. I called Joey's name but got no answer, then saw the
interior was dark and barren, lit only by the light from the open
door, and on the floor a broken clay pot and rusty tin cup.
Whatever else of life's things the Ryans once owned had been
removed by scavengers. Sunlight shone across the large blood-
stain on the dirt floor where Toddy Ryan bled his profuse last.

I considered what I should do in this place, then stepped fully
inside, closed the door, and shut out the day. The room became
blackness of a deep order. I breathed the smell of earth and tried
to imagine the life of the Ryans in this tiny room, then tried to
imagine them living in a ditch with their wagon as a roof. Poor
as we Quinns had been (and we had gone weeks without money,
our food all charity from relatives), never were we dirt poor, nor
ever before had I understood the meaning of that phrase: to live
day and night inhaling the odor of raw earth. I felt like a bur-
rowing animal, and thought how the Ryans must have cursed
all things and people that had brought them to this condition,
and how they must have envied all who lived above it.

I stepped back into the sunlight and saw that Toddy, the
wagon, the recruiter, and his crowd were all gone. I followed
the lane and fell in line soon enough behind the wagon, the
recruiter now seated and holding the reins but still hailing
all gawkers with his spiel: "Hullo and listen to us now . . .
look here on the corpse of Toddy Ryan . . . killed for being
Irish . . . clubs for all at the foot of Lumber Street . . . we'll
show them who we are . . . we'll send them to blazes . . ."

We passed Patroon Street, several dozen of us now in the
growing parade with Toddy's wagon, and we moved north on
Broadway in the warming sunlight of the morning. I could see

the crowd of men looming ahead of us, twice as large as the group I'd seen on the hill. These were young men, mostly hatless and in shirtsleeves, vibrant in their gestures, anticipating the greater vibrancy of battle. A dozen or two smaller boys were fighting mock duels with the promised clubs that were being handed out from a wagon. I knew a few of the men: Walter White and Petey Carey from Van Woert Street; Midge McTigue, who had worked at the lumberyard with my father. I guessed that my father would have been with these men had he been alive. I could not find Joey Ryan but I saw Emmett, still unshaven, probably sleepless, and looking gravely upset as he grabbed two men by their shirts. I heard his words: "It's madness to fight uphill . . . madness to fight at all this way."

"Too late for that jabber, Emmett," one man said, knocking Emmett's hand from his shirt.

Emmett pushed through to the head of the crowd to yell to them all, "Don't do this, men . . . we'll have a dozen corpses among us before the day is out . . ."

One hoarse voice called out, "By the Christ, let's get on with it," and at that the men, numbering sixty at least, strode forward up Lumber Street, some of them pocketing stones as they went. And then came the rap of the clubs on the cobblestones in steady tattoo: rap, step, rap, step, rap, step, rap—this in march cadence, which the men's feet found compatible; and they moved to it. Emmett saw me, came to me, grabbed my arm.

"You're not in this, boy. I say you're not."

"I was looking for Joey Ryan. He's out to get Alfie Palmer."

"That puny little thing after Alfie?"

"He wants to cut his head off."

Emmett shook his head. "Madness everywhere," he said. Then he looked at the men moving up the hill. "I've got to get with them."

"Are you going to fight, Emmett?"

"Not if I can help it. But maybe I can do some good."

"I'll go with you."

"No."

"I want to see it."

"Then see it, but stay on the sides."

I had no animosity toward Alfie Palmer, whom I didn't know; nor did I feel it my responsibility to champion the cause of Toddy Ryan beyond keeping track of Joey. I walked with Emmett and we caught up with the men as they turned a corner. Spectators joined us: old men, young men, women and children—all on the run from other streets as word of the battle spread; and we moved like a Roman parade, marching the gladiators to the arena. The men kept themselves a tight body as they marched, but when they sighted the enemy waiting two blocks up Colonie Street hill, some behind barricades, their cries went up: "Kill the bastards . . . go now . . . get 'em," and they broke ranks and with wordless screams ran forward.

The Ryans, doing themselves no favor running uphill, ran into a hail of stones and paving blocks. They returned them in kind, but the Palmers, galloping downhill with the help of gravity and raised clubs, flung their bodies at the uphillers and felled sixteen into varying states of unconsciousness, losing only half a dozen of their own number in that opening charge. The smack of fists on flesh, the whap of club on skull collided with the curses and whoops of the warriors. Iron bars came into use, though the dominant fashion was the club, either of these tools cumbersome in close combat and some quickly discarded so as to allow fighting with fists and teeth, the battlers rolling and tussling into the proper position to gouge an eye, chew an ear. The battle opened itself and tumbled down new streets and into the pasture that sloped toward Van Woert Street, the growing mob of spectators ringing the fighters, moving with the most vicious, cheering them on to ever grander gouging and bashing.

There exists in the spectacle of a mass of men in fistic battle a love of punishment and pain, a need to be smashed in the mouth by life or else risk losing sight of what is necessary to survival. In the war I would see much worse, but I'd seen nothing before to equal the violence of this day: the ripped shirts, the bloody faces, the noses and ears bitten half off, the torn and bloody fists with their naked bones, men spitting out teeth, men unable to stand, one man shot but the pistol never found, a dozen men stabbed, two dozen with fractured heads, and some to die of these things and be buried in secret, one of the Palmers stabbed in both arms and never the same after. I saw Emmett remove from the fray the man who did that stabbing, a Ryan, but one not to Emmett's liking, and so he punched him, but once, on the side of the head, and the man fell like ten pounds of liver. Emmett took the man's dirk from his hand and rolled him down the hill.

Women ministered to fallen battlers, blotting their wounds, pulling them to safer turf. I spied a man whose face was the color of a ripe tomato, a scorch in full bloom, and I wondered, is this Alfie Palmer? The raw look of him just might have come from a bath in boiling tea. (How had the Ryans boiled their tea in that closed shack? I saw no chimney, nor any opening for one. Did they live amid smoke?) Such was Palmer's face (and it *was* his) that it could not have heretofore eluded me, and I concluded he was a latecomer to the battle. But that face was known, and when it appeared, it magnetically convened the Ryan lust for vengeance, Alfie quickly ringed by more men than could possibly reach him with club or fist. He knocked down two Ryans with his club before he went under: under by choice, I must now think, for what reasons other than guilt, or suicidal madness, could have compelled him to enter this battlefield of hate as a willful target?

He went down and felt the rain of kicks by Ryan brogans until a group of Palmers moved in for the rescue. But rescue the principal Palmer of the day they could not; for while other Ryans beat the Palmers back, a man all in Albany would come to recognize from this instant forward as Horse Houlihan, a lumber handler of immense size and girth, picked up the inert Alfie and, with great strength and unerring method, broke both his arms and both his legs, cracking each arm over bent knee, stepping on each leg and then snapping it upward, the reverse of its natural flex. The pain of the first break revived Alfie into a scream, but he then lapsed back into his coma and accepted the other fractures without a whimper.

The battle moved in splintered struggles away from the useless Alfie, the last of his reduction being the gob of spit Horse Houlihan loosed on him. And there he lay, a man of spoiled body and soul, a testament to what? To an incomplete understanding of the forces that had been unleashed through his loss of job and death of son; of even less comprehension now of what he himself had released with his random vengeance on the tragic Toddy.

Madness was insufficient designation for what had come of it, for what arose among the battlers was not pathology but something more conscious of itself: the final horrific begetting now blossoming in Joey Ryan, who came out of the crowd after the spectators had shifted with the flow. He found himself standing alone, moving slowly forward and then kneeling to perform with stunning malice the final coda of Alfie's saga: pummeling the near-dead face of his father's murderer with his slungshot as he shouted "Bastard man, bastard man" over and over, until I pulled him away and was, myself, struck by inadvertence with the weapon, no less painfully for Joey's lack of intent. My intervention came too late, for the slunghot had created bloody craters on Alfie's face and permanently blinded his right eye, a total blinding having been Joey's intention from the moment he espied the inert form.

I cuffed Joey and flung his weapon away from him, pulled him by the arm off the battlefield in the general direction of the mansion, and we left all Ryans and Palmers behind us. The Ryans, after several retreats, regroupings, and two hours of blood, finally routed the Palmers. Alfie Palmer survived to become the half-blind cripple of Arbor Hill, spent four years in jail after confessing the murder of Toddy Ryan, and lived out his remaining days as drunken beggar and infamous martyr to the unfathomable rhythms of rage.

Newspapers reported on the battle, calling it a feud between Papists and Americans, between the Irish and the Know-Nothings (who numbered in their political ranks the enraged nativists and assorted hybrid-haters bent on shaping a balance in this republic of equals by expelling the unequals). Will Canaday, in a departure from reasonableness, noted that a number of probable deaths, and an unmeasurable maiming of heads, had been effected in the battle, and he concluded: "It is not enough. Let them keep at it until there are no more of their heads to be broken." Will's view was widely shared, for it had been brought home to us all that the mob at fury's peak has no politics, no ethnic allegiance, no religion, but is a rabid beast with bloody claws, and must be neutralized.

On the Monday after the battle I went with Dirck to hear Lyman Fitzgibbon as he mounted a loading platform on the wharf of his foundry and delivered his gospel to the work force at the hour of high noon. He announced he would sustain the cost of repairing Alfie Palmer's bones but would otherwise leave the fool to his fate; that he would, with great heart, give moral and financial support to the widow and children of Toddy Ryan; that his foremen would hereafter monitor all comparable battles and would note, for purposes of effecting terminal discharge from foundry employ, the name of any worker involved; that he would write his will to encourage his heirs and assigns to do likewise; that he believed in his soul that we are here on this earth to court peaceful ways in the name of the good Christ, and may those who choose otherwise boil forever in the fluid caldrons of hell.

The silent men, surely not persuaded into pacificity by any such pietisms, began the antcrawl back to their furnaces, boilers, puddles, and moulds to ponder the vagaries of existence. Then, in this peculiar ironbound world under one benevolent God, the making of stoves was resumed, for now and forever, amen.

Lyman held forth later that evening in the drawing room of the Staats mansion, eulogizing Dirck, about whom, he said, he felt a certain guilt, but also recollecting with heartfelt agony the probable stirrings of Petrus in his grave over Dirck's book and the furor it generated in this city; for he knew Petrus feared that precisely such, as did, would occur: that Dirck would fall victim to the low pursuit of the word and with mischievous results.

Hillegond corrected Lyman, saying Dirck's pursuits were in no wise low or mischievous, but of a high moral order such as others rarely reach. It is true, she said, that he is peculiar and ill-clad (and she eyed my own attire with disdain); but Dirck was also kindly, courageous, and brilliant, and she was proud of him.

"Yes, of course," said Lyman. "We are all proud of the boy. Proud, proud, proud. But his father would have loathed the publication of that ruinous book. Didn't your son know that his father was a founder of The Society?"

Dirck promptly stood and wrote his answer at the inkstand under the portrait of Petrus in his senescence, wrote with unerring speed of quill, after which I, with rounded vowels, read his words to all: "Of course I knew. Masked man who ordered my tongue cut, and also ordered against my murder, was giving obeisance to power of Father's residual status in The Society."

"Yes, yes, yes," said Lyman, addressing his remarks to me. "But I'm suggesting you apologize on behalf of your father for what you wrote. If you do, I myself will resign publicly from The Society on grounds that this once splendid brotherhood's high moral aim has fallen into low estate, corrupted by latter-day scoundrels."

Dirck exploded into a furious quilling of counterthrust, then stood beside me and said through the medium of my voice that he considered Lyman "great man, great friend of family and of father, but I will never retract one word, for book cost me eternal voice, and what recanting will return that? Neither apology nor resignation will change Society, an evil needing violent overthrow." Then Dirck sat down in a swim of silent passion.

Lyman stood and shook his fist at me, saying he could not resign "without history's awareness that The Society was *not always* vile, and that *all* present members are not villainous men."

Dirck scratched out his reply and I read: "Well enough. Then *you* put Society in historical niche. Please reveal secret dogmas of yore that have led to crucifying of men and slitting of their gizzards to create pasture for rats. For I do not understand such moral evolution."

Lyman said that nothing he could say would reveal such progression, and that no matter *what* he said, "it would not clear the name of Petrus for having founded the local chapter of The Society. The words of Dirck Staats are required for that."

Dirck, dismissing this remark with a wave of his hand, wrote his conclusion: "Am not dead father's keeper. Nor yours either."

The sociality of the evening deteriorated with that remark and before long we took to our beds. All that had passed weighed on my brain, but shining epiphanically through it all was the face of Maud. With her visit to Saratoga approaching within weeks, I knew a decision loomed: one that would also involve my bronze disk, which had been recurring in my dreams. On this burdened and sleepless night the disk's face spoke to me in a pair of cryptic phrases: "Under the arches of love," it said, and then "Under the banner of blood," neither phrase holding intimate meaning for me. Only an intuition persisted that one day I might find the grand significance of this oracular object, as well as how it related to Joey Ryan and his slungshot, to the bumblebees in Maud's script, to the bleeding wrist of Joshua the fugitive slave, and to the exploding soldier's melancholy dust. The message emerging from my febrile imagination during these tumultuous days was a single word: "linkage"; and from the moment I was able to read that word I became a man compelled to fuse disparate elements of this life, however improbable the joining, this done in a quest to impose meaning on things whose very existence I could not always verify: a vision, for instance, of a young girl holding a human skull with a sweetly warbling red bird trapped inside, the bird visible through the skull's eye sockets.

In an earlier day I would have dismissed such a tableau as nightmare. But now I was propelled into an unknown whose dimensions grew ever wider and whose equal in spanning them I knew I was not. But even as I knew this I knew also I might never be their equal, and that remaining as I was, out of deference or timidity, would keep me ever distant from Maud. My life would then, I knew, fall into desuetude, like the lives of so many men of my father's generation, men who moved through their days sustained only by fragments of failed dreams, and who grew either indolent in despair or bellicose in resentment at such a condition.

And so, on a morning not long after the peaking of these pressures, I rode in silence with Will Canaday and Dirck to the *Chronicle-Paddle*, and when I saw the pair of them together in editorial conference beside the woodstove, I summoned the courage to present them with my decision, saying, "If you please, sirs, I think I must resign from this job and leave Albany." They regarded me with silent surprise.

"Leave for where?" Will asked.

"For Saratoga, to the north."

"I know where Saratoga is. Have we treated you so poorly here?"

"No, sir. I feel very happy here. Nobody is more grateful than I for what I've been given, but I have to meet someone."

"A relative?"

"No," I said, almost adding, "not yet."

Will sat down in the chair beside Dirck and stared at me with what I took to be incomprehension compounded. I believe he felt me bereft of common sense. "When does this departure take place?" he asked.

"About two weeks," I said.

"You'll stay in Saratoga? Live there?"

"I'm not sure."

"How long will you be gone?"

"I really can't say."

"Do you plan to look for another job?"

"I was hoping," I said, "that you would help me figure that out."

"Ah," said Will. "So I'm to be an accessory to your flight."

"I would rather work here for the *Chronicle* than anywhere else in the world. But I have to help this person."

Dirck scribbled a note and handed it to me. It read: "Maud?" I nodded and handed the note to Will.

"Then your journey is really a romantic quest," said Will.

"She asked me to meet her. She seems desperate," I said.

"Of course you're fully equipped to solve all the random cares of desperate young women."

"Probably not any of them," I said, "but I promised to try."

Will and Dirck then listened with mock solemnity while I spoke about Maud's life with La Última and John the Brawn. But the more I talked the more I saw how ignorant I was of everything about Maud except her desire to be stolen by me. I did not say this. I said in summary that I couldn't be sure when I'd return to Albany. At that moment I saw in Dirck's face his realization that he was losing his voice yet again. I had become adept as his surrogate, but surely others could replace me; and I couldn't say the same for Maud's role in my affection, or mine in hers.

Will raised the question of my disk and I said I'd leave it in his safe, but he said no. What if they burgled the safe? What if the place caught fire? What if he died? No. We needed proof of my ownership, and then safekeeping for the disk in a bank vault, in my name. As usual, Will was thorough.

During subsequent days my departure was much discussed, especially by Hillegond, who couldn't believe I was going off on my own. She stared me up and down and said, "If you are going to be an adventurer, you must stop looking like a crossing sweeper," and she summoned a tailor to the mansion to measure me for wool and linen trousers, dress coats (the wool coat had a velvet collar), two silk damask waistcoats to match and contrast with the dress coats, and a long gray frock coat for cold weather. She personally took me to the city for dress shoes and shoeboots, six new shirts, six cravats, two pairs of braces, and an abundance of stockings and undergarments. All this was topped off with a tall black hat that I thought somewhat silly, but that Hillegond insisted was the true mark of a young gentleman.

"I only wish Dirck had been like you," she said to me.

When we had done with clothing she took me to the stationer's and fitted me out with a writer's travel kit that included a writing box, a portable lamp, candles and holder, two everpointed pencils, a dozen pen points with pen, ink, and inkwell, and a roll of writing paper.

"Now you are a writer," said Hillegond.

"I think I will have to write something first," I said.

I came back to my room in the mansion, marveling at all my acquisitions. But one may be an acquisitor for only so long, and then the emptiness of it comes to the fore. And so I went down to the kitchen to see Matty and Capricorn, who had become my friends. I always wanted to hear their stories of Negro life in old Albany, and their tales of fugitive slaves, which sometimes were happy stories of escape, sometimes tragic with death and separation. I wanted to know what had happened to Joshua, and so

I asked them how he was getting on after his ordeal and where he was. This won me a profound silence and brought our talk of slavery to an abrupt end.

Two mornings before my leave-taking I was breakfasting in the dining room with Dirck when he placed a message alongside my plate as we finished our tea. I read:

Daniel,

Our society seems ever to be confessing its flaws to you, just as you seem to have been born to witness tragedy and to elevate people from trouble. I owe you my life. My banker is setting up an account in your name and will be here today to talk with you. You will now have an income for the next fifteen years of your life. By then you should be wealthy in your own right.

Luck,
Dirck

When I realized what he had written and raised my head in grateful wonderment, Dirck was gone. As good fortune embraced me, baleful new shadows fell upon the Ryan family. The young Molly erupted with sores and boils over her entire body, a disease of no ostensible origin that was finally ascribed to the terrors that had taken seed in her upon her witnessing Toddy's murder. Joey Ryan was set upon twice as he ventured little distances from the mansion, and one boy sought to pluck out his eyes. Hearing this, Margaret Ryan ran to Hillegond and fell prostrate on the parlor rug, cursing the enemies of Ireland, cursing America, cursing God and His mother, cursing the murderer of her husband and all his heirs and ancestors, cursing the curse that was on her and her children. She stopped cursing when Hillegond patted her head and cooed at her; then she sat up and swore she would leave Albany for a new place, swore it on the suffering body of Molly Ryan, on the threatened eyes of Joey Ryan, on the hate that lived in her own body and which was the blood, fire, and venom of her will to survive this hell of black devils.

Lyman Fitzgibbon rescued the Ryans from family dementia by finding Margaret a charwoman's job in a Syracuse orphan asylum, where her children could find haven away from Albany; and so one day they were gone from the mansion, yet frozen forever in my memory as paradigms of helpless, guiltless suffering. I sensed in the days after they left that a life such as theirs would probably not be my lot; that any troubles befalling me in later days would emanate more from my own willfulness or sapheadedness; that I was not destined to be a passive pawn of exterior forces. One exposes great hubris with such confession, but there was truth in my intuition.

On the day I was to leave, Hillegond supervised the farewell breakfast, for which she baked bread from an old Dutch recipe. Laden with cheese, raisins, sugar, and walnuts, the bread, for Hillegond, was symbolic of plenty, her parting wish for me. Dirck kept his farewell as brief as he could, but his handshake was as strong as a bear's trap as we separated.

Will, who had already given me a letter recommending me as a gracious, trustworthy young soul of plentiful talent and potential, an effusion of praise I was sure no one would believe, came to pick up Dirck and report to us that Lyman had sent him a letter, to be printed in the *Chronicle*, publicly repudiating The Society and resigning from it.

Will gave me his personal copy of Montaigne's essays, telling me it contained enough wisdom for several young men like myself, and he urged me to read it constantly and in small doses. He also gave me some agates of advice. Sitting at the end of the dining-room table, where Hillegond and I were eating alone, holding his hat in one hand and his walking stick in the other, he delivered his message to me in words whose precise shape I cannot reconstruct, for I felt terrible leaving Will's newspaper, which had become the home of my soul; and the thought of departure clouded my memory severely. Though I searched for those precise words all the rest of that day, my findings fell far short of Will's impromptu eloquence. What he said, as best I could reconstitute it, was this:

"Remember, Daniel. The only thing worth fighting for is what is real to the self. Move toward the verification of freedom, and avoid gratuitous absolutes."

I confess I did not know what he meant by the two final words, but which are exact, for I recorded them indelibly on my memory because of their strangeness. Will also added that I should be wary of marriage "before the age of comprehension," which he placed at twenty-five. "No man younger than that has any idea what women are all about," he said. "And while after twenty-five they have even less, they are somehow readier for the game."

His speech brought tears to Hillegond's eyes, for it made my departure increasingly real to her: yet another adventure of the heart taking its leave. She gave me quite contrasting counsel as to matters of love.

"I know you and Maud saw what happened on the night Magdalena came back from the dead," she said. "I did not see you there, but John did, and he enjoyed the audience. I won't apologize for what you saw, but I do say that life is never what you think. We seem to discover love in the most awkward places, and not always with the appropriate people. But Daniel, young dear of our hearts, love is better than wheat. Love is worth what it costs to find it, and I do know you've found it. I also know you know everything that I say before I say it. You are such a smart boy—smarter than Dirck was at your age, and he was smart as a Dutchman's thirst. I shall miss you, Daniel Quinn, and I *demand* that you come back as soon as you can and make your home here. Bring Maud if you like, and if not her, then another. But you have made yourself valuable to the Staats family, and you shall never want again as long as we live. God bless your good sense and Godspeed on your new journey."

I had my train ticket in hand and was packed and ready for departure well before the appointed hour. Emmett Daugherty came to pick me up, and said we'd have to watch the Irish circus before I left, a comment that confused me. But he explained that today was the departure day as well for the new immigrants: homeless Irish who had come to Albany to find life, and finding none, were being ushered elsewhere—driven, really, from the city by authorities unable to cope with the mounting cases of Ship Fever the newcomers had brought with them. It was widely held that fever could not prosper in open spaces, and so the immigrants were being sent to the western plains, where they could build cabins, and forage in the outdoors for their lives, becoming as one with the wilderness, safely distant from the fetid city, where fever seeds wax strong.

I embraced Matty and Capricorn in turn, vowing I would see them both again, then was smothered in my final enfolding by Hillegond and her abundant bosom, which made me weep with love for the woman to whose open arms I swore anew that I would filially return.

I climbed onto the seat of Emmett's open wagon as he threw my baggage aboard, and I turned my final gaze upon the mansion, its shrubbery, its turrets, its gables and conical towers, its sprawling porches and beautiful lawns of intense verdancy, its acres of bosky slopes, and that vast metabosky terrain I had always judged to be the Staatses' primeval forest, and along which their road coursed toward the city. All this I surveyed with saddened eye, for I knew that this time I was truly leaving, perhaps never to return, despite my avowals, and sensing in my most anxious reaches that this was all slipping away forever, even before I had begun to command power over its lushness. This was no longer mine, and I was to be alone on the road, a waif in gentleman's clothing, aimless and homeless, pointing myself in the vague direction of an even more vaguely defined duty to a stranger I barely knew but loved with unquestioning fervor.

I wept openly upon my separation both from the grandeur of this vision and from Hillegond's chest full of heat. And then, as I accepted the unknowable emptiness of my future, Emmett clucked his horse into motion.

And so goodbye.

We saw signs of Emmett's circus as we neared the railroad station: mobs of people being herded out of the city by constables and sheriff's men on horseback. I sat beside Emmett in his wagon and we watched them pass.

"Pay heed to these people and remember what you see," he said to me, and I remember him as vividly as the rest, his great wavy mane of black hair crowning him with handsome abundance, his eyes as strong as nuggets of iron. And so in memory I heed him as much as I heeded that troubled throng. Here came a man with two children on his shoulders and three more in tow, a woman nursing slung babies at both naked breasts as she walked along. The day was chill, but some men walked barechested, galluses holding their trousers, their feet in rotting boots. A man with a bull terrier under his arm had grown neck whiskers like a dog collar, his face otherwise clean of hair. A boy in a small cart drawn by a jackass played on the pennywhistle a Gaelic air I remember my father whistling, and naughty women with chemises visible and skirts flying threw visions of hip and thigh at men and women both (one of them eyed me), taunting in the Irish tongue all who watched the parade from windows and doorways. One man wore no shoes, his feet wrapped in cloth. Another carried a short club, the Irishman's gun, ready for impromptu battle. Men wore hobnail boots, hats of straw and felt, caps of leather and fur, tall hats, plug hats, sailor hats, vests. Women wore bonnets and shawls or nothing on their heads, sweaters, tattered coats, threadbare cloaks, long skirts. They carried brooms, and straw boxes, bags and valises tied with rope. Their stockings were rolled, their hair in buns or loose to the middle of their back like my mother's, some of the loose-haired ones loose as well with affection to the men who pawed and pat- ted them as they walked, those patters clad in tailcoats and knee britches with holes in the knees, men carrying pails and whiskey bottles and a small pig in a basket. One man pissed like a horse in the street, and an entire clustered family of six gripped one another's hands in fearful dignity.

Emmett told me stories of some of these people. He had been moving among them for a week to hear their tales, discover news from Ireland, help where and how he could. His concern for them was missionary: he had been one of them himself when he came here. His fervor to work for their betterment would grow in him with the passing years and affect my life profoundly. He told me of one man who stole a sack of horsehides, was arrested trying to sell them back to their owner and went to jail for it, leaving his family destitute. He told of a man long off the whiskey who came home drunk and singing and urged his sullen wife to sing with him, but she would not, and so he beat her with a crock and went to jail for it, leaving her destitute.

"They're lost, most of them," Emmett said to me. "And who wouldn't be? They've left all they knew, and all they've got is what they can wear and carry. But if lost it is, then some say this is the land to be lost in, for it all comes right again here. Would you agree to that, lad?"

I nodded my head yes, but I thought of Dirck and his absent tongue, and of lost Joshua and his fugitive life, and of the dead Swede who could no longer agree life would come right again;

and it remained to be seen whether the lives of the Ryans would ever again be other than a tissue of days with open sores.

"Look at them," Emmett said to me. "Study the face and the eyes and the gait of the walking misery that's come to visit."

They passed on then, the last of them, and Emmett followed their steps with his horse and wagon. Ahead we could see them climbing into the railroad carriages that would take them west, the carriage windows down, some wet wash and portable bedding already getting the air, the children barefoot and on holiday, racing on the cobbles and gravel, a snarling dog clubbed by a militiaman's rifle, a piglet dropped and running loose beneath a carriage. I scrambled under the car to catch it, but the pig could run faster than I could crawl, and it ran into the tall grass by the tracks, lost forever to the old man who dropped it.

Thirty-four cars they occupied, not the longest train I ever saw but the one whose memory is vivid still. We watched until they were all on board. A man of middle years, his shirt in tatters, a half-eaten chicken leg in his hand, stood alone on the steps of the train and began a song in the Gaelic, that strange tongue rendered brilliant by the man's plaintive voice. Silence came onto the crowd and we listened to the minstrel, I with a growing wonder in my heart at all the joy and misery that simultaneously commanded so many unknown lives. The train whistle interrupted the sound of the song but not the singer, and as the cars moved out, his voice reached us in fragments, audible between the whistle blasts, a fervent melody struggling to be heard. And then it was gone.

While we waited for my train Emmett and I talked of Ireland, and of family, and of my future, and of how I was always welcome at his home, which I well knew, and then my train was there, bound for Saratoga.

I boarded knowing, with every willful step, that I had once and for all obliterated the image of myself as helpless, hapless orphan, tossed off a canalboat like so much offal. Nor was I a greenhorn victim, not anymore. I still do not know why I knew this so firmly, but it was true. It remained to be seen whether fate would again ravage my life, but at the moment luck was with me, and I felt an extraordinary rapture, full of the music of sunrise. As I waved farewell to Emmett, I and my train moved northward with that same boiling energy that we had, at the dawn of the light, stolen from the gods.

THE DUMB CAKE

Saratoga

Spring
1850

WHEN MAGDALENA COLÓN stepped onto the stage at Utica, her first public appearance after leaving Albany, her overarching impulse was to tell the audience of her death and resurrection. But with John's words strong in her brain, she stifled the urge. What John had said to her was, "You talk of that and they'll think you're daft as a bloody owl."

By Syracuse Magdalena could stifle herself no longer. In a voice reverberating with all the humility of a heavenly choir's frailest angel, she stepped delicately to center stage and offered her thanks to God for resurrecting her from the dead. She told her story of the child at the bottom of the river who had welcomed her to the birthplace of dreams. She expatiated on her pleasant time under water in the land of luminous dolls and, with a great surge of her mystical wisdom, told her listeners they should not fear crossing over into death, because it was so attractive over there. "Also," she said, "there is always the chance of turning around and coming right back." She concluded by saying, "I can't imagine a more pleasant experience than dying."

She then went into her performance: a song first, then her famed Spider Dance, in which she shook off an attack of imaginary arachnids that were climbing her skirts and bodice, and in so doing revealed more flesh than was generally provided to American audiences outside of brothels. Alas, her report on the beyond had taken its effect. The audience tittered at her dancing, and her vaunted sinfulness was paled over with an aureole of humbug sanctity.

A Syracuse newspaper reported on Magdalena's disquisition:

DANCER CLAIMS RESURRECTION

The Spanish dancer Magdalena Colón, who calls herself La Última, performed for an overabundance of spectators last night but failed to arouse either the condemnatory or the lascivious reactions her dancing has produced in other cities. After evoking the Deity by describing Him as a small female child clutching a doll, the dancer spoke of her own experience drowning in the river and of being resurrected from death at a much later hour by the ministrations of love. It might be said of her performance that while it, too, perished, resurrection was not a consequence.

* * *

Magdalena, undaunted, repeated her tale to a Rochester audience. By then the word of her bizarre story, and not her sensuality, sold out the house. Hearing the laughter and hooting that met her remarks about resurrection, Magdalena swirled in frenzied pirouettes across the stage and fled into the wings. Witnessing this, hearing the hoots, Maud walked onstage and faced the hostile audience, whose derision subsided at her advent.

"Only fools and martyrs laugh at death," she said to them. "Which are you?"

She then asked the orchestra leader to play the music for the Spider Dance, and in learned emulation of her aunt she whirled about in recklessly flying skirts, her wild abandon silencing all hooters, and at length provoking them into cheers and long applause as the curtain fell. She took no curtain call. Backstage the wounded Magdalena embraced her, saying, "What a wonderful child you are."

"I'm not a child any longer, Auntie. No child could.dance as I just have."

"Whatever you are, Maudie mine, I love you."

[144]

"You needn't go on about that. Go out there now and sing your songs or the theater manager will deny us our money."

Thus began the stage career of Maud Fallon.

La Última, in subsequent days, experienced a falling off, an attack of despair that prevented her from venturing on to Buffalo. She stopped eating and faded languidly into a vale of melancholy.

"I have lost the voluptuary in me," she kept saying. "My life is a bore, and in boredom I shall surely die."

She did not say this to John McGee, especially when he was providing her with the only kindness he fully understood: the thrust of his pelvic appendage. She received his thrust with artificial passion, but such politeness also bored her, and so she eventually accepted John's largess in immobilized silence.

"You had more life when you were dead," John told her.

She arose one day from her passionless bed to perform the usual ablution, and the coolness of the water between her legs seemed to renew her spirit. The idea of the healing power of water, so capable of assuaging even the agony of death, preempted all her thought.

"I must have a lake," she said to John.

"A lake, is it?"

"I must lie in a lake and recover my passion," she said.

"By the Jesus, I'm all for that," said John.

And so Saratoga Springs, famed for its lake and its healing spas, famed also as a place where voluptuaries were as commonplace as clover, became the destination of Magdalena, of John the Brawn, and of that chrysalid creature of the future, Maud Fallon.

Upon arriving in Saratoga, Daniel Quinn bought a newspaper and read of the cancellation of Magdalena Colón's performance that night at the Union Theater. The brief story referred to unexplained noises in the theater during an earlier performance. Quinn went to the theater and found it closed. He went to the print shop where the newspaper was printed and confronted its publisher, Calvin Potts, a small man with a white pigtail, who was wearing an apron stained with a generation's worth of ink. Potts was working at a type cabinet, a stick of type in his hand, when Quinn introduced himself and handed him the letter Will Canaday had written on his behalf.

"A man of substance, Will Canaday," Potts said. "You must be worth a scrap of something if he thinks well of you. Did you ever set type for him?"

"Setting type isn't what I want to do," said Quinn, and he groped for the word that would define his goal. Editor? Not likely. Writer? Too ambitious. "I think just now I ought to learn how to be a paragraphist," he said.

"You'd best learn to set those paragraphs in type if you want to earn a living, boy. Words are flimsy things. Type is solid and real."

"I can see that," said Quinn. "But paragraphs are also real in their way. I've seen how they can change things."

"Ah, so you're out to change things."

"No, sir. I just want to write paragraphs and see what happens. I thought I might write one or two for you about Magdalena Colón, the dancer. I know her quite well and I saw this story about her in your newspaper."

"Did you read that about those noises? Folks think spirits made them."

"Yes. Magdalena is quite good with the spirits."

"You talk to spirits too, do you?"

"No, sir. I talk only to living people."

"A blessing if you want to be a reporter."

"I don't know where to find Magdalena, though."

"She's out at Griswold's place, but I don't know as they'll let you in out there."

"I'm expected," said Quinn.

"You certainly do come equipped," said Potts, and he told Quinn how to find Griswold's. "I'll look at your paragraphs, if you write any," he added, "but hold down that spirit nonsense. People want real stuff, not all that folderol about spooks."

Quinn nodded as he went out, not quite agreeing.

Calvin Potts gave Quinn directions to the home of Obadiah Griswold, the carriage and sleigh manufacturer at whose home on the shore of Saratoga Lake Magdalena Colón and her entourage were guests. Obadiah had become smitten with Magdalena after seeing her dance in New York, and offered her the run of his mansion, his stables, his vast acreage, and his lake whenever she cared to visit. In her melancholy period at Rochester she remembered Obadiah and wrote him, accepting his invitation.

Obadiah welcomed his guests with one proviso: that Magdalena alone occupy the room next to his own. He kept her constantly in his sight during the first days of her visit, catering to her every whim. Magdalena accepted him as an oddity, a foppish middle-aged widower who frequently wore an ankle-length robe to hide his bowlegs, a descendant of English Puritans who had long ago rejected all Puritanical inheritances. Anticipating Magdalena's early capitulation to his desire, Obadiah took her on a tour of his secret third-floor room that housed his erotic sculpture, paintings, etchings, and pornographic books dating to the dawn of printing. Magdalena relapsed into melancholy at the sight of so many erect phalluses and lubricious vaginas, and she retreated to her room, insisting that only Maud and John the Brawn attend her bedside.

Obadiah took up a vigil outside Magdalena's door and left it only to eat, sleep, and perform bodily functions, a gesture of concern that so bored Magdalena that she sent John theaterward to book her a performance as soon as possible as a means of escape. John returned, accomplished, but warned her the theater manager would brook none of her humbuggery.

"Just keep mum on what you found at the bottom of the river," John told her, "or he'll throw us all out in the alley."

And so Magdalena performed as she had prior to her death: a blithe entrance to the orchestral melody, several pirouettes of restrained torsion, then a medley of French and Spanish songs. She followed with her interpretation of a Viennese waltz, *andante*, and concluded with the Spanish tarantela, her spectacular Spider Dance, *allegro*—oh yes, quite. Hisses, hoots, wild applause, and huzzahs, the miscellaneous wages of Terpsichore, followed her performance.

On the next night Magdalena had barely begun her Spider Dance when a thunderclap shook the theater, vibrating orchestra seats, rocking the boxes, loosening plaster dust from the ceiling, and spilling oil from the burning wall sconces into running pools of fire onstage. Maud, standing in the wings, swiftly smothered them all with a piece of canvas.

Magdalena was convinced an earthquake was in process, but then calm returned, audience panic and screaming subsided, and except for a few who fled at the threat of fire, people returned to their seats. Magdalena signaled the orchestra to resume, and she began her dance anew. At her initial steps another noise erupted, smaller of force, but formidable even so; and then another, and another. Magdalena stood frozen, and the orchestra trailed off. The booming from above, fixed in no single area, seemed to be a storm floating free inside the theater. The concussions came yet again, four this time, and rhythmic; then three more, and rhythmic. Such noises were man-made, were they not? Earth had never quaked in regularized tempo, had it?

Magdalena knew only confusion in that moment, and then she saw Maud walking onto the stage and staring up at the theater's stormy ceiling. Maud clapped her hands four times, then three. The noise instantly echoed: four sounds and then three, all subdued in keeping with the softness of Maud's clapping. Maud clapped twice more, then once, and the source of the noise responded in precise kind.

"What are you doing?" Magdalena asked.

"I'm having a conversation with the noise," said Maud.

People in the audience began to clap their hands, but the noise would not echo them. When audience clapping subsided, Maud looked toward the nearest ceiling and wall from which the noise seemed to come, and said, "Are you a human being making these noises? If you are, then rap once."

No rap followed.

"Then are you a spirit? If so, rap twice."

Instantly two raps were heard, along with gasps from the audience and the swift exodus of the timid and the incurious. But most of the audience stayed, fully as transfixed by Maud's performance as was Magdalena, who atavistically blessed herself.

"Good Lord, Maudie, what's going on?"

"How many letters in my first name?" Maud asked the wall.

Four raps followed, and Magdalena immediately told the audience, "That's true. Her name is Maud."

"How old am I?" asked Maud, and thirteen raps followed.

"Correct again," said Magdalena.

"Now, how old is La Última?"

"No, no," said Magdalena, but there followed then a rapid series of raps like the long roll of a drum (forty-one in all) and the audience exploded with laughter. At this Magdalena shook the front of her skirt, exposing her saucy response to mockery, and won applause from the crowd. But from the wings came another response: the hisses and wild fulminations of the theater manager, demanding a resumption of music and dance. Non-plussed by the condition of life around her, Magdalena gestured her agreement. Maud shrugged, nodded to the audience, and walked off the stage. The orchestra resumed the music of the Spider Dance, but before Magdalena could begin, a thunderclap descended with more power than at first, swaying the chandelier in a dangerous arc and scattering the audience beneath it. The thunder clapped a second time, then a third, and more of the timid folk took their exit. Only when Maud walked back onstage and clapped three times at the noise did it clap thrice in return. *Lento*. Politely *lento*.

Thus began the spiritualistic career of Maud Fallon.

Throngs came to the theater on subsequent nights to hear the indoor thunder, but after three nights of only pregnant silence the crowds dwindled and the accusation of humbug again attached itself to Magdalena. She cancelled all performances and reluctantly retreated to Obadiah's lakefront sanctuary.

Four days after the first onset, the noise returned, this time at morning in Obadiah's plant-ridden conservatory–breakfast room. Maud paused in the midst of her shirred eggs and told the noise to mind its manners and not interrupt her and her aunt's breakfast.

The noise desisted but returned at midafternoon, sliding an empty chair across the porch and thumping lightly on its wooden back. Maud spoke to it in French and Spanish, and the noise responded in a way Maud found unintelligible. The following day the noise returned while Maud was in the kitchen talking to the cook and the scullery maid. She told it to go away and stop bothering people, and it exploded with a thunderbolt that broke four teacups.

Word of all this spread through Saratoga and crowds con-

verged on the Griswold property, cluttering the road and carriageway, many asking to see Maud in action. Obadiah posted
servants outside to deflect the crowds. He also invited the mayor,
the constable, two bankers, four judges, the head of the women's
auxiliary of the county orphan asylum, and asked them to help
define the nature of this visitation.

It was at this point that Quinn arrived at the mansion. Having
left his traveling bag at Mrs. Trim's rooming house on Phila
Street, he hired a cab to take him to Obadiah's home, his first
expenditure of money from the Dirck annuity. He arrived quite
the young gentleman, thinking of himself for the first time as a
journalist of independent mind and means, in debt to no man,
woman, or relative, and full ready to carry out the task at hand,
the nature of which eluded him utterly.

To the servant who answered his knock he said he was a
friend of Magdalena and Maud. The servant summoned John
McGee to establish Quinn's validity, which John did with a
middling smile and a lifted brow.

"Damned if it isn't Danny me boy."

"I'm no boy of yours, and that's the truth of forever," said
Quinn.

"Does he know Madame Colón?" the servant asked.

"He does. She knew him in Albany. We all knew him when
he had no hat."

At this Quinn doffed his hat and the servant made way for
him to step inside. The servant took him to Obadiah in the
library, where Quinn introduced himself as an emissary from the
newspaper of Calvin Potts. Obadiah instantly recruited him as
a witness to the proceedings upcoming with Maud the wondrous,
who could converse with the insubstantial air.

"Do you believe she can do that?" inquired Obadiah.

"I believe she can do anything she sets her mind to," said
Quinn. "I believe she has the magic."

"The magic?"

"Yes, sir. The magic."

Here is what Maud was thinking as she entered Obadiah Griswold's drawing room to face eleven witnesses, including one
woman who would make a body search of her prior to her planned
conversation with the voluble dead.

First came the vision of Daniel Quinn, whom she saw as soon
as she entered the room, he sitting there with a broad grin on
his young face, wearing well-tailored clothes, new boots, and
waving his new hat at her, the ninny, as if she hadn't seen him
the instant she walked into the room. She nodded her awareness
of his presence but refrained from smiling, for when one con-
verses with the dead, one must observe proper decorum.

Second, she had the moving image of a tall, emaciated man
riding a horse across an open field. Here is what she was seeing:
When the man becomes aware of the two carriages coming rap-
idly along the road he is nearing, he leaps down from his mount
and, at a run, climbs a slight incline. He halts in the center of
the road so that the deadly onrush of horses and vehicles will
run him over.

Third was her thought on the cause of this image, which was
a mystery, for it was neither memory nor dream, but a fully
developed panorama, even to the brightness of the sun and the
brilliant green of the hills behind the oncoming carriages. It
arrived in her brain in all fullness at the moment she saw Quinn
enter the drawing room of the mansion. Quinn was none of the
men in the image.

Maud nodded at Quinn and turned her mind to her inquisitors,
who all looked to her to be believers in the plausibility of conversing with a spirit. Maud felt lost in such a world of belief.
Her classics teacher in Madrid had spoken of enantiodromia; the

ancient Greek concept of running in contrary ways: believing in the unbelievable, for instance. Maud could not so believe. She believed in noise but not in spirits. Dead is dead, she believed. Noise came from the living. Minds were as noisy as the howling of a terrifying windstorm. Minds made noise: the collision of minds—hers, Magdalena's, Quinn's across the room, the ninny. I love him and his mind.

With her vision of Quinn came the continuing visual story of the emaciated man, who was climbing now to the road as the horses bore down on his life. The noise came then, rappings synchronized with the thudding of the horses' hooves, growing louder, louder, louder.

"Enough!" yelled Maud, jolting her witnesses in their silent seats.

And so began the séance.

Talking with spirits can be tedious, and so Maud quickly devised a code: one rap is yes, two is no, spell out the rest with numerical equivalents of the alphabet. The noise quickly understood this, and while Maud was establishing her rules, witnesses left their seats and sought out hidden rappers or rapping devices. They moved furniture in their search, kept vigil in rooms adjacent to, above, and below the drawing room, and they found nothing at all.

"Can you see this spirit?" Obadiah asked Maud.

"Not a shred of anything," said Maud. "But it is sending me pictures." And she told them of the emaciated man.

"There he is in the road," she said, "and the horses are coming at a fierce gallop. The man is facing the horses and won't budge. Now the driver of the oncoming carriage is veering the horses to avoid running the man down and the carriage wheel strikes a rock on the rough ground. The right carriage door, it's flying

[153]

open, and oh, a woman, a woman is thrown to the ground. Now we're on the road again, and a second carriage and pair are coming at a furious pace, directly behind the first. The second driver reins in his steeds and comes to a stop just where the emaciated man is standing with his eyes closed. The man is standing there between the frothing mouths of the second team of horses. There, now, there comes the driver jumping down from the second carriage. He grabs the emaciated man by his shirt collar and drags him from between the horses. He punches him once in the center of his face, and the man falls backward and rolls down the incline. Now I can see the first carriage, halted in the distance. The punched man is rolling toward where the woman was thrown from the carriage and he bangs his head on a stone. Oh. Oh, oh, oh, the poor woman is impaled through the chest on a protrusion of rock. Oh dear, oh dear. She is dead."

Here is what Maud and the spirit said to each other:
"Are you the dead woman?"
No.
"Are you one of the men in the vision?"
Yes.
"Are you the emaciated man?"
Silence.
"Was the dead woman your wife?"
Silence.
"Do you want to talk about this or don't you?"
Yes.
"Then tell me something. Are you the driver who punches the man in the road?"
No.
"Then you must be the emaciated man."
Silence.

"Goodbye, then, whoever you are."
Yes.
"You are the emaciated man?"
Yes.
"You're not proud of that."
No.
"You were trying to kill yourself."
No.
"Then what was it?"
L-o-v-e.
"Love. Pish-pish-pish, as my aunt would say. Love indeed."
L-o-v-e.
"You were chasing the woman because you loved her?"
Yes.
"And you tried to kill yourself because of her?"
L-o-v-e.
"Because of love."
Yes.
"Instead of killing yourself, you killed her."
Silence.
"Didn't you?"
L-o-v-e.
"Yes, I understand the motive. But you can't escape the facts. You killed the woman you loved."
THUNDER.
Long rapping on walls, floors.
THUNDER.
"It upsets you to hear the truth. I can see that. Did you kill yourself after this?"
Silence.
"So. You didn't. You couldn't. Am I right?"
THUNDER.
"Do you tell this story to many people?"

No.

"Why me?"

L-o-v-e.

"Ah. So you love me the way you loved the dead woman."

Yes.

"Then I'd better watch out."

No.

"Suicidal people don't care who dies with them. My mother was that way. She left me alone when I was an infant and when she tried twice to kill herself, I almost died both times."

THUNDER.

"Maybe you stood in front of the carriage because you wanted it to go off the road and kill someone."

THUNDER.

"I don't believe you. I think you're lying."

THUNDER.

THUNDER.

THUNDER.

And down came the chandelier, only inches from Maud's head.

"I knew it," said Maud, and she left the room.

Here is what Quinn eventually decided he was thinking as he watched Maud conversing with the spirit of the emaciated man:

Her frown belongs to the devil.

Her frown is paradise lost.

Her left eye sees through brick and mortar.

Her mouth is cruel with love.

Her mouth is soft with invitation.

Her lips exude the moistness of temptation.

Her glance will break crystal.

Her nose is imperious.

Her eyebrows are mistrusting.
Her hair is devilishly angelic.
Her eyes are golden beauty.
Her eyes are as hard as Satan's heel.
Her teeth are the fangs of a devil bat.
Her cheeks are the pillows of a kiss.
Her cheeks are the soft curves of abandon.
Her hair is full of snakes.
Her hair is a bed of warmth.
Her hair is a tiara of desire.
Her throat is the avenue to passion.
Her face is a white tulip.
Her face is a perfect cloud.
Her face is virginal.
Her smile is an oriflamme of lust.
Her smile is paradise regained.

Quinn, studying Maud's face as she conversed with the spirit of the emaciated man, wondered whether all her talk, all her responses were an effort to create a reality superior to the one she was living.

If so, Quinn feared Maud was a candidate for madness.

You cannot talk to spirits.

Dead is dead.

Maud's face is a dream that cannot be imagined.

Maud insisted on dining alone with Quinn in the gazebo of the upper gardens so they could speak without fear of being overheard. Together they left behind the witnesses to the séance, who were babbling with great verve. Maud refused to talk about the spirit with anyone, including Quinn. Instead, she talked to him of the decline of Magdalena into solitude, depression, and prayer of a peculiar order: asking God for the return of her lost lust, that electrovital force that made people pay to see her dance.

She prayed that when it returned she would no longer lust for men seriatim, for she was weary of sex and longed to give her body a vacation from friction.

"How do you know these deeply personal things about her?" Quinn asked Maud.

"She confides in me," said Maud. "She wants me to understand men."

"And do you understand them?"

"I don't understand what she has against friction."

"Neither do I," said Quinn, who did not understand why anyone would be interested in it to begin with. All it did was cause things to wear out, or break, or burst into flame. Even so, he perceived that Maud was learning things from Magdalena that he was not learning from anybody. Women handed their wisdom on to each other, but boys were supposed to discover the secrets of life from watching dogs fuck. Quinn listened to Maud with as much patience as he could tolerate, and then refused to hear another word about Magdalena.

"No more of that," he said. "I want to kiss you."

"It's not the right time," said Maud.

"Then until it is the right time, we'll talk about how I'm going to kidnap you."

"I can't be kidnapped now," said Maud. "There are too many interesting things going on."

"You mean like talking to spirits?"

"There are no spirits," said Maud.

"Then who were you talking to?"

"I don't know. I might have been talking to myself."

"You mean you made it all up?"

"That's a possibility."

"How do you do thunder? How do you make a chandelier fall?"

"I don't know. Maybe I didn't do that."

"Then how can you say it wasn't a spirit if you aren't sure you did it?"

"There are no spirits."

"That well may be," said Quinn, admiring how deftly he was getting back to the point, "but even so, I want to kiss you. I didn't move to Saratoga to be rejected."

"You're absolutely right," said Maud.

She stood up and took his hand, and they walked across the lawn in the early darkness. They saw Magdalena sitting under an arched pair of trellises at the entrance to the lower gardens, with John the Brawn and Obadiah Griswold both seated facing her. They could hear John say, "All he wants is a bit of a look. He's been a proper gentleman, and very accommodating, if I might say so."

"No," said Magdalena. "I can't be immodest."

"You can be the bloody whore of Babylon when you put your mind to it," said John. "Give him a look. Go on. Get it out."

Maud and Quinn watched as Magdalena stood up and, by the light of the early moon, and swathed in the shadow of a great weeping beech tree, undid her buttons. Then, holding her dress open with both hands, she allowed the men to violate her with their gaze. As she undulated her body ever so slightly, John the Brawn leaned back in his chair to take in the view of his eminent domain. Obadiah, seeking a more proximate vista, leaned closer to the subject at hand. Magdalena swayed on. Obadiah's right hand moved toward her *vestibulum gaudiae*. Magdalena backed away, closed her dress around her, and sat down.

"That's enough of that," said Quinn, and he grabbed Maud by the arm and moved away from the tableau, down the long, sloping lawn toward the lake.

"She's such a fool," said Maud.

"She seems to have a body that men desire."

"Men desire any woman's body if it's naked."

"Would you ever be naked like that?" Quinn asked.

"I can't predict what I'd do. I'm not ready for that. But I am ready to kiss you."

She stopped at the edge of the dark water and turned her face to Quinn's. Obeying an inherited impulse, he put his arms around her waist, thrust his face toward hers, and placed his lips upon her lips. They kissed, just as they had in front of the dusty soldier's coffin, with lips tight. Then, with the lips loosened somewhat, with tension rising, with everything new and the pressure of each kiss increased, with Quinn's teeth and gums turning to sweet pain, they broke apart, came together again, tight, loose, looser; and then Maud's lips parted and she eased the pressure totally, without breaking the kiss, and Quinn found his own lips growing fuller and softer and wetter. Then Maud's mouth was open, and so he opened his own, and here came revelation. He tasted her tongue. This so undid him that he stopped to look out over Maud's shoulder, out at the lights playing on the dark water, and to whisper into her ear, "This is a terrific kiss. This is the best kiss I ever had."

"Keep quiet and open your mouth," said Maud, and she pressed her lips again to his.

At this point Quinn fell in love with the secluded night.

Obadiah decided the only way to lay hands on the flesh of Magdalena was to dance with her. He could hold her hand, perhaps stroke her neck, or, given the proper gown, even stroke her shoulder. He could press himself against her bosom, feel the full whirling weight of her body as they moved about the dance floor. And so he arranged for them all to attend the weekly ball given by the Union Hotel.

A month had passed since the séance, and Maud's fame as a spiritualist had spread, fueled at first by a report on her behavior written by Quinn for Calvin Potts's newspaper and reprinted by

Will Canaday. Horace Greeley's *New York Tribune* sent a reporter to talk to Maud and to the witnesses to her séance, and
in time published a lengthy story on the "miracle at the spa." A
scout came to hire Maud for P. T. Barnum's museum of freaks,
but upon discovering Maud's lack of belief in the very spirit with
whom she had talked, the scout decided such skepticism was
commercially useless.

Magdalena received offers to perform in many places, and she
sensed a rebirth of both her passion and her talent for seduction.
Wriggling into the shoulderless pink dress Obadiah had bought
her for the ball, she counseled Maud on the display of a bodice.
"Precisely three inches of cleavage is proper," she said. "Two
inches is denial, and four is basely vulgar."

Magdalena insisted that Maud and John the Brawn attend the
ball, and Maud chose Quinn as her escort. The five alighted from
Obadiah's splendid barouche and moved with sartorial elegance
into the hotel's vast lobby, where fashion ruled tyrannically and
ostentation at its most fulsome was the crowd's principal pleasure. John looked overdressed in cravat and tailcoat, Obadiah
was original in black silk trousers and opera cloak, Maud virginal
in white frock, and Quinn felt brand-new, wearing, for the first
time, the gray dress suit Hillegond had bought him.

A group of men and women turned their full attention to our
group upon a remark by one of the women. "There are those
fraudulent spiritualists," she said in stentorian whisper. "We saw
them at the theater and nothing happened at all. They're all
charlatans."

"How," asked another woman, "are such low people tolerated
here?"

"Ignore them," said Obadiah to Maud and Magdalena. But
John had already turned to address the insult.

"If I was you," said John, "I'd keep that kind of talk to meself,
ya old pissbats."

A man whose brawn matched John's, who wore a full beard

and a dress suit, stepped in front of the women. "Hold your tongue, you pup," he said to John.

"Hold me fist," said John, and with the right jab Quinn had seen him deliver so often, the punch Quinn called The Flying Sledgehammer, John caught the whiskered man on, as they say, the button. The man fell like a wet sock, his legs betrayed by his devastated brain. On his back, the man found it difficult to believe such a thing had happened.

"No man knocks down Michael Hennessey," he said.

"This man does," said John the Brawn, "and if Michael Hennessey stands himself up from the carpet I'll knock him down again."

"He knocked Hennessey down," said another man's high-pitched voice from the crowd that suddenly surrounded the group.

"You knocked Hennessey down," said the owner of the voice, a nattily dressed runt who grabbed John by the hand and shook it. "You put Hennessey on his back."

"I see that I did," said John.

"Do you know he's the champion?"

"No."

"Well, he is."

"Champion of what?"

"Of the world entirely."

"Is that a fact?" said John.

"It's a positive fact," said the runt.

Hennessey was up then, and smiling.

"You've a grand right hand there, bucko," he said.

"I don't deny it," said John.

"There's damn few right hands like that," said Hennessey.

"There's none at all that I know of," said John.

"There's one or two," said Hennessey, extending his own right hand for a handshake. The two men shook hands and smiled at each other. Then Hennessey swung a left and caught John on, as they say, the button, and he went down like a wet sock.

"You see what I mean," said Hennessey. "They're here and there, and sometimes they're on the other fist."

John smiled and picked himself up.

"If you get rid of those old bats you're with," said John, "I'll buy you the best drink in this house."

"You're a drinkin' man, are you?" said Hennessey.

"It runs in me family," said John.

"What a coincidence," said Hennessey. "It runs in me own as well." He clapped a hand on John's shoulder and the two men went off to the bar, leaving the ladies and the younger folk to fend for themselves in this argumentative world.

At the ball Quinn and Maud danced all dances that required no special skills, since Quinn had none. They danced what they knew until boredom ravaged their legs, and then they sat. At this point, and with ritual avuncularity, Obadiah asked Maud to pursue a schottische with him, and she accepted. As she danced with Obadiah, Maud realized she had never been alone with him in the months they had lived at his house. She looked at him and saw a skull being abandoned by its hair, revealing bony lumps that had the fascination of a mild deformity. Obadiah was a creature unlike most. Maud thought he would be much at home in an aquarium. He danced much worse than Quinn, and he told her she was a remarkable child, that few in this world had her gifts.

"Such people as you make the world spin on its axis," he told her.

"You're very nice to say that," said Maud, "but I am not a child. I'm thirteen years and two months old."

"Well, of course you are. But in a way—"

"Not in any way," said Maud.

"Of course not."

They danced in silence. Maud saw Magdalena dancing with

[163]

Quinn and talking to him with her eyes closed, and jealousy rose up in her.

"There is a difference between a child and a woman," said Maud. "I can't say I'm a woman yet."

"When do you become a woman?" Obadiah asked.

"When I make love to a man."

"Have you chosen the man?"

"I may have."

"I presume young Mr. Quinn is the lucky one."

"He may be."

"If he is not . . ."

"If he is not I will find someone equally exciting."

"Yes," said Obadiah with a sigh. "Exciting. I'm not sure I was ever exciting."

"What an unusual thing to say," said Maud.

"What?"

"That you were never exciting. People don't say that about themselves."

"They do if they are me."

Obadiah was a uniquely homely and boring rich man, but his abnegation thrilled Maud, gave her gooseflesh. She said to herself: I love Obadiah. I love what shall not be. I am never what I was. I am always new, always two. I am, and I am, and so I am.

After Maud accepted Obadiah's invitation to dance, Quinn, obligated in the breach, asked Magdalena to dance. He found his feet not nearly so bored, and Magdalena floated in his arms. He told her as much and she told him he was a sweet boy. She apologized for John the Brawn's throwing him off the canalboat like a sack of oats. Quinn's newly assured self had already decided to relegate that event to useless memory, especially after watching John knock down the world champion, and so Quinn smiled and said of his canalside odyssey, "It was nothing. I just walked home and it was fine."

The dimension of this lie convinced Quinn he had a future as a confidence man. He'd always felt bound for hell, convinced of it by his early confessors, and also by his great maiden aunt from Ireland who told him he was "a devil dog if I ever saw one," when what he was doing—cutting his dead cousin's hair with his father's knife—was not devilishness but tidiness, for the boy's hair was full of nits and cockleburs. And what way was that to bury anybody?

"You are becoming a reporter for the newspaper, I understand," Magdalena said.

"I'm trying," said Quinn.

"I, too, write," said Magdalena.

"I thought you were just a dancer."

"Dancers have souls with myriad planes," she said. "Every step of the dance is like a line from a poem."

"I didn't think of that," said Quinn.

"I write poetry that dances."

Quinn nodded and danced on, fearing she would recite to him.

"Would you like to hear some of my poetry?" she asked.

"Oh, that would be fine indeed."

Magdalena cleared her throat and prepared to recite and dance all at once.

"The moon followed me home," she began, her grip on Quinn tightening.

"But a cloud covered it

"And I made my escape."

Quinn nodded and smiled. Magdalena needed no more.

"If a butterfly

"Turned into a caterpillar,

"Where would be the loss?"

Quinn narrowed his smile, spinning with Magdalena as he did so, wondering how to respond.

"Those are quite short poems," he finally said.

"I never write long poems," said Magdalena. "My longest was about my trip to the bottom of the river." She closed her eyes, straightened her neck.

"Four gleaming clamshells

"Danced for my pleasure.

"The mud fairies made me a shawl

"Of luminous eelgrass.

"I died of death

"Until the sword of the sailor

"Pierced my heart,

"And I ascended again

"Into the land of sorrow."

"Someday I must write about your poetry so people will know you are more than a dancer," Quinn said, shamed by his deception, pleased by his politesse. He wanted to be as honest with Magdalena as she was being with him. Perhaps he *would* write about her. She was a striking woman. He could even write of her body, of which he had had privileged sightings, in the *Dood Kamer* and under the garden arch.

"That would be very kind of you," Magdalena said to him. "When are you going to kidnap Maud?"

"What's that?"

"I know she's asked you. Hasn't she?"

"She told you?"

"She didn't have to. She's been asking men to kidnap her ever since she was eight years old."

"No."

"Everybody knows that about Maud."

"I didn't know it."

"She doesn't tell her kidnappers."

"She's been kidnapped before?"

"Never."

"I don't understand this."

"She doesn't want to be kidnapped. She only wants to talk about being kidnapped. That way she doesn't have to make any decisions about the future. When things get difficult she invites someone to kidnap her."

"That seems madcap."

"Yes, doesn't it?"

"Has Maud always been madcap?"

"As long as I've known her."

"How long have you known her?"

"Since she was born."

Maud Lucinda Fallon was born in 1837 of a twin and a tenant farmer, and distinguished herself at the age of two by reciting the Ave Maria in its entirety, in Latin. Her mother, Charlotte Mary Coan, and her father, Thomas (Thomsy) Fallon, both denied having instructed her, and both claimed utter ignorance of Latin.

Maud began a diary at age four and filled notebooks with poetic language her parents could understand only marginally. The source of her gift was made suspect by the parish priest in Athlone and her writing was not encouraged. When she was five her notebooks were sent to a schoolmaster for evaluation and Maud never saw them again.

Maud's life lost what little formal structure it had when her father joined a tenant farmers' rebellion and was arrested and shipped to an English prison. He escaped en route and found his way to Canada, from where he sent money back to Charlotte, a young woman of spirit, whose gift was for music and dance.

Charlotte, in short order, took herself and her child to Dublin, resolving to wrench them both up from the depths into which Thomsy Fallon's arrest had plunged them.

Charlotte joined a traveling theater company, became its principal dancer, the lover of two of its actors, and by the time the troupe reached England, she was its sensual public flower. From London she was whisked to Paris by a plutocrat in the July monarchy of Louis Philippe, changed her name to Lila Márquez to distinguish herself from the French, and was kept in circumstances proper to her burgeoning ambition.

Maud grew to be an encumbrance on her mother's *vie amoureuse*, and so Charlotte-Lila sent the child to Spain to live with Maud's aunt (and Charlotte's twin), Magdalena Colón, that surname a gift from her most recent late husband. Like the intrepid general who refuses to die in battle but is thwarted in the charge by having his horses repeatedly shot from under him, Magdalena had bid farewell to three husbands at graveside and was on the brink of acquiring a fourth when Maud arrived in Spain and changed her life, generating in it the wise child's mystery, and giving Magdalena new vistas beyond sensuality and security.

While Charlotte-Lila abandoned the Parisian plutocracy to pursue the devil amid the royal resplendency of Bavaria, Magdalena imposed tutors, dancing masters, and dolls on the five-year-old Maud, who became trilingual in a trice, and at six could also emulate her aunt Magdalena in the flamenco and the tarantela (which Magdalena had learned from a Zincali Gypsy queen).

In 1848, as revolution swept through Europe, Magdalena saw her fortunes fading in Spain and, upon the advice of a cosmopolitan lover, turned her attention to the United States of the New World, a nation only moderately cultured and given to irrational frenzies toward beautiful dancing females.

And so it came to pass in the summer of 1849 that Magdalena, known as La Última after the death of her third husband, arrived at New York with serving maid and Maud, now twelve, and began a theatrical tour that included a capsizing and sudden death in the icy river at Albany, a spiritual communion in Saratoga, a reluctant companionship with John McGee (a well-hung lout), an empty dalliance with Obadiah Griswold (a generous fool), and a dance in the arms of Daniel Quinn (a boy of compelling charm).

Maud, witness to this, adolescent savant-seer, child of the emotional wilderness, discovered one night in Obadiah's mansion at Saratoga the presence of bloodstains on her bedsheet and fell instantly into raptures at their significance, judging them to be the geography of a long-awaited unknown. She sought counsel from Magdalena in coping with the flow.

"Well, Maudie, it's about time," said Magdalena. "Your body is several years late in catching up with your mind, but here you are, at last. Maybe now you'll understand what your auntie is all about."

Poor Quinn. Consider him. He saves a life, discovers love, finds it reciprocated, is obsessed and rightfully so, alters his life to yield to his obsession, finds worlds beyond worlds that he cannot understand, finds the object of his obsession to be madcap, takes her home, kisses her, all but swoons with confounded desire, goes to his rooming house, fails to sleep, rises, lights his writing lamp, plucks from his writing case his pointless pen, finds a point, imposes it upon the pen, unrolls his paper, uncaps his inkwell, poises his pen above the well with the intention of wetting the point and writing, refrains from dipping because his condition allows no clarity of thought, puts down the pen, paces up and down in his bedchamber, takes up his collection of Montaigne's essays, opens it, and finds two passages underlined: "What causes do we not invent for the misfortunes that befall us? What will we not blame, rightly or wrongly, that we may have something to fight with?" and also this: "And we see that the soul in its passions is wont to cheat itself by setting up a false and fanciful object, even against its own belief, rather than not have something to act upon," and piqued by this, turns back to the beginning of the essay, which is called "How the Soul Relieves Its Feelings on the Wrong Objects, When the Real Are Wanting," reads it through, then resumes his pacing, considering the current state of love, of men and women, of his life past and future, wondering what will become of himself, a novice in all things, now that he is lost to love and probably about to set out in several wrong directions, linked as he is to a radical child, a deluded poetaster, and John McGee, a scurvy bastard, but who did knock down Hennessey with Quinn as a witness, and at that memory Quinn picks up his pen, dips it in his ink, and writes one sentence: "They call him John the Brawn and he doesn't know enough to pull his head in when he shuts the window, but he knocked down the best fighter in the world," and having written that, puts down his pen, smiles, walks up and down the bedchamber, and understands that he has just changed his life.

Quinn's mood elevated once he discovered his control over the word. He envisioned a thrilling future for himself, sitting alone in hotel rooms, ruminating on epic events, then imposing his conclusions on paper for the world to read in the morning newspaper. He felt a surge of power and also vague intimations of wealth. He made plans to hire a carriage and take Maud to the High Rock, the Iodine, and the Empire Springs, whose multiple chlorides, bromides, sulphates, phosphates, and bicarbonates of magnesia, iron, soda, strontia, and lime had been vitalizing and restoring the health of multitudes since the age of the Indian, most notably the health of the "high livers," whose love of good food, abundant drink, and nocturnal revels was a proven ravagement. Quinn did not consider himself a high liver, but he intuited that he might become one; and Maud, too, though of a different order. Quinn's intuitions about Maud had all the fixity of a cloud in high winds.

Quinn's plan was this: hire the open carriage, promenade through the city to the springs, stop at an appropriate place for tea, and, while the carriage waited, stroll with Maud through the first available park, lead her into a wooded grove, throw your arms about her, kiss her passionately with lip and tongue, declare your eternal love for her face, her form, her brain, her soul.

Upon Quinn's invitation to an outing at the springs, Maud brooded on the uncertainties that had been keeping her wakeful during recent nights. Most disturbing was the dream that had arrived after her talk with the emaciated man. Walking by a lake she saw a living, pulsating, disembodied eye sitting on a large rock. The eye was her own and when she reached for it to put it back in its socket it slithered through her fingers into the sand. She cupped it in the palms of her hands and as she lowered it into the water to rinse it, the eye swiftly melted into corrupt slime.

Maud read this as an omen of confusion, especially in regard to Quinn. It was true that only he and she would do each other justice in this life. But what but a proper botch would they make of an adolescent marriage? It was a peasant dream, laughable. Furthermore, Maud was mutating: communicating with herself through the techniques of Mesmer, willing herself into states that were alien to her waking self. Become a loveless Japanese wife, she would tell herself. Become a sibyl in the Delphic mode.

Become a child of slaves at the auction block. Become an actress who works with Shakespeare himself. She would allow herself to pass hours of waking and sleeping in these foreign moods, and come away from them only reluctantly, and with written messages she could not reconcile. "The sadness of bumblebees and the longitude of pity exist only for lovers," she wrote to herself. This poetic turn she found to be at odds with her pragmatic self, and pleasingly so. But her ability to communicate with the emaciated man was a disturbing extension of the condition, for it existed outside what she deemed the realm of the possible. She therefore disbelieved it, albeit hollowly: full of mocking echoes.

I must decide what to do about Quinn, Maud told herself, and so she fasted for the rest of the day, then set about making a dumb cake, as Magdalena's Zincali Gypsy had taught her. She waited until Obadiah's household was asleep and then in the kitchen she created her cake from eggs, salt, flour, and water in which she had lightly bathed her privities. She sat in silence with her back to the stove until it was time to take out the cake. She then revealed her breasts to the cake, covered herself, drew her initials with a knife on the top of the cake, and set it on the hearthstone in front of Obadiah's drawing-room fireplace. She opened the front door of the house and left it ajar, sliced out a small piece of the cake for herself, and walked backward with it up the stairs to her room.

She put the piece of cake on her bedside stand, took off her dress, and unbuttoned her underclothing. She then ate the cake while standing, awaiting the spectral double of the man she would marry to enter the drawing room, carve his own initials on the cake downstairs, and perhaps then come up the stairs to pursue her with phantom hands. The loosening of her shift would allow her to free herself from such a grasp. He might get her underclothing, but not her. She would fall upon the bed at such an attempt, thus banishing him from the house.

The charm drugged her into sleep, and upon waking, and after inspecting the cake on the hearth at morning, she dressed herself and awaited the arrival of Quinn and his carriage.

Quinn walked through the village streets with Maud, envying the behavior of other strolling couples, all of whom seemed to be either in complacent love or in varied stages of flirtation. None seemed to exude the intensity of what he himself felt, and yet he could not touch Maud, not even her hand with his fingertips. Nor could he take hold of her arm to guide her; and so they walked as strangers along the grass-trimmed sidewalks, out of the area of stores, shops, hotels, and onto a street of stately homes and private gardens. At a wooded area past the last of the homes, Quinn stopped to regard the residue of a careless pic-nic: bits of bread, a strew of paper, a chicken bone, the core of an apple, a cork, a cigar butt, a woman's handkerchief with a hole burned in it. An irrational sadness overtook Quinn.

"Look at that mess," he said, shaking his head.

"The remnants of beauty," said Maud, nodding.

Quinn and Maud were entering a new condition. Despairing of more intimate conversation, Quinn told her of a story he was writing about John the Brawn and that Calvin Potts was interested in printing in his newspaper.

"You will be very good at what you do," Maud said. "I myself am riding horses again for the first time since we lived in Spain. Obadiah has wonderful horses."

"I've never been on the back of a horse," Quinn said.

"It's a majestic experience," said Maud.

Quinn nodded, uncertain of the meaning of "majestic," and how riding a horse could be conducive of that.

"We ought to walk through the woods," Quinn said, and in a gesture that defied the static present tense of his life he grabbed

Maud's hand and stepped over the pic-nic leavings and onto a path that led he knew not where.

"You want me to walk in the woods?" said Maud.

"Are you so delicate?"

"I'm not at all delicate."

"Then we'll go into the woods," said Quinn. "I don't like what's been going on with you today."

"Nothing has been going on with me."

"Nothing indeed, and more nothing. What I expect from you is something. I expect you to love me as I love you. I expect you to want to kiss me and hold me as I want to kiss and hold you." Quinn thought he might have stolen this line from a poem.

"Yes," said Maud. "I understand that. But what happened is that I spent the night baking a dumb cake to find out how to behave with you."

"Why would you bake a dumb cake? Why wouldn't you bake a smart cake if you wanted to know something?"

"All cakes are dumb."

"I think I always knew that."

"The true dumb cake helps you discover who will be your husband."

"Ah, I see," said Quinn. "More spirits."

"If you like."

"What do you do with a dumb cake after it's baked?"

"You put your initials on it, you eat some of it, and you wait for your future husband's double to come and also put his initials on it."

"And that's it?"

"No," said Maud, and she paused. "You also show your breasts to it."

"You show your breasts to a cake?" said Quinn.

"That's part of the ritual."

"It would make more sense if you showed your breasts to me, if I'm going to be your husband."

"My breasts are too small to show to anyone. Especially you."

"Am I so much less than a cake?"

"It's not less or more, you ninny. It's what must be. I didn't invent this ritual."

"I'm glad to hear that," said Quinn, and he grabbed her hand and pulled her along. Suddenly he stopped and threw his arms around her and kissed her with lip and tongue, but could say nothing. He finished his kissing and pulled her toward the street.

"Your face is very rough," Maud said to him, stumbling along behind him. "You should shave."

"I don't shave," Quinn said. "People who are lower than cakes don't have to shave."

"You're not lower than a cake, Daniel," said Maud. "You don't understand my situation, and you don't understand me."

"It's true I don't."

"If you shave I'll tell you everything."

"Then we'll go to the barber right now."

"No, we'll go back to Obadiah's. I'll get you John's razor."

"I don't know how to use a razor. I'd cut off my nose."

"Of course you wouldn't. If a primitive like John McGee can use a razor, so can you."

"John also knows how to use his fists and knock out the champion of the world, and I don't know how to do that."

"Then it's time you learned," Maud said, stepping up into their hired carriage.

Quinn stood before the mirror of the shaving stand in an upstairs bathroom and looked at himself. His shirt was hidden under the towel Maud had tucked into his collar. She had fetched all of John's shaving gear: soft-bristle brush, mug of soap, bone-handled straight razor, also a jar of alum to cauterize cuts—medical wisdom she had come by while watching John shave. Maud opened the razor and put it in Quinn's hand.

"You know how it's done, don't you?" she asked.

"Of course I know how it's done. I saw my father shave a thousand times."

"Well, don't cut yourself in any vital spots. Go careful till you get the knack of it."

"I don't need to be told."

"Then I shall tell you no more for now. Ta ta."

And she left.

Quinn touched the razor to his right cheek, a fly's weight on the skin, and moved it gently downward. Some of the dry, soapless stubble gave way before the razor's formidably sharp edge, but with the pain of snagged hair. The truth was that Quinn had never seen his father shave. The man wore a beard. Quinn now looked at John's brush and soap as hostile objects, for if you cover your face with soap how will you see what you're supposed to cut? He continued his dry shave. It hurt. Still, he had not gouged himself. He pressed on. It hurt.

Eck.

A cut.

Reluctantly he wet his face and soaped one side of it and around the mouth, making small dabs with the brush, using the circular motion he remembered from watching a barber work. He moved his lower jaw to the left and puckered his lips as he lathered his right cheek, moved jaw to the right and made opposite pucker when lathering left. With his first finger he wiped his lips clean of soap, picked up the razor and began anew the elimination of his downy whiskers. Blood was coloring the soap on his cheek, but he tried not to watch. He shaved on.

Eck.

Another cut. More blood.

He pressed on, carefully, learning to let the razor glide over his skin, shearing the whiskers with newfound ease as the blood flow intensified. He finished, rinsed his face in the now pink water, then set about applying alum to the cuts as Maud had instructed him. His blood stopped leaking but he felt new pain from the alum's stypticity. He dried his face and stared at himself in the mirror. He concluded he would have to shave regularly from now on, a relentless obligation. He would, in spite of all, develop an awesome talent for shaving himself. He could feel that. He would be very good at what he did. Maud had predicted that.

Life does seem to conspire against the lofting of the spirit, does it not? Quinn came down clean-shaven from the bathroom and looked for Maud. He asked the footman if he'd seen her and the man said he had not.

Quinn went to the veranda and sat in the largest wicker rocker in North America. In the waning sunlight of the afternoon he mused on beauty, wealth, women, and the brilliance of the person who had invented shaving soap. He studied the architecture of Obadiah's veranda with its twisted columns and the perfection of its paint, which seemed ever new. He relished the rolling symmetry of the lawn and gardens, the trellises and arches, the beds of roses and lush stands of mature trees. He felt a profound serenity overtaking him and he began to doze. He was awakened by the footman, who asked if he cared for tea. Obadiah had seen him napping and thought the tea might brace him. Quinn smiled and said yes, tea would be pleasant.

He rocked, no longer worrying where Maud might be. He knew she would be along, probably in a new dress, or in a peculiar costume, or with a new hairdo. Whatever her look, her mood would be the reverse of what it had been when they parted. She would be effusive, flirtatious. She would open her mouth and pretend to kiss him. She would tell him stories of old Spain, or of majestic horseback riding, or of her mother and the King, or she would reveal arcane secrets of love that Magdalena had passed on to her.

Quinn equated Maud with his Celtic potato platter: both of them agents of change and illusion, both of uncertain origin and significance—the platter waiting underground for another generation to unearth it, quantifying its own value and mystery in the shallow grave; and Maud propounding mysteries of the cosmos with every Maudbreath. Buried, they eluded. Resurrected, they grew lustrous.

The footman brought tea and cucumber sandwiches. Quinn apologized for not liking cucumbers and asked was there an alternative. The footman said he would speak with the cook, and returned with caviar canapés, diced celery, and raw peppers. Quinn tasted and loathed each in turn, an awareness dawning in him that something was amiss. It was unlikely that so many foods chosen by a chef should all displease him. Negative matter was being imposed on him. He wondered if Maud's spirits were stalking him. He saw dusk settling on Obadiah's landscape and imagined himself starving to death while the footman brought him an unending stream of food samplers: lamb's eyes and bull's testicles, goat fritters and fried pigskin. These would be perfectly cooked, elegantly offered. Quinn would reject each, and passersby would soon notice his weight loss.

Obadiah sat down in the rocker next to him.

"Enjoying yourself?" Obadiah asked.

"I enjoyed the tea, but I wonder what's keeping Maud."

"No one has seen her since last night. She's not in her room."

"I was with her today. We took a carriage ride and came back here so I could shave with John McGee's razor. I sat here to wait for her. She's a girl of a different sort."

"A different sort exactly," said Obadiah. "No one has seen her since last night."

"I was with her today. We took a carriage ride."

"If you say so."

"What do you mean, if I say so?"

"Well, you're a young lad."

"I *was* with her."

"If you say so."

"I do," said Quinn.

"A horse is missing. From the stable."

"A horse?"

"One of my horses. A horse."

"Where did it go?"

"Well, that's certainly a question. Where *did* it go?"

"Do you think Maud took the horse?"

"It's been suggested."

"Maud wouldn't steal a horse."

"Perhaps she's only out riding. But she's been gone since last night and so has the horse, and no one has seen either one of them."

"I have. I was with her today. We took a carriage ride."

"So you've said. That's quite extraordinary. But no one has seen her since last night."

"I have. We took a carriage ride."

"I think you should stop saying that."

"It's the truth."

"It's your truth. It's certainly not my truth. I wasn't out for a ride with anybody today."

"I didn't say you were."

"But you keep contradicting me. The fact is that no one wants you around here. You come in and use the razor and sit on the veranda and reject my food and now you tell me I'm a liar."

"I didn't say that. Where is Maud, anyway?"

"We would all prefer it if you went somewhere else and asked your questions."

"I want to see Maud."

"You'll have a long wait. She's run away with my roan stallion."

"She knew I was waiting for her."

"She took her bag."

"She took her bag?"

"No one has seen her since last night."

"I have. Where is Magdalena? Where is John?"

"They don't want to see you. You better go along now, like a good fellow. My carriage will take you to the village."

"How do I know Maud is gone?"

"No one has seen her since last night."

"I have, we took a carriage ride."

Obadiah stood up. Quinn resisted standing, but here was the man ejecting him from his home. Quinn stood.

Two days later he returned and asked for Maud. The footman said she had not been seen in three days. Quinn asked to see Magdalena and John but was told they were not at home. The footman told Quinn he was no longer welcome at the Griswold estate.

Quinn returned to Mrs. Trim's rooming house on Phila Street and stood looking out of the window of his room at people walking and talking with one another on the sidewalk. He grew irrationally jealous of these amiable strangers and decided to lie upon his bed until the jealousy passed. He lay there, staring at the ceiling, until he felt the energy of his hostility wane. He perceived that he was not angry with Maud. He dwelled on that and felt humiliated, abandoned, and lost yet again. This condition sickened him, an emetic to his soul.

He went back to the window and looked down at the people on the street. They had become normal. He liked them now, liked the way they preened in their finery: fashion on the hoof, style on parade.

He framed Maud's face in his memory.

This girl, he said to himself, is beyond your control. She has excluded you from her future. Well, so be it. Forget her. This part of my life is over and I will suck up to no one. I am done with all the tattered nonsense of first love. The word itself caught in my throat: love. In the years ahead I would be unable to abide all the fatuous love palaver that would assault my ears. Humming "Kathleen Mavourneen," I packed my bag. But I caught myself humming and knew what it meant. I stopped humming, thinking: Done. Yes. Done.

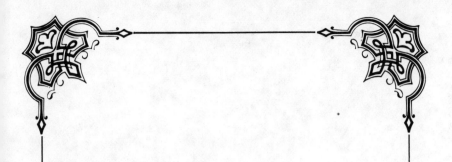

Book Two

The malevolent and terrifying thing shall of itself strike such terror into men that almost like madmen, while thinking to escape from it, they will rush in swift course upon its boundless forces.

—LEONARDO DA VINCI

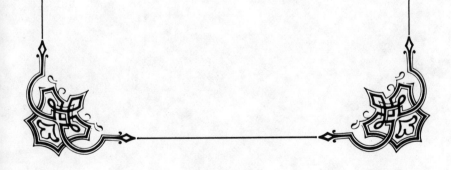

A BAZAAR
OF ENTICEMENT

Albany

Summer

1864

WE WILL NOW TALK of events that take place in fact and memory after Daniel Quinn, that orphan of life, now twenty-nine years of age, arrives by train at Albany from the mudholes of hell. Quinn, for more than two years, has been traveling with the Union Army, interviewing generals, captains, and soldiers of the line, writing about their exploits at Spotsylvania, Cold Harbor, Monocacy, and elsewhere, describing their casualties, camp life, army food, the weather, incompetent surgeons, Southern women.

The day in Albany is intermittently sunny and overcast, and the clerk of the weather says no rain is expected, that Albany's long drought will continue, and that passing rain clouds are merely illusory elements in a dry world. Quinn has already bought a horse and saddle, the mode of travel that has become part of his being, and is riding, at an ambling gait suited to the slowness of his mind, toward the Staats mansion of revered history. The waters of the Staatskill course toward him as he ascends the hill, arousing in him thoughts of time spent near other water . . .

He was then riding with the Forty-fourth out of Albany, camped on one bank of the Rappahannock, with rebel troops camped on the other. For two days men of both camps swam in the river under an unspoken truce. Jim Lynch from Saratoga broke the silence when he swam to the rebel shore and yelled to the nearest reb, "You got a newspaper we can read?" The reb waved one at him and Lynch waded to shore, naked, took the paper and thanked the reb, swam back with one hand high, and gave the paper to Quinn. It was from Richmond, only days old.

In a day's time the swimmers were killing each other. In three days' time Quinn, walking the battlefield seeking survivors among the dead thousands, heard a wounded reb ask for water. Quinn gave him his canteen and let the reb drink his fill. Then he wet the reb's leg wounds with the remaining water. Quinn considered this a fair exchange for the Richmond newspaper. The reb could not move, but he would not die of his leg wounds. The water will cool, it will loosen, it will cleanse. It will be interesting, important to the reb. But do not touch him.

The reb thanked Quinn by telling him of his optimism before battle. Such optimism was an inversion. It was based upon the vision of his wife beckoning him into the barn with their secret love gesture. The reb knew this was a temptation sent to him by the devil. He knew the barn was death and that his wife would never invite him into death's hayloft.

The reb was of North Carolina stock, strong of face and form, and Quinn knew he had farmed all his life. He revered Longstreet and grieved over the outcome of the battle. He had not known defeat in two years of war. Quinn covered the reb's legs with a blanket taken from a dead reb's bedroll, then found a rebel canteen and filled it for the reb in the river. He filled his own canteen and rinsed the taste and touch of the reb from its neck. He walked across the darkening field, where the broken artillery was strewn, but found no other survivors. Six horses stood hitched to a limber, all with limp necks, all erect in harness: twenty-four legs in an upright position, dead.

Quinn patted the neck of his new horse of the Albany instant, thankful for its life, trustful of its strength. It may be that I am coming out of death, he thought, though he sensed this was untrue, or at least a confusion. Probably he was still in death's center and losing ground. But even the possibility of leaving death behind cheered him, and always there was the banal reality: he had survived and others had not. Such a thought made him as optimistic as the wounded reb before battle. Rubbing elbows with optimism calmed Quinn and he rode on toward the mansion.

At first glimpse he knew the mansion had grown. More rooves and towers rose up from it, more porches spanned its new girth. A Chinese roof topped one new wing and on another rococo carvings spun and curled upward and around new doors and archways, new pillars and dormers. Hillegond and Dirck are manic builders. Lost in a house suited for multitudes, they create yet more space for their solitary comings and goings.

Quinn circled the mansion to see what had become of the structures and gardens of his memory. Amos's tomb and the pump and boat houses were as he remembered. A small, elegant structure was new (this was the shooting villa), but the gazebos and trellises looked as they always had, and today were brilliant with flowers, though the lawns that surrounded them were brown from the drought. All buildings were newly painted in the uniform colors of yore—a rich brown with beige trim—and all the brickwork was that same pale, rusty red.

In replenishing his vision of it all, Quinn sought not what was new but what was not: the elusive thing that endured unchanged in spite of growth. He tethered his horse in the front carriageway and knocked at the portal of first entrance, the carved wooden door looming before him with the same majesty it owned on the night he arrived a fugitive from the wild river. He stood on the same spot where he had stood then, feeling the strength of ritual rise in him. Repetition of past gestures suddenly seemed to hold the secret of his restoration to . . . to what? He could not say. He would not repeat a single day of the known past, would he?

Would he willingly relive the days in which Maud was revealed to him, full knowing that the brink of that ecstasy gave onto a chasm of loss and waste? He had kissed Maud and known love, and then descended from beauty into the valley of putrefaction, where lay a generation of blasted sons: seven thousand dead in a single battle, dead in a great wedge of slaughter, their brains and bowels blown out of them, and they then left to rot on a field consecrated by national treachery and endemic madness. And the killing moved on to greener pastures.

The front door opened and Quinn recognized Capricorn, hair gone to white, skin gone to leather, eyes waning. The old man did not recognize the long, lean Quinn in his soldier's shirt (he was not a soldier), his riding breeches and boots, and the wide-brimmed slouch hat beneath which he had lived so long. But when Quinn took off the hat to reveal dense waves of hair the color of earth, then the old man's eyes remembered history.

"You're Mist' Quinn."

"Cappy, you've kept your wits intact, unlike most of us."

Quinn entered a house refurnished: gone the cherrywood sofa on which the widow Ryan and her terrified children had sat, replaced by a resplendently huge oval settee; gone the music-room portraits of Petrus and Hillegond, the walls covered now with huge tapestries; gone, too, the foyer's Dutch colonial chandelier, and pendulous now in its place one of crystal, twice the size of the old one and exuding thrice the former elegance. This place does not shrink in memory. It waxes in breadth, and its opulence thickens.

"Is Dirck home?" Quinn asked.

"No more. He marry that singer and he move to Sweden. That's where he live now."

"Sweden. I remember his wife always wanted to go back there."

"Said he didn't wanna be here no more. Sold the house to Mr. Fitzgibbon and went away."

"Sold the house? What about Hillegond?"

"Mist' Quinn, Miss Hilly's gone."

"Gone where?"

"Gone. Killed. They strangle her. Wire her neck. They say she musta died right off."

Quinn took off his hat, ran his hand through his hair, falling into the void, groping for a word.

"When?"

"Last Feb'ary sometime. Six months now. Worst thing ever happen in this house." Capricorn sighed mightily and his voice broke. "They do my Matty too. Killin' women like that."

"Who did? Why? What is all this?"

"Don't really know. Some thinks they knows. But nobody knows why they do my Matty too."

Capricorn was near tears, and Quinn motioned the old man toward the east parlor.

"Can we sit and talk about this?"

"Capricorn don't sit in there. New butler, he don' allow that."

"A new butler. Everything's changed. What about the porch?"

"Don' think so."

"We won't go to the kitchen. All right if we walk?"

"Walkin' is fine."

And so they walked on the road under a relentless sun, with Capricorn immediately talking of the great wealth of the new owner, Gordon Fitzgibbon, son of Lyman, and passing on then to Hillegond. Sadness smothered Quinn with each vision of her that came into his memory, and he knew he would have to turn the conversation away from her. He would find out the details of her murder from Will Canaday, read all the stories Will must have written about it. Quinn could drown in such evil but he would not. He would survive Hillegond's death as he had others in the war: move past them; control the power of grief and anger to destroy the vessel. But he could feel the impetus for control weakening with each new death that touched him, his survival drive waning like Cappy's eyesight. Soon there may be no drive.

And Capricorn talked on.

"This woman, she open her house to colored folks. She feed them, help them go to freedom. She save Joshua from jail, then give him money so's he can bring other coloreds up from Carolina. Joshua's woman stop here too. Miss Hilly a sainted lady. She in heaven for sure. She be a queen up there."

"I was here the night Joshua came in as a prisoner, manacled to the Swede," Quinn said.

"I recollect."

"After that I asked you about him, but you wouldn't tell me anything."

"I recollect that too."

"I saw Joshua in New York."

"We ain't seen him here. How that boy doin'?"

"Long time ago, but he was all right then." Quinn the liar.

"Aw, that's fine."

"He was working in John McGee's saloon. You remember John? The fighter? John the Brawn they called him."

"Nobody forget *that* man once they meet him."

"Joshua had a new name first time I caught up with him. Called himself Mick the Rat."

"Go on. Mick the Rat?"

"That's it. He was handling rats for John."

"Handlin' rats?"

"A special show to bring people into the saloon. They see the rat show free, then maybe they drink and gamble some. Joshua had a bag full of rats. He'd catch a fresh bunch every night at the slaughterhouse. Throw a light on them and while they stared at it he'd grab 'em with long pincers and drop 'em in the bag."

Capricorn shook his head. "Joshua do that? Joshua?"

Quinn nodded. "Then he'd bring the rats into John's place and put one into this pit in the back of the saloon. People all around the pit watching, and then somebody'd put a bull terrier in with the rat. Terrier'd kill it quick. Then Joshua'd put two rats in and the terrier'd kill them too, sometimes just one bite apiece. Then they'd put a Mexican hairless in and Joshua'd dump in four rats and the Mex'd get them all. Then five rats, then six. The rats had no chance. It was a matter of time."

"Can't say as I like that game."

"No. But Joshua needed money. He was hiding two fugitive slaves and trying to move them north."

"He always doin' that."

"Asked me to help him. He didn't really know me, but he trusted me. Said that was his talent, knowing if he could trust you."

Joshua told Quinn the bounty on one of the runaways was three hundred dollars, which made his work of hiding the pair doubly difficult. The second slave had no price on his head, being possessed of only one eye, the other destroyed by the lash of a whip from his master's hand, marking him as an evil-eyed source of ill luck to all. Joshua had led the slaves from Philadelphia to a farmer's cabin south of Kingston that was only marginally secure; and when he learned the slave hunters were closing in he put the problem to Quinn: We need a white man. Quinn said he was a white man.

Joshua had allies, but the known local abolitionists were of no value in this situation. Quinn, a stranger, could bring the necessary word to the inns and the grogshops where the deadliest gossip thrived and where the slave hunters had been biding their time to hear it. The slavers were also a pair, not from the South (by their accent) but Yorkers, clearly. They came equipped: ropes, manacles, rifles, pistols, money to loosen tongues. They called each other by name—Fletch and Blue—and made no secret of their ambition: "Catch niggers."

And so when Quinn sat in the Eagle Tavern and ordered his whiskey toddies and grew garrulous, dropping the news that he'd seen niggers moving around near a cabin up the pike, then repeated his performance at the Bump Tavern at the next cross-roads, well, it came as no surprise when Fletch and Blue turned up at his elbow, inquiring about particulars.

"You hunt niggers, is that it?" Quinn asked them.

"We take property back to its rightful owners," said Fletch.

"A wonderful thing," said Quinn. "Man owns somethin', he shouldn't oughta have to give it up, just on accounta the thing he owns don't want to be owned no more. Man could lose all his cows that way."

"Cows," said Fletch, and he thought about that.

"You think you could show us where you seen them niggers?"

"Can't really tell it," said Quinn. "Don't know the names of none of these roads, don't know where nothin' is, rightly."

"You figure you could show us?" asked Fletch.

"I s'pose." And Quinn mused on the possibility. "What's the profit for a fella like me shows you what you're lookin' for?"

"You want profit, is that it?"

"Most folks do."

"We'll give you profit."

"That case, we probably got us a deal."

"Then let's go."

"How much profit you figure we're talkin' about?"

"We give you two dollars. You can buy a new horse with two dollars."

"Not no kind of horse I'd wanna ride." And Quinn fell silent.

"We'll give you three," said Blue.

"We'll give you five, never mind three," said Fletch.

"All you gonna give me is five? I was thinkin' twenty ain't a bad price for a couple of niggers."

"Twenty; all right, twenty. Let's go."

"I'd like to get the feel of the twenty 'fore we go," said Quinn.

"Give him twenty," said Fletch. And Blue opened the flap of his shirt pocket and took out a fold of bills.

[194]

"You ready now?" Blue said when Quinn took the money.

"I'm ready," said Quinn. "You ready?"

"We're ready," said Fletch. "But if'n we don't get no niggers I'll be lookin' to get back that twenty."

"Fair's fair," said Quinn, and he led the way out of the tavern, mounted his horse, and headed north on the turnpike.

Wrapped in blankets, the fugitive slaves squatted on the earth in a pit under the floorboards of the cabin, their retreat in times of threat. Planks covered their heads. Long slivers of light from the oil lamp in the second room of the cabin found their way down between the boards and into the soft clay cubicle of the slaves' secret dwelling place.

Joshua added wood to the fading fire, the first time the stove had been used in the eight days the slaves had been here, for smoke is a traitor. In the second room of the cabin sat two white men with blackened faces, each with pistol and shotgun. When they heard the horses approach, the men took up prearranged positions and Joshua stood by the cabin door, carrying no weapon, and waited for the visitors to knock.

Quinn rode to the rear of Fletch and Blue when they neared the cabin and in his mind heard the music the two banjos made when the cadaverous dancer at The Museum sang his ditty:

> Dere's music in de wells,
> Dere's music in de air,
> Dere's music in a nigger's knee
> When de banjo's dere.

And then Fletch was telling Joshua that they were working for the federal marshal to track runaway slaves. Joshua spoke in a voice foreign to Quinn, whining and mewling.

"I's a free man," he said. "Don't know nothin' 'bout no 'scaped

[195]

slaves. Lived here all my days. You don't believe that, go ask anybody here'bouts."

"Ain't you we're lookin' for," said Fletch. "We're after two niggers got only three eyes between 'em."

"Don't know nothin' 'bout three eyes," Joshua said. "You wanna come in and look, you can. I ain't fightin' no federal marshal. But ain't nobody here but Mick the Rat, and that's me, and that's what is."

"We'll have a look," said Fletch. He dismounted and tied his horse to a bush, and then with Blue behind him and Quinn bringing up the rear, the three entered the cabin. What Quinn saw was a long shadow of a man in the second room, and Fletch and Blue both drew their pistols and moved toward it. Joshua backed into the room ahead of them and turned toward the shadow, which was made not by a man but a coat and hat on a stick, at which Fletch and Blue pointed their guns. As they did, the shotguns of the blackfaced men rose out of the shadows to the level of their faces, and both slavers dropped their pistols.

"You lookin' for us niggers?" said one of the blackfaces. "You wanna take us to Virginia?"

Fletch shook his head.

"Thought you did," said blackface.

Joshua drew a knife from the scabbard on his belt and with deft strokes cut the belts and waistbands on the trousers of Fletch and Blue.

"Sit," said Joshua, and Fletch and Blue sat.

"Take off your boots," said Joshua, and they did.

"Stand up and drop your pants," said Joshua, and they did.

Joshua left the room, lifted the planks, and helped the slaves up from their pit as the blackfaces led Fletch and Blue to the pit's edge. The slaves huddled by the stove and watched as Joshua and one of the blackfaces tied the arms and ankles of the slave hunters. Fletch wore long underwear to his ankles. Blue's went to his knees. Neither man wore stockings. When the slavers were bound, Joshua and one of the blackfaces rolled them into the pit.

"We gonna be leavin' now," Joshua said to them. "But thinkin' about how you gonna be all alone down there, we got you some company."

Then from a corner of the cabin, he dragged out a canvas bag the size of a small child. He undid its drawstring, then upended it, dropping two dozen live rats into the pit. The men yelled, the rats squealed. Fletch and Blue kicked at the rats and backed themselves into a corner together.

As Quinn raised the lamp to see what was happening, a courageous rat began climbing Fletch's bare foot.

Fletch kicked it, and the rat flew against the wall and rolled over.

Then it righted itself, undaunted.

Quinn, at this point, let the twenty dollars he had taken from Fletch and Blue flutter back down to its rightful owners.

Capricorn was laughing so hard that tears were on their way. "Oh, that Joshua, he wicked. That man, he know how to do it. How all that come out?"

"Joshua took the horses and they all rode north," Quinn said. "I guess they made it. I never saw any of them again, except Joshua. Never did know those fellows in blackface."

Quinn and Capricorn turned toward the house, walking past the pond Petrus built for the wild ducks, six of which were in residence. Quinn looked toward the house and saw Hillegond in the window fourteen years before, and he thought: Queen mother of compassion, I loved you.

But he would not weep.

He would not be diminished.

Joshua, a saint, could diminish Quinn, but not death, not even the death of queenly love. The war, wondered Quinn, astonished anew at his toughness—has it turned my soul into a lump of lead? He pictured the city of corpses where he had lived, and a fear gripped him. He was growing strong because of that city, preening with survival. One by one the corpses struggled upright, began a ragged march in his direction. He remembered his Celtic disk and he imposed its memory on this vision, raised it before his eyes like a monstrance, like a shield. Protected from corpses, he breathed deeply and walked toward the mansion.

As he approached his tethered horse he saw a coach and four coming up the carriageway from the new turnpike that now passed the Staats property, and Capricorn said, "That's him now. Mr. Fitzgibbon."

And so it was: Gordon Fitzgibbon, son of Lyman, a man Quinn knew by name but had not met. Beside him in the carriage Quinn saw a woman.

Then he saw it was a woman of love.

Saw Maud.

He could not have suspected or even intuited her presence here, and yet neither was this coincidence. We could call it Quinn's will to alter existence, to negate life's caprice and become causality itself. This was not the first time he had willed history to do his bidding, but it was the first time history had obeyed him. He'd come here seeking not Maud's presence but the ethereal fragrance of her memory, all he could hope to find. Given that, he felt he would be able to trace her. Now here she arrives, and so begins a new confluence for these two strangers of love.

The coach halted at the mansion, and the coachman leaped to the ground, opened the door. Out first stepped Maud Fallon, dressed in black and white silks, her abundant auburn hair upswept into a crown encircled with a white ribbon, her skin exquisitely white; and upon seeing Quinn she said, "Daniel, I feared you were dead," and gave him her hand, which he took and held.

"I seem to have survived," he said, "but it may be an illusion."

Maud turned then to Capricorn and said, "Cappy, will you bring in my boxes?" Then, nodding once at Quinn, she entered the mansion. Gordon Fitzgibbon approached Quinn with extended hand.

"You're Quinn," he said.

"That's a fact," said Quinn.

"I've heard about you and read your writing. You're quite a famous fellow."

"I think you exaggerate."

"Not at all. Everybody knows Quinn."

"I would have thought almost nobody knows him."

"I'm a true admirer. You've projected me into battles and set me alongside those wounded soldiers. I could feel the weight of their haversacks. You have a talent for creating the vivid scene. Won't you come into the house?"

"I was just leaving. I came to see Hillegond."

"Poor Hillegond. But at least they caught the villain." Gordon nodded sadly and, without waiting for Quinn's response to his invitation, strode purposefully into the mansion.

Quinn debated whether to follow, stunned by Maud's brusqueness, then decided he had not exhausted his fate's capacity for surprise (and that's why they call it your fate). Also he wanted to hear more about the villain, and so he left his horse and followed Gordon into what he now was forced to think of as the Fitzgibbon mansion. In the drawing room Gordon offered him whiskey, Quinn's first under these multiple rooves. The two men then settled into facing armchairs, a table between them, and on it a bowl of grapes and apples. Gordon positioned himself so that he was framed from behind by his own enormous portrait: a figure of abundant black hair, strong of jaw and dark of eye, wearing a cloak flared over one shoulder, holding a sheared beaver hat in his right hand, and standing in boots and breeches on the steps of his newly acquired mansion: arrived—for the ages.

"A very good likeness, that," said Quinn, perceiving the jaw in the portrait to be stronger than the jaw beneath it. Of Gordon's past he remembered only Yale law school, but he would come to know the man as the successor to his father in running the family foundries, a serious churchgoer who abandoned his father's Presbyterian life for the Episcopal high church, who translated Vergil's *Aeneid* from the Latin and then dramatized the story of Aeneas and Dido for the stage; a man of many interests. One too many: Maud.

"It's only been up a week," said Gordon of his portrait, "but I am pleased with it. The artist worked on it five months. He began it even before I took title to this place."

"You were very sure of yourself."

"Once I heard Dirck was selling it, I had to have it. I bought it for Maud, really. She's mad about being here."

"It was quite a surprise to see Maud."

"She's spoken of you, but then again, who hasn't? She's here only a few days and then we're going to Saratoga for the racing. She has a relative up there."

"She looks well."

"Indeed she does. She's dazzling. We'll be married soon."

"Now, that's a surprise, Maud married," Quinn said, reaching for the grapes.

"She's trepidatious about it."

"Maud is always trepidatious about relationships," said Quinn, popping grapes into his mouth.

"We're solving it," said Gordon.

"You're a sturdy fellow," said Quinn.

Quinn popped his final grape, then stood up and drank his whiskey in a gulp. "I must be going," he said, "but first tell me about Hillegond."

"The killer went upstairs and found her sleeping, looped the garrote around her neck and dragged her from the bed with it. It was clear she died in a moment and did not suffer."

"Some suffer in a moment what takes others twenty years to feel."

"I'm sure you're right," said Gordon, and his voice was receding for Quinn, only sporadic words registering: ". . . strangled Matty . . . the stairs . . . she fought . . ." For Quinn there was only Maud's coldness, and he silently recited the old Irish poem of warning:

> Wherefore should I go to death,
>   for red lips, for gleaming teeth? . . .
> Thy pleasant mien, thy high mind,
>   Thy slim hand, O foam-white maid,
> O blue eye, O bosom white,
>   I shall not die for thy sake.

Repeat it now. Repeat.

For this is your fate.

". . . the fellow was shameless . . . dressed like a priest . . . Hillegond's young lover, can you imagine? . . . But he shows up in no records as a priest . . . Did you know him?"

"Who?" asked Quinn.

"The priest fellow. Finnerty, if that's his name. It's what he went by in the theater. A bad apple, to say the least."

"What about him?"

"Aren't you listening, Mr. Quinn? He's in jail. They've charged him as her killer. He had her jade ring. He said she gave it to him."

"Hillegond?"

"Damn it, Quinn, are you all there? I took you to be acute. Are you ill, or what ails you?"

"I'm distracted, forgive me," and he turned to leave, turned back. "Thank you for the whiskey."

"I hoped to hear of your war experiences."

"Another time."

[201]

"Perhaps tonight if you're not busy. Join us at the Army Relief Bazaar."

"Perhaps," said Quinn, straining.

"It's for the sick and wounded, you know. I'm chairman of the thing. I've been so involved with the war that my father considers me a practical amalgamationist. I actually recruited an entire company of army volunteers out of our two foundries. A good many were Irish."

"That's very patriotic," said Quinn.

"You *must* come to our bazaar," said Gordon. "We'll lionize you if you'll let us."

"I doubt I could handle that."

"We'll be going at seven. We could pick you up. Where are you staying?"

"I'm not sure."

"You mean you don't have a place? Why, stay here, then."

"That's generous, but I think—" and Quinn, in this instant, could not think at all.

From the doorway Capricorn intruded on the hesitational moment. "Mr. Quinn, Miss Maud say she got a letter she want you to read. She be upstairs in the sittin' room."

Quinn turned to Gordon, who was smiling.

"It's pleasant in Maud's sitting room," Gordon said.

Quinn returned Gordon's smile, feeling the sudden urge to stuff several grapes up the man's nose. Then he followed Capricorn out of the room and up the stairs.

As he walked, Quinn perceived that with a brusque offering of her hand, with a summons to come hither for a letter, with a decorous public invitation to chat in proper confines, Maud again proved herself a creature of quixotic ways, social fits. Quinn made the first turning on the mahogany staircase, that broad, expansive work of art that rose out of the foyer into the mystery of the mansion's upper labyrinths, and he measured the distance from his last meeting with Maud: six years—the year 1858, when, as journeyman paragraphist and sometime essayist on sporting events, theater, crime, and judiciality for Will Canaday's *Albany Chronicle,* he was present as Maud made her debut in *Mazeppa.*

This was a hippodramatic spectacle, an innovation within a hoary melodramatic theatrical corruption of a Lord Byron narrative poem that had been inspired by a passage in Voltaire's history of Charles XII of Sweden; and it proved that Maud Fallon not only possessed a singular body but was willing to demonstrate said fact to the world at high risk to that very same singularity.

Lo, the poor Mazeppa. A Tatar foundling who comes to young manhood in the court of the King of Poland, he shares love with the King's daughter, who is abruptly promised to the Count Palatine. Professing his love for the princess, Mazeppa assaults and wounds the Count in a duel and for his effrontery is strapped supine to the back of a wild horse. The horse is then lashed into madness, loosed upon the Ukrainian plains, and runs itself to death. Grievous torture is the lot of Mazeppa during this wild ride, but he survives, is discovered near death by his father (what a coincidence is here), who is the King of Tatary. And Mazeppa soon returns to Poland with the Tatar army to wreak vengeance on Poland and marry his beloved.

In early years of the play the Mazeppa ride had been accomplished onstage with a dummy athwart the live animal, the dummy role in time giving way to intrepid actors. But not until Maud's day had the intrepidity been offered to a female, this the idea of Joseph K. Moran, Albany's Green Street Theater manager and erstwhile tenor turned theatrical entrepreneur, who invited Maud (a horsewoman all her life, as well as a danseuse with acrobatic skills and risqué propensities—her famed Spider Dance, for example) to impersonate the male hero, ride supine and bareback upon Rare Beauty, a genuine horse, and to rise, thereon, up from the footlights and along four escalating platforms to a most high level of the stage, and to do this as well at a fair gallop while clad in a flesh-colored, skin-tight garment of no known name, which would create the illusion of being no garment at all. And so it followed that Maud, barebacked, perhaps also barebuttocked and barebusted, and looking very little like a male hero, climbed those Albany platforms to scandalously glamorous international heights.

Witnessing all this on opening night in 1858, Quinn confirmed his suspicion that he and the truest love of his life (whom he had not seen since she disappeared from Obadiah's home in Saratoga eight years previous) were at this moment incompatible; for who could marry a woman of such antics? That raucous lasciviosity of the audience would madden Quinn in a matter of weeks. And so he called upon Maud in her dressing room, waiting for the wildness of her success to subside into a second day, to tell her as much.

"My God, Daniel, you're my savior," she said when she saw him, hugging him vigorously, talking as if only days and not years had elapsed since their last meeting. "You've come just in time to rescue me from this dementia. Can you imagine what this will do to my life?"

Quinn, nonplussed as usual, sat next to Maud, bathing in her presence and her gaze, and could say only, "You are quite spectacular. I love you incredibly. I'll always love you."

"I know that," said Maud. "Never mind that now. How am I going to get out of this? They want me for as long as I'll stay. They want a contract. They think they'll draw capacity houses for weeks, or months. They say I'll be rich in a trice."

"Money is nothing," said Quinn.

"Don't be a nincompoop, Daniel," said Maud. "Money is everything to me. How am I to live without money? I've schemed for years to accumulate wealth but it eludes me. I'm incompetent."

"I'll take care of you," said Quinn.

"How much do you make?"

"Twenty dollars a week."

"I'll make four times that tonight," said Maud.

"Then marry your horse," said Quinn, and he left her.

Quinn made the second turning on the grand staircase, contemplating the nature of love and money, inquiring to an unknown authority whether there was such a thing as pure love, or was it as much an illusion as Maud's sham nudity? If there was such, he wondered further, was it what he now felt? And if what he now felt was *not* love, could the real element ever be begotten by his like?

He repeated to himself:

> *I shall not die for thy sake,*
> *O maid with the swan-like grace . . .*

And then, trepidatious, he entered the sitting room of Maud the Brusque, and encountered her in a pale pink dressing gown, her auburn hair now flowing to her shoulders, her pink chemisette visible beneath her gown, and beneath that, three visible inches of cloven line between her breasts. Never before had Quinn seen this much of Maud's flesh. Never before had he known it to be so abundant; and the sight of it stopped his movement.

"You have a letter for me?" he asked.

"I do," said Maud, "but that's not why I invited you here. I thought you might like to see my breasts."

"Ah," said Quinn, "have I at last become the equal of a cake?"

Maud loosened the belt of her dressing gown and moved closer to Quinn.

When she saw Quinn standing tall by the door of the mansion, Maud assumed he was a spirit, so certain had she been of his death; for she had seen in her mind how he crumpled when hit by the cannonball, and how he lay still. And from then forward she received no further visions of his distant life. She thought often of him, and wept always at the memory of his face, his infectious smile of the so-white teeth. And yet there he stood, not a spirit at all, so she knew she must act quickly.

From the first landing on the staircase she watched him as he talked with Gordon, ready to call his name if he started to leave. When she saw him enter the house she knew she had gained time, and so came to her rooms, found the letter she had written him in 1858, and prepared herself to greet him in the manner she had so long imagined. With the help of her serving maid, Cecile, she stripped off her clothing, then donned the chemisette and the robe, placed the letter on the long table, lighted the candles in the two candelabra to frame the letter (and in due course, herself), drew the drapes so the room would not be visible from the upper porch, and sent Cecile away.

She sat on the green velvet sofa, thinking of how angry with her Quinn would be after his talk with Gordon. But that anger would pass and she would impose on him a *geis*. He would then, in due course, be hers, never again to talk of money. They would live together, or separately, it would not matter, for they would be equals in love, something they never had been since love began.

When he came into the room she saw his expression was a stone of feigned wrath, which only made him more handsome, more appealing. Maud always saw through Quinn's masks. He threw the cake up at her when she spoke of her breasts, but she pacified him by offering herself to his eyes. He will not resist me, was her intention. But one must not dismiss Quinn's dispositions too easily, for he is a willful man and at times must be cajoled into the behavior he most desires. With him love must be sat upon, like an egg. It will hatch with warmth, with envelopment. On its own it could rot.

She let her robe fall open, revealing the chemisette, the same order of undergarment Magdalena had worn the night of her death in the river of ice. It clung to Maud from shoulder to middle thigh. Maud imagined herself floating to the bottom of the icy river, snared by John's hook, lifted aboard a skiff, then dragged, bitten, and bounced through the night toward this mansion, which Maud ever since had known as a place where the miracle of love rises gloriously out of death, relinquishes its scars, and moves on to the next order of fulfillment.

She opened the tie of her robe, cradled her breasts with both hands, removed them from constraint, and introduced Quinn to her matured bosom.

He stared.

He almost smiled.

He looked at her eyes.

He looked again at what was revealed.

He kissed her on the mouth.

He held her shoulders.

He stepped back from the kiss.

He touched her left nipple with his right fingertips, lightly. It was the color of cinnamon sugar.

He put his lips on her left nipple, tasted it.

He lifted her left breast in his right hand, moving it slowly from east to west, then west to east.

He attended her right breast with his left hand.

He put his lips on her right breast.

He lightly bit the nipple of her right breast.

He kissed her on the mouth, holding both her breasts in both his hands.

He stepped back from the kiss, levitating both breasts, moving them from west to east, north to south, and so on.

He kissed the cloven line between her breasts.

He licked the line and tasted her salt.

He held both her breasts with both his hands and pressed their softness against both sides of his face.

He raised his face to hers and kissed her on the mouth.

"Do you like me?" she inquired.

"That's the most ridiculous thing I've ever heard you say, and I've heard several."

"Have you known a lot of women?"

"A fair number. It's been a bazaar of enticement, you might say."

"I've had six men."

"A round number."

"And several hundred suitors."

"The fellow downstairs is one of the privileged half dozen, I presume."

"He is not."

"Has he ever put his mouth on your body?"

"Never. But even so, he is quite jealous. We must hurry. I want you to see all of me."

"You're very determined."

"Only fools are otherwise."

She picked the letter off the table and stuffed it into Quinn's trouser pocket, then moved the candelabra farther apart and sat on the table.

"Do you remember how John came to Magdalena when she was dead, how he raised her clothing?"

"I remember it vividly."

"I want you to do the same with me now. My breasts are blushing. Can you see?"

"I can."

"I feel a sharp rush of blood to them when I get excited."

"I could feel their pulse when I touched you."

"They make the rest of me function. They're the brains of my sex."

"I'll remember that."

"Now, I want you to look at me, but you must be precise in what you think. I'm accessible to the man who knows exactly how he loves me. No voyeur will ever reach me."

She lowered herself into a supine position on the table, freeing up her robe and chemisette. Quinn, seeking precision but astonished by Maud's behavior, could only watch with awe her reenactment of Magdalena's posture, the array of her apparel before resurrection.

"For God's sake, hurry up," Maud said, and Quinn folded her robe and chemisette upward to reveal the inversely triangulated center of his dreams, more striking than he had imagined, more symmetrical, the auburn crest of it an arc, an emerging sunrise of irresistible invitation. Maud closed her eyes and let her arms fall into the same position as Magdalena's of yore. Quinn put the palm of his hand on her sunrise and she opened her eyes.

"No," she said. "We're not ready."

"Who says we're not?"

"My blood."

"Why are you with him?" Quinn said.

"I have to be with someone once in a while. He's bright."

"And he's rich."

"That doesn't matter."

"It used to."

"Why are you talking about money when I'm in this position?"

"You should leave him."

"Why don't you take me away from him?"

"I wondered when you'd get around to kidnapping."

"Look at me, Daniel," she said, and she spread herself.

Quinn looked. "You are a most willful woman," he said.

"Everyone has a right to a willful life," said Maud. "I dare you to take me away."

"And so I shall," said Quinn. "But first I must know. Have you ever done this in front of a cake?"

She sat up and covered herself, moved the candelabra to where they had been before her ritual, snuffed the candles, opened the drapes to the upper porch, and sat on the velvet sofa precisely where she had been prior to Quinn's arrival. Gordon then knocked on the door of the sitting room.

"Maud, may I come in?"

"Of course," she said, and Gordon entered, smiling.

"I have to change for this evening," he said, "and I wondered whether we should prepare a room for Mr. Quinn. I invited him to join us at the bazaar tonight."

"What a good idea," said Maud.

"I guess it would be valuable to see it," said Quinn.

"It's quite a spectacle for Albany," said Gordon.

"Albany has spectacles and spectacles," said Quinn.

"Then I'll have them go ahead with the room."

"If it's not too much trouble," said Quinn, "I wonder could I have the one I used to sleep in. Next floor up, opposite the stairs."

"We have much grander rooms than that," said Gordon.

"There's grandeur also in repeating history."

"Then you shall have it. I'll have Cappy bring up your things and stable your horse." Gordon looked at Maud. "You seem to be in your nightclothes."

"I'm about to bathe," said Maud.

"We'll meet at a later hour, then," said Quinn, moving toward the door.

"An excellent idea," said Gordon, standing pat.

My dearest Daniel [Quinn read, lying in the bed he last lay in six years earlier, the careful handwriting before him composed six years earlier also], I am appalled by your unfeeling ways. You are a man of mercurial moods, and if you do not change, I shan't promise that our love will survive, which would be lamentable. I have never ceased of loving you, but when you came into my dressing room and I hugged you as a savior, I felt something I had not felt since our kiss by the shore of Saratoga Lake (and I have known certain compelling intimacies with men in the intervening years). I conclude from this feeling that I have an enduring element in my makeup, one that, unlike most mortal characteristics of our species, resists change. Poets have talked of this but I have never credited them with propounding anything except romantic twaddle, and yet I must now confess they knew something I heretofore did not.

But you left me in such haste that I did not even gain the moment to tell you what led to our separation in Saratoga. I saw all that happened to you on the veranda that afternoon. I did not ride off on the roan stallion, as some thought, but created the ruse of my departure by convincing a stableboy to take the horse to a neighboring farm. I then hid in the hayloft with my bag and observed all events, for I was in need of time to think what I should do. Intuitively I knew you would never accept my solution to the situation in which I found myself that afternoon after our return. I was, of a suddenness, sorely pressed to provide for Magdalena in light of John McGee's decision to leave us and pursue a career as a prizefighter.

Magdalena, headstrong of course, decided to depart Obadiah's farm immediately and resume our life on the road. She thought of accepting an offer from a New York producer who wanted her to travel and dance and then meet with visitors curious to observe her beauty up close. She was to charge one dollar for each personal handshake. But I was fearful of her health, and knew it would worsen with travel. She was in a most sorry and withdrawn condition and I felt it my duty to bring her to a less grueling fate. This I achieved by shifting Obadiah's obsession from Magdalena to myself. I discovered he was a man of peculiar predilections, obsessed by the backs of women's knees, and so I agreed to make such parts as I owned available for his periodic scrutiny in exchange for his solace and support for the dwindling Magdalena, and a curb on his attentions to her.

In short order Magdalena grew easeful and serene, and in

time I hired a woman companion, a French immigrant girl named Cecile, and began my life as the sojourning spiritualist, which afforded me small income and much danger from malevolent Catholic Irishmen. During one visit at Troy a group of them sought my destruction, thinking me an apostle of Satan. I eluded them and struck out from those shores soon enough to become the successor of Mother and Auntie, which is to say, I became the daring danseuse, which I remained until you saw me in my triumph as Mazeppa. This, I fear, will be the bane of my days, as well as my financial salvation. A new life opens before me now, with bookings everywhere. I do loathe these particulars, but I am comforted by the memory of our last embrace, and I send you my fondest caresses.

Until we meet again, I remain, your truest love, Maud Fallon.

In the carriage Maud asked Quinn's permission to practice aloud what she would be reading later in the evening: excerpts from Scott and Keats; and from her handbag she took a slim volume, *Marmion* and *The Lay of the Last Minstrel*. The reading, she explained, was her contribution to the Army Relief Bazaar. Tonight she would take no fee for her work, which, of late, she had been doing in salons and temples where the arts flourished.

"Elocution in the salon has replaced horses in the hippodrome for Maud," Gordon said.

"Elocution in the salon. Exotic in the extreme," said Quinn.

"I needed something less convulsive than an upside-down horseback adventure every night of my life," said Maud. "I crave tranquillity."

"We seem to crave that as we wind down," said Quinn.

"Winding down has nothing to do with it," said Maud in miffed tones. "I'm winding neither down nor up. The problem was boredom and physical torture. I'm sure my body has suffered more than Mazeppa's."

"She was a tapestry of black and blue," said Gordon.

"A tapestry," said Quinn.

"I had to wear long sleeves and high collars," said Maud.

"What a shame," said Quinn.

"It was punishment without sin," said Gordon.

"I hope you were well paid," said Quinn.

"I loathe money," said Maud.

"My romance with money is enough for both of us," said Gordon. "That's why I took her over."

"I hardly think I've been taken over," said Maud.

"You shall be," Gordon said with a smile.

Maud then decided not to practice her reading and said nothing for the rest of the ride.

When he entered the bazaar Quinn experienced a rush of black wisdom and felt himself moving toward the crags of a new nightmare. This was irrational and he knew it. Tension rose in his throat and chest. He followed Gordon's lead, walking beside Maud, threading himself through handsomely dressed crowds, breathing in the bright and busy oddness of this peculiar building: a sudden upthrust built in two weeks and designed in the shape of a double Grecian cross.

They walked beneath the elevated orchestra stand, from where a waltz by Strauss energized the evening. Arches festooned with flowers and evergreens led Quinn's eye to booths celebrating England, Ireland, Russia, Schenectady, Troy, Saratoga. Hundreds of flaming gas jets imposed brilliance on the bodies below, which exuded in their finery a light and power that for Quinn paralleled the luminous battlefield dead. Irrational. Quinn knew it.

"It's a veritable palace of Aladdin," said Gordon. "And all these fair ladies, why, they seem like the nymphs and graces of mythology."

[213]

"By and large, dumpy and frowzy," said Maud, who explained that one of the graces was really doing public penance by working here since her husband was in jail for selling horseshoes to the rebel army.

Gordon ignored Maud's remark and led the way to the Curiosity Shop, explaining that they would see Myles Standish's pistol, carried by Myles on the *Mayflower* and purchased by Lyman Fitzgibbon after his genealogist discovered a link between Myles and the Fitzgibbons.

"It's merely on loan from Father," said Gordon. "Not for sale, by a long shot. A curiosity of history, as they say."

Quinn looked at the pistol, wondered how many savage breasts its power had pierced, then moved along to the writing bureau owned by George Washington, upon which George had signed Major André's death warrant. He saw Madison's cane, Lafayette's pistol, Grant's autograph, and the Bastille model (made from the Bastille's own stone) that Lafayette had presented to George Washington. Such lovely revolutions. Such a grand Civil War. We must not forget how they are done. He noted a pair of leather shoes that had been made for Union troops by prisoners at the Albany penitentiary. Five hundred and six prisoners were busy making the shoes. Half of their number were Negroes.

Then Quinn saw and quickly found focus on handwritten words in a locked cabinet, under glass, difficult to read: ". . . gradual abolishment of slavery within their respective limits . . . the effort to colonize persons of African descent . . . upon this continent . . . all persons held as slaves within any state, or designated part of a state . . . shall be then, thenceforward, and forever free . . ."

Quinn read the related sign explaining that one might, for one dollar, purchase a ticket and perhaps win, and thereby own forever, this document donated by the President to the Albany Bazaar, and described as the

> ORIGINAL DRAFT
> of the
> PRESIDENT'S FIRST
> EMANCIPATION PROCLAMATION
> dated September 22, 1862

Whereupon Quinn fumbled in his pocket for a dollar and purchased a ticket from one of the nymphs.

Maud took Quinn's arm and said, "I must show you something at the Saratoga booth," and Gordon, noting this, followed in their wake. Crossing the transept Quinn sensed an easing of his tension at the touch of Maud the cynosure. Then he saw Will Canaday standing by the Irish booth and he felt a surge of joy at the convergence of the two people he valued most in this life, and he moved Maud toward the Irish booth. When Will saw them he grasped Maud's hand and kissed her cheek; then he embraced Quinn, neither of them speaking.

"You didn't say you were coming home," Will finally said.

"I wasn't sure until I actually got on the train," said Quinn.

Six years had passed since Quinn last saw Will, who was more stooped than Quinn had ever seen him, and walking with a limp. He had always carried a handsome walking stick but now a stout cane supported his steps.

"What happened to your leg?" Quinn asked.

"Aaah, they knocked me around one night and shattered a bone."

"Who did?"

"A few of the boyos. I didn't know them."

"The Society?"

"It could have been. I've all sorts of new enemies as well, and they didn't identify themselves."

Will's reputation for being the scourge of the city had not

abated since Quinn left Albany in 1858 to test out New York and expose his soul to other than clement weather. He left with an invitation from Will to write anything he pleased, and so he had, until he hired on at Greeley's *Tribune*. Even then, Will reprinted all that he recognized as coming from Quinn's pen.

"And yourself," said Will. "Are you well?"

"I wouldn't say that," said Quinn.

"I'll introduce you here tonight. You'll say something about the war, I understand."

"I don't think so," said Quinn. "I have nothing to say."

"Then no one else on earth does, either. It can be brief. Everybody here knows your name."

"I'm not up to it, Will."

"You'll do it. People need the war's reality."

"They do? You can't mean it."

"I mean it."

"I'm the wrong choice. I wouldn't know reality if it knocked me down. And it did."

"Just a few minutes will do," said Will. "And how are you, Maudie? You look thunderously beautiful."

"I wanted to show Daniel the Saratoga booth, and our old friend."

"Oh yes," said Will, "our friend." He looked at his pocket watch. "We'll be ready for your reading in about five minutes. Are you doing the Keats?"

"Yes, and I may also do Scott," said Maud.

"Scott is always a pleasure."

"Perhaps 'Lochinvar.' "

"Splendid," said Will, and he winked at Maud.

Will left them then, and Quinn saw what had been shielded from view by Will's presence: a photograph of General McClellan framed in marble, and beside that a huge morocco-bound Bible donated to the booth by Mr. R. Dwyer, superintendent of the County Idiot Asylum. Quinn moved closer to a large framed

photo of a military unit and saw it was the Irish brigade, led by
Batt Connors from Wexford. Quinn had ridden with them for
two days and told a bit of their story: wild men all, daredevil
heroes their superiors thrust into lost or impossible causes. Using
a steady supply of replacements off the boat, the brigade reca-
pitulated the fate of ancient Celtic warriors: they went forth to
battle but they always fell.

At the Saratoga booth Quinn found the usual antiques and art
objects, as well as photographs and sketches of the great hotels,
the ballrooms, the long porches, the ladies in promenade, the
parks, the springs, the pines. What was new to him was a sketch
of jockeys on racehorses, and an excited throng rising in the
grandstand of the new racecourse that was opening this week.

"This is what I wanted to show you," Maud said to Quinn.
"Do you see who owns it?"

Quinn then saw a photo of a man standing beside a chestnut
filly called Blue Grass Warrior. The man was well dressed, with
a full black beard.

"That's my horse," said Maud.

"Really? Well, you always loved horses."

"It was a gift from a suitor. Not one of the six, to anticipate
your question. He's from Kentucky. I met him at Saratoga just
before the war, and he gave me a horse and a slave girl as gifts."

"I hope you kept the slave girl too."

"Of course. And I sent her to Canada in case he changed his
mind about her."

Quinn read the printed matter explaining the photo.

"Why that's John," he said. "John McGee."

"It took you a while to notice."

"It's his beard. I never saw him with a beard."

He studied the most recent incarnation of John the Brawn,
handsome figure of substance and money, as wealthy as he is

hairy. The last Quinn had seen of him was in 1863, when, as always, John was leaping into a new future, linking his fistic notoriety to the politicians who ran New York City, using his name as a draw for gambling parlors: John the Brawn becoming John the Grand and John the Mighty, his power and his fortune as expansive as his chest.

"He owns the track?" Quinn asked.

"He's one of the principals. A handful of millionaires."

"Our John has truly risen."

"He's wonderful to Magdalena," said Maud.

"Isn't she living with Obadiah?"

"She married Obadiah five years ago. But you know Magdalena. She was never content with one man."

"That seems to be a family trait."

"It's stupid that you're jealous," said Maud.

As Quinn smiled his skepticism, it became evident to him that his possessiveness stemmed not only from desire and love but also from seeing Maud as the instrument by which he would rid himself of death and war, put life once again on horseback. He had felt such rumblings of possibility for himself on Obadiah's veranda, anticipating Maud's arrival after his first shave. He'd reveled merely in waiting for her there amid the architecture of dynamic serenity, that vast, sculpted lawn sloping to the lake, leading him to the edge of all that was new, centering him in a web of escalating significance. And in such privileged moments his life became a great canvas of the imagination, large enough to suggest the true magnitude of the unknown. What he saw on the canvas was a boundless freedom to do and to think and to feel all things offered to the living. In Maud's presence, or even in waiting for her to arrive, the canvas became unbearably valuable and utterly mysterious, and he knew if he lost Maud he would explode into simplicity.

"Ah, there you are, cousin," came a female voice, and here toward Gordon, with hand outstretched, came a handsome woman in her thirties, artfully coiffed, regal in maroon silk dress, its hoop skirt bouncing as she came.

Gordon took her hand, kissed her cheek. "Phoebe," he said.

"We expected you for tea," Phoebe told Gordon. "But here you are, all bound up with an entourage."

"Two friends," said Gordon. "Miss Maud Fallon and the war journalist Daniel Quinn."

"A pleasure indeed, Mr. Quinn," said Phoebe. "You've educated us all on the terrible battles you've seen. And how quaint to meet you with clothes on, Miss Fallon. You're usually naked on horseback, aren't you?"

"I was born naked," said Maud.

"How charming," said Phoebe. "We'll look for you at tea tomorrow, Gordon. Please come alone."

"Excuse me, madam," Quinn said to her, "but you have the manners of a sow," and he took Maud's arm and walked her away.

Will Canaday found them browsing at the Shaker booth and led Maud to the elevated platform in front of the booth of Military Trophies. This, the focal point for the bazaar's public moments, was crowned by Washington's portrait, crowded with cannon, bristling with crossed rifles and muskets, and grimly but passionately brilliant with the regimental flags and the colors of the nation from before the Revolution to the present Civil War. Many of these proud silks had been reduced to gallant rags, the most notable being the flag of Albany's Forty-fourth Regiment, shredded with eighty bullet holes, and for whose constant elevation in battle twelve standard-bearers had died and eighteen more had been wounded.

"A peculiar place for a poetry reading," said Quinn.

"A perfect place for it," said Maud.

"Why are you doing these readings?"

Maud cocked her head and considered a reply before ascending the stairs ahead of Will. "I suppose," she said, "that one's brain also craves distinction."

Will addressed the crowd then, explaining Maud's international renown as an actress and how in recent years she had been a popularizer of the great poets as well as a woman asserting an intellectual stance on behalf of all womanhood. "And," he added, "if any of you have had the pleasure of talking with our Maud, you know the keenness and originality of that mind of hers," which, he concluded, was tonight a gift to the bazaar, and that after her reading a basket would be passed for donations.

Maud smiled and stared out at the crowd, found men's faces beaming at her, many women scowling. At what did they scowl? At the dancing spiritualist? The sensual horsewoman? The actress who reads poetry? The woman of fame who represents the power of the intuitive life? Well, whatever it is, Maud, they are scowling at you: you who merely by breathing in, breathing out, grow ever more singular.

Maud looked down at Quinn and saw neither the boy nor the young man (however briefly met) that she once knew. She saw a pacific smile and knew she was the cause of it, but saw, too, the trouble that lay behind it, had noted that trouble the instant she saw him in front of the mansion. It was the war, of course, and so she would begin with Keats, telling Quinn that he was perhaps half in love with easeful death.

"Thou wast not born for death," she read, and eyed Quinn secretly, finding his smile gone, his face at full attention. Her *geis* was functioning. He was in the spell of her suggestion about the kidnapping. When they talked later she would invite him to Saratoga as her and Gordon's guest. And once there . . . and once there . . . ?

She opened her second book and told the audience she had not publicly read this poem before this moment, and then began:

O, young Lochinvar is come out of the west
Through all the wide Border his steed was the best;
And save his good broadsword, he weapons had none,
He rode all unarmed and he rode all alone.
So faithful in love, and so dauntless in war,
There never was knight like the young Lochinvar . . .
But ere he alighted at Netherby gate,
The bride had consented, the gallant came late:
For a laggard in love, and a dastard in war,
Was to wed the fair Ellen of brave Lochinvar.

Maud read with great verve and sensitivity the next four stanzas, banishing male beamings and female scowls and replacing both with rapt attentiveness to the narrative, wherein Lochinvar avows to the bride's father that he has come only to drink one cup of wine with the bride denied him and, when it is drunk, to have but a single dance with fair Ellen. And they do dance, as parents and bridegroom fume, and as bridemaidens watch approvingly. Then does Lochinvar assert himself:

One touch to her hand, and one word in her ear,
When they reached the hall-door, and the charger stood near;
So light to the croupe the fair lady he swung,
So light to the saddle before her he sprung!
"She is won! we are gone, over bank, bush, and scaur;
They'll have fleet steeds that follow," quoth young Lochinvar.
There was mounting 'mong Graemes of the Netherby clan;
Forsters, Fenwicks, and Musgraves, they rode and they ran;
There was racing and chasing, on Cannobie Lee,
But the lost bride of Netherby ne'er did they see.
So daring in love, and so dauntless in war.
Have ye e'er heard of gallant like young Lochinvar?

Maud descended the stairs to stout applause, perceiving with pleasure that Quinn's was the stoutest of all.

"Will Canaday has suggested I talk of the war's reality," Quinn said to the audience. "These cannon here look like reality to me . . . and these flags all full of holes. And those things over there in the Curiosity Shop made by rebel prisoners at Point Lookout: rubber buttons turned into rings, and carved with the word 'Dixie.' You could walk right over there now and buy a rebel button and that might qualify as reality. Albany boys in rebel prisons down in Carolina and Alabama are making things too, carving pictures of Abe Lincoln and the flag out of kindling so the rebs can buy them and pitch them in the fire.

"Reality in this war is not always what you think it is. Take the fight at Round Top, when the Forty-fourth from Albany was part of the brigade trying to take that hill. Just a hill like a lot of others in this world, but ten thousand of our men went after it, and only twelve hundred came out alive. A pile of dead people, that's the reality I'm talking about. The bigger the pile, the bigger the reality. We did get that hill before the rebs, and that's reality too. A lot of hand-to-hand fighting. When it looked like our boys might get their tails whipped, our batteries opened up and dropped a whole lot of cannon shot on top of everybody—the point, of course, being to stop the rebs. Fact that our boys were mixin' it up with the rebs wasn't all that important, and so they got themselves killed by their own cannons. Reality.

"Then there was the major that the general wanted to see but nobody could find him. This major, he was from Buffalo. He was one nice fella, and I knew just how good a soldier he was. The best. We didn't want him to get into trouble, so we all went out looking for him. I found him under a bridge, having what some folks like to call carnal relations—with a brown chicken. That may not seem like it, but that's reality."

Several women exchanged glances at this remark, rose instantly from their seats, and left the gathering. Men snickered at one another and some squirmed. Quinn fell into a natural pacing up and down the platform as he talked, unintimidated by the task for which he claimed to be so ill suited.

"This reb from Texas," he went on, "when our boys got him in their sights at Round Top he called out to them, 'Don't shoot me,' and threw down his rifle. Soon as he did, one of his fellow Texans shot him in the back. Reality coming up from behind.

"And the attack at Cold Harbor, where seven thousand of our boys died in eight minutes trying to break through Lee's line. Couldn't do it. Our dead boys were spread shoulder-to-shoulder over about five acres. You could hardly find any grass wasn't covered by a dead soldier. That was unnatural reality down at Cold Harbor.

"I remember a letter I helped a young boy from the Forty-fourth write. He wrote what an awful mistake other boys back home had made by not joining up with the glory of the Forty-fourth. He died of inflammation of the brain, somewhere in Virginia. There was also a measles epidemic that killed a bunch of our lads before they ever had a chance to get themselves killed by reb muskets. Sort of a reductive reality, you might call that.

"Then there was this close friend of mine from Albany who was a captain, and we used to talk about things that were real and things that weren't, though we never put it quite that way, and one day I heard he got shot three times in less than a minute. Shot sitting down and so he stood up, and before he could fall over he got shot again, and then on the way down they got him again, and he didn't die. Still kickin' after twenty-three battles, and that's one of the nicer realities I ever heard of in this war.

"I got my own reality the day I was hit by a spent reb cannonball. Just touched by it, really, and it wasn't moving very fast. But it knocked me down, broke my leg and made me bleed, and I thought maybe I'd die alone there on the battlefield. I couldn't even give a good explanation of why I was hit. The battle was long over and I wasn't a soldier. I was just out there looking for survivors and some reb cannoneer maybe figured, why not wipe out that Yankee bastard? He let one go I never paid any attention to, and it got me. I might be out there yet, but then along came this grayback doctor and I see him working on hurt rebs. I called out, 'Hey, doc, can you stop my bleeding and set my leg?' And he said, 'I cain't set no laigs. I got soldiers of my own dyin' here.' And he went on helping rebs. So I called out and said, 'Hey, doc, I got money I can pay you if you stop my bleeding and set my leg.' And the doc looks me over and says, 'How much you got, son?' and I say, 'I got twenty-five dollars in gold I been savin' for my retirement,' and he says, 'Okay, I can help you retire.' And he comes over and looks me up and down and says, 'Where's the gold?' And I fished in my money belt and showed it to him, and he smiled nice as peach pie at me and went ahead and stitched me up and put a splint on me, and then he wrapped that leg so fine I got right up and started to walk. I gave him the gold and says to him, 'Thanks a lot, doc,' just like he was a human being. And he says, 'Don't mention it, son, but don't put too much pressure on that leg,' just like I was a goddamned reb."

The squirmers in the audience, spellbound since the mention of bestiality, were at last roused to indignation by the profanity, and a dozen or more men and women rose from their seats, a few shouting out to take Quinn off the platform. But as they left, Quinn moved to the platform's edge, pointed after them and shouted, "Do you know the reality of Eli Plum of Albany?"

He stopped some in their exit and riveted the hardy remainder. Then he genuflected in front of them all and blessed himself with the sign of the cross.

"We called him Peaches Plum," said Quinn, "and he was never worth much in any context you might want to discuss. He was one of your neighbors, and he and I went to school together here fifteen, twenty years ago. We were in Virginia, and we heard the drum corps beating a muffled Dead March in the woods near us and we all knew what was coming. Before long, orders came down to form with the whole First Division, and the Forty-fourth moved out onto elevated ground, facing an open field. The men formed a line, division front, facing five fresh graves.

"That, my friends, was a fearful sight. Also very rousing somehow, with all those brass buttons and rifles shining in the sun, and kids watching from trees, and older men alone on horses, or on top of rooves, and everybody's eye on Peaches and four other boys as they came walking: two, two, and one. Peaches was the one, walking behind the drum corps, and followed by the provost guard, fifty of them with bayonets fixed. Five clergymen walked along, too, reading scriptures, and thirty pallbearers carried five new coffins. The procession went up and back the length of the whole line of battle and then the pallbearers stopped at the fresh graves. The five prisoners stopped, too, and stood there with their hands tied, a guard alongside each one of them. Then those five young men sat down on their coffins.

"I never got to talk privately with Peaches, but I dug up his story, once I saw it was him. Never wrote it, though, and I'm only telling it now because Will Canaday says you folks are hounds for reality.

"Peaches was a bounty jumper who joined the army eighteen times. You only got a fifty-dollar bounty for joining up when Peaches started his jumping career. Used to be there was enough henpecked husbands, and third sons, and boys who got girls in trouble, who were glad to go to war and improve their outlook. But the war kept on going and volunteers fell away to a trickle, and so the price of bounties went up, all the way to a thousand dollars, which is what they're paying right now. Peaches, he made lots of money enlisting but he never got to keep it. When he'd light out he'd always bring the cash back home to his pa, like he was supposed to. Then one day after the draft came in, Peaches's pa told him, 'Go join up the army again, Peaches, only this time don't come back because you're going in place of your brother.' This brother was a lawyer, a son the father couldn't do without, the way he could do without Peaches.

"All those times Peaches joined up he never got close to a battle. He'd just disappear during the night off a train, or on a march toward some regiment, then head back home to Pa. But this time Peaches finally went to war. He saw a lot of corpses and didn't want to become one of those, so he drew on his talents and his instincts, and he took out for points north. And he ran right into another unit and got court-martialed for desertion along with the four other boys who ran with him. They were all found guilty and the President approved they be shot as a warning to cowards and mercenary men in the army. I guess we all know how many good soldiers have the impulse to run, but somehow don't, either out of fear, or good sense, or because they want to kill rebs. One youngster told me, 'I'm stickin' because we got justice on our side.' Lot of rebs think the same way, but that doesn't matter. Death's all that matters, and I know you all want the reality of that, just like the folks back home in the real olden days who wanted to know how their war was going. And their soldiers would collect the heads and genitals of the enemy and bring 'em back home for inspection to prove the army was doing its job. Peaches never got into any of that kind of fun. He was just one of those poor souls who fumble their way through life, never quite knowing the rules, never playing by them even if they think they know them, always fated to be a pawn of other folks.

"Poor Peaches. Grizzled men around me were crying as the provost guard took up its position, ten guardsmen for each of the five prisoners, rifles ready, standing about fifteen yards away, while the captain of the guard read the five orders of execution out loud. The clergy came by and talked to each of the prisoners for a few minutes, and then the officers started putting those white blindfolds on the chosen five.

"I could see Peaches really clear, see him crying and quaking, and before I knew what I was doing I'd called out, 'So long, Peaches, and good luck,' which wasn't very appropriate, I admit, but that's what I said. Peaches looked toward my voice and nodded his head. 'Okay,' he yelled. Then his blindfold was on, the black cap was placed over his face, and it was ready, aim, fire. Four of the prisoners fell backward onto their coffins. Peaches took the bullets and didn't let them knock him over. He crumpled in place and I never felt more an outsider in this life. All that pomp and panoply in service of five more corpses. It's a question, I'll tell you. But that's all that's left in me—a kind of fatal quizzicality, you might call it. I hope my sharing it with you has been of some value."

And Quinn left the platform.

QUINN, THAT FORMIDABLE FOLKLORIST, walked along amid throngs of other souls like himself and he took sight of a picture photograph that revealed how a man will sometimes stand alongside of a horse. Quinn then said to himself, "I have a horse, but not so fine a horse." This was a truth that served no purpose for Quinn, and yet he felt a goad. He went to his friend the editor, who wrote wisely about the great warps and goiters people must bear in this life, and his friend said to him, "I think it is time you took up with your platter."

Quinn then went with his friend to a place where they met a man with chinwhiskers who opened a great door and took out from it The Great Platter of the Unknown that Quinn had long ago found at the bottom of a birdcage.

"This is a great thing," Quinn said when he felt the heft of it. "I wish I knew what it was."

"Well, you'll never know that," said his friend, "for you're not smart enough."

"I'm smarter than many," said Quinn.

"We'll not dispute that. Just carry it with you and it won't bother anyone at all that you don't know what it is."

And so Quinn went to the slaughterhouse and bought a pig's bladder and blew it up like a balloon and then soaked it in whiskey until it was strong and put the platter inside it and slung it over his back with a thong.

"You're on your way," said his friend.

"I am," said Quinn.

"Do you know where you're going?" said his friend.

"I do not."

"Will you know when you get there?"

"I might," said Quinn, "or I might not."

"Then I'll go with you," said his friend. "I'm going in that direction myself."

And so the two rode their horses, one each, and found themselves at the house where the woman known as The Great Mother had lived until she was done in severely. As they entered they heard the voice of an archangel in the music room. They stopped where they stood and Quinn said, "It is a man's duty to sing."

"And when one man sings," said his friend, "it is another man's duty to listen."

So listen they did until the song came to a full stop. Quinn knew then that the archangel was a fellow named Moran.

Quinn and Will Canaday walked into the music room and saw that Maud was sitting at the pianoforte, looking into the smiling eye of the Moran fellow, and Quinn saw more in her eye than a beam of light. He resolved to tell her of this.

"I'm so glad you came," Maud said. "We've been waiting for you both."

"We didn't know we were coming until we got here," said Will.

"That's true," said Maud. "But don't let it bother you."

"You're dressed in mourning," Quinn said to her, and she was: hair upswept and bound with a black ribbon, wearing a severe black bombazine dress with long skirt and half sleeves, the severity relieved by a descending bodice line designed for provocation.

"We're having a wake," said Maud.

"Who died?" Quinn asked.

"Hillegond."

"Again?"

"Six months to the day. We're remembering her, aren't we, Joseph?"

"We are," said Moran, "and I remember this fellow as well. He can't sing a note."

"You've a good memory," said Quinn, and the two shook hands even though Quinn was of a mind to knock him down. He had not seen Moran in six years, which was also the last time he'd seen Maud. The man's face was prematurely ravaged, probably by drink, which was what had done him in as a performer. In his cups he mocked his audiences and drove them away, making himself a pariah with theater managers. And so he gave up the drink and became a manager himself, of the Green Street Theater, establishing a reputation for recognizing talent by casting Maud as Mazeppa.

"Joseph was just singing to Hillegond's memory," said Maud, and she gestured toward the Ruggiero mural of Hillegond seated at the same pianoforte at which Maud now sat, Hilly in the obvious midst of supernal music. Quinn looked at the opposite wall, to find the matching mural of Petrus Staats totally covered with a tapestry of a brilliantly white unicorn on a field of golden flowers.

"I'm glad to see Hilly out in the open again," said Quinn. "But why is Petrus still out of sight?"

"Gordon covered them both so they wouldn't haunt him," said Maud, "but I had him uncover Hillegond. I couldn't stand her being completely gone."

"You did well," said Quinn. "And where is the master of the house today?"

"At the foundry," said Maud.

"I thought you were down south dodging musket balls," Moran said to Quinn.

Quinn regarded Moran's large, flashing, and breakable teeth, then put his sack on the table in front of his chair.

"I gave that up," said Quinn.

"You're right to come back here," said Moran. "I love this place."

"We all love this place and we love one another, don't we, Joseph?" said Maud.

"Love lasts forever," said Moran, staring at the portrait. "I loved Hilly."

"Who didn't love Hilly?" said Quinn.

"The fiend who murdered her," said Maud.

"Ah now, that's a truth," said Moran. "Bad enough to kill one woman. An act of passion, perhaps. But to turn on Matty."

"Murderers have their logic," said Maud.

"Who is the killer?" asked Quinn.

"Ah," said Will Canaday. "There's a question."

"Finnerty," said Moran. "Ambrose Finnerty."

"Joseph brought him to Albany," said Maud.

"I saw him in Boston," said Moran. "I never heard a more stirring orator."

"He's in the penitentiary," said Will. "He claims innocence and says he's an ex-priest, but nobody can find the truth of that yet. He traveled with a woman and babe, his wife and child, oh yes. But she's a known cyprian who says she's a nun and that Finnerty, her confessor, plugged her up with child in the convent. She loved him all the same, and he her, and they knew the world was good and the church wasn't. So they went into theater with their peculiar love of God, and their hatred of all true priests and Catholics. And may the rightful Jesus and all his saints stand strong between us and the likes of such faith."

"The Catholics have a lot to answer for," said Moran.

"As do the heathens and Hottentots," said Will.

"Finnerty could sing, too," said Moran.

[231]

"Bawdy songs about religion," said Maud.

"He kissed and fondled his wife onstage," said Will. "In their nun's and priest's costumes."

"It was very effective," said Moran. "We filled the house twice a night for three weeks at thirty-five cents a ticket. Think of it."

"Hillegond was in bed," said Maud, "reading Gordon's play about Dido. Joseph was going to produce that at his theater, too, with some help from Hillegond, weren't you, Joseph?"

"I had hopes," said Moran.

"She was wearing her rose-colored nightdress," said Maud, "and her worsted stockings, too, because there was a chill in the air. And her silver earrings. She would never be caught without her earrings, even in sleep. It was near midnight when she looked up from her book and heard the step outside her door."

"How do you know she looked up from her book?" Quinn asked.

"I have my ways."

Quinn nodded and opened his satchel. He took out his bronze disk with the angry face. Was it a fat man with a round tongue? Was it a walrus? Was it a bespectacled woman screaming? Quinn put the disk on the table in front of him.

"What is that?" Moran asked him.

"It's a thing of a kind. A round sort of thing," said Quinn.

"I can see that."

"Quinn puts tubers on it," said Will.

"Hillegond," said Maud, "had come to the part of the play where Dido pleads with Aeneas to stay in Carthage with her, but he says he cannot. I'm so sick of self-sacrificing women, immolated by love."

"How do you know where she was in the play?" Moran asked.

"There are things one knows," said Maud.

She stood up from the pianoforte bench, walked across the room with regal poise, and sat in a cushioned chair that gave her a vision of both Hillegond's portrait and her own listeners.

Quinn rotated his disk so that its face had proper perspective on Maud. He did not know why he did this but he did it. Why should I have to know why I do what I do? he said to himself.

"Finnerty was intriguing to Hillegond," said Will from his own plush bench. "She invited him to dinner one night to hear his full story and he admits they had a dalliance."

"More than a dalliance, I'd say," said Moran.

"They found her jade ring in Finnerty's rooms," said Will. "That's what did him in."

"He said she gave it to him," said Moran. "But there's no proof. His wife said he was with her that night, but that's a wife talking."

"Hillegond took fright at the footstep," said Maud, "for it was heavier than it should have been. But when the door opened and she saw him she gave him a smile. 'Ah love,' she said to him. 'Look at you, sneakin' around like a nighthawk.' "

"You even know the words she used," said Moran.

"It's quite remarkable what I know," said Maud.

"You used to do that sort of thing all the time," said Moran.

"She made her living at it," said Quinn.

"She moved sideways on the bed to let him sit beside her," said Maud. "He kissed her gently on the forehead, then on the lips—not a real kiss, which she expected—and then he took off her spectacles and kissed her on the eyes. When he had closed both her eyes with his kisses he put the garrote around her neck and tightened it. She flailed but she wasn't strong. She was big, but age had drained her and she soon stopped her struggle. He continued twisting the garrote and pulled her off the bed with it. Her feet knocked over the ewer pitcher with the tulips on it."

"A pair of owls are roosting in Hillegond's room," said Will.

"I would like to see that," said Quinn.

"They'd be asleep now," said Moran. "Owls sleep in the daytime."

"Even so," said Quinn.

"I see no reason not to see them, even if they're asleep," said Maud, who stood up from her bench and led the way out of the music room. Quinn put his disk into his sack.

"Are you coming, Joseph?" Maud asked at the foot of the stairs.

"What is the point of looking at owls?"

"Indeed there is none," said Will.

"But they must be a sight to see," said Quinn.

"They're quite beautiful," said Maud.

"I have no objection," said Moran.

And so up the great staircase they went to Hillegond's room, whose six windows offered a view of the river and the sunrise, and where the pair of owls were asleep on the valance above the glass doors to Hillegond's balcony. The room was a vista of peace and order. Murder was nowhere to be seen, though the aroma of villainy hung in a vapor alongside the lushly canopied bed, and all four visitors to the room walked 'round it.

They stood by the glass doors and stared up at the sleeping owls, which were two feet tall, one a bit taller, being female. The birds were both solidly pale gray, great soft puffs of matching and matchless beauty, both feathered to their talons and sleeping side by side, facing into the room with closed eyes.

"They'll die in here," Quinn said.

"They go out to eat," said Maud. "The servants open the doors for them at dusk and again at dawn. They know no one lives in this room anymore, and we all welcome their presence."

"An owl can turn its head completely around and look backward," said Moran. "I once made a study of birds."

"The room isn't quite like it was," said Maud. "The Delft vase and the double-globed lamp with the lilacs were both broken when Matty came in and fought for Hillegond's life."

"I thought they found Matty on the stairs," said Quinn.

"The struggle carried out of the room. Matty fought fiercely. She was a strong woman and she loved Hilly."

"She heard the fighting going on?" asked Quinn.

"She only heard the pitcher fall and break," said Maud.

"You know it all, don't you?" said Moran.

"Yes," said Maud. "I also know it wasn't Finnerty."

"You can hold these owls when they're asleep, and they won't wake up," said Moran. He carried Hillegond's baroque silver dresser bench to the glass doors and stood on it. He reached up and grasped the sleeping female owl with both hands and stepped down from the bench. The owl slept on.

"That's quite a trick, Joseph," said Will.

"Not a trick at all if you know anything about owls," said Moran.

Maud opened the double doors to the balcony and the breeze of summer afternoon came rushing into the room. Quinn studied the behavior of the owl held by Moran and observed that owl sleep is comparable to coma, a step away from death. He studied the behavior of Moran and marveled at the man's concentration on the bird: eyes as hard as iron spikes. Quinn felt his old resentment at Moran's ability to differentiate himself from the normal run of men.

"Joseph and I became lovers during my time here as Mazeppa," said Maud. "Everybody knew, didn't they, Will?"

"Joseph tends to boast about his conquests," said Will.

"He was very attentive in those months," said Maud, "but I don't think I made him happy. As soon as I left the city he began to court Hillegond."

"Assiduously," said Will. "It was peculiar."

"Which of your six was he?" Quinn asked.

"Number three," said Maud, "and the only one in theater."

"Joseph wanted to marry Hillegond," said Will, "and she considered it for a time. But finally she wouldn't have him."

"We remained great friends," said Moran. "May we change the subject?"

"He loved this mansion," said Maud, "and all that went with it. And all that went with Hillegond."

[235]

"Then he saw he couldn't have it," said Will.

"Hillegond came to think it was ridiculous, the idea of them marrying," said Maud.

"It was not ridiculous," said Moran. "Profound aspirations must not be mocked."

"How lofty of you, Joseph," Maud said.

"I admit error."

"The news will thrill Hillegond in her grave."

"It's a great pity," said Moran, "all this plangency so close to the heart."

"Closer to the throat," said Maud.

Quinn pondered these remarks and concluded that for some men a fatal error is the logical conclusion of life, and may not really be an error at all but the inevitable finale to an evolutionary evil. He watched as Moran the covetous sat on the bench, holding the owl aloft above his lap. Suddenly the bird was awake and staring, and Moran instantly released her upward. Perversely, she settled downward and sank her talons through his trousers and into the tops of his thighs. He screamed pitifully as he fell backward, and at the sound of flowing blood the male owl's eyes snapped open. Soundlessly he flew down from the valance and, in an act of providential justice, drove his talons into Moran's face and neck.

TAMBO & PADDY
GO TO TOWN

Saratoga

August
1864

Horseless now, I, Daniel Quinn, that relentless shedder of history, stepped aboard the horsecar, the first of three conveyances that would take me to Saratoga Springs and Maud and the others who had gone before me, and I sat beside a Negro man in whose face I read the anguish of uncertainty, an affliction I understand but not in Negro terms. The man was bound for a distant place, his bundles and baggage revealing this fact, and I began to think of Joshua. I then tried to put Joshua out of my mind and opened the satchel containing my disk. I studied the disk rather than people who would take me where I did not want to go again. I discovered the disk looked Arabic with all that cursiveness in its design. Were the Celts really Arabs? Perhaps they were Jews: the lost tribe of Tipperary. The lost tribe of Ethiopia, some say. Go away, Joshua. I will remember you when I am stronger. I concentrated on my disk and it changed: convexity into concavity—a fat tongue into a hollow mouth; and in this willful ambiguity by the Celtic artist I read the wisdom of multiple meanings. Avoid gratuitous absolutes, warned Will Canaday. Yes, agrees Quinn, for they can lead to violence.

How had Maud known about the violence to Hillegond? Well, she knew. Psychometry is the most probable. How did she make the chandelier fall? Psychomagnetic pulsation, most likely. Quinn has neither of these gifts. Quinn is a psychic idiot. Quinn experiences everything and concludes nothing. *Tabula rasa ad infinitum.* Still, when the owl tore out Moran's throat there was a purgation of sorts. Quinn perceived that he himself had wanted the mansion as much as Moran did, but so hopelessly that he did not even know that he wanted it. What good is your brain, Quinn, if you can't even read your own notes? Yet, once free of secret covetousness, Quinn moved outward: another leaving off of false roles, false needs. In beginnings there is all for Quinn, a creature of onset. Will Quinn ever become a creature of finalities?

For this newest onset I was, as usual, unprepared except financially. I'd used less than a thousand dollars of what Dirck had given me over the past fifteen years and had allowed the rest to mount up in Lyman Fitzgibbon's bank; and so for a reporter I was a modestly wealthy man, without need of work for hire.

Freed from the history and the penury of war, at least for the moment, Quinn was about to embark on a life of thought, or so he thought. And there he went, west on the train to Schenectady and north on another to Saratoga, crowding his brain with unanswerable questions and banishing unwanted memories that would not stay banished, especially since he was about to enter the gilded and velvet parlors of John McGee, the gambler who could fight, and would, and did, and whose life is not separable from Joshua's anymore.

John never gambled when I first knew him, preferring to store up his savings for drink. But we find new targets for our vices as we move, and when he knocked down Hennessey, the champion of the world entirely, John's life entered an upward spiral that took him into bare-knuckle battles in Watervliet, Troy, the Boston Corner, White Plains, Toronto, and home again to Albany. I wrote John's ongoing story for the *Albany Chronicle* until the Toronto bout, Will Canaday then deciding not to finance expeditions quite so distant. I grew audacious enough to tell Will he was erring in news judgment, for John McGee and his fists had excited the people of Albany and environs like no sportsman in modern memory.

"Sportsman? Nonsense," said Will. "The man is loutish. No good can come of celebrating such brutes."

It is true that John's brawling was legendary by this time, his right hand a dangerous weapon. He knocked over one after the other in his early battles and in between times decided to open a saloon in Albany to stabilize his income. He set it up in the Lumber District, an Irish entrenchment along the canal, and called the place Blue Heaven. Over the bar he hung a sign that read: "All the fighting done in this place I do . . . [signed] . . . John McGee."

A brute of a kind John was. Nevertheless, he was a presence to be understood, as even Will Canaday perceived when John fought at Toronto. In that fight, ballyhooed as Englishman against Irishman, John knocked down, and out, in the twenty-eighth round, a British navvy who was Canada's pride. John escaped an angry crowd, bent on stomping his arrogance into the turf, only with the help of the fists, power, and guile of the man who had been his sparring mate, and whose talent for escaping hostile pursuants was also legendary. I speak of Joshua.

And so it thereafter came to pass that John the Brawn was, at the age of thirty years, polarized as the heroic Irish champion of the United States, and matched against Arthur (Yankee) Barker, the pride of native Americans. The fight took place on a summer afternoon in 1854 at the Bull's Head Tavern on the Troy road out of Albany, a hostel for wayward predilections of all manner and scope, where, as they say, cocks, dogs, rats, badgers, women, and niggers were baited in blood, and where Butter McCall, panjandrum of life at the Bull's Head, held the purse of ten thousand dollars, five from each combatant, and employed a line of battlers of his own to keep excitable partisans in the crowd from joining the fight, and whose wife, Sugar, kept the scrapbook in which one might, even today, read an account of the historic fight taken from the *Albany Telescope,* a sporting newspaper, and written by none other than Butter himself, an impresario first, perhaps, but also a bare-knuckle bard, a fistic philosopher, a poet of the poke.

Wasn't it a grand day [Butter wrote], when we all twenty thousand of us gathered in the Bull's Head pasture to witness the greatest fight boxiana has ever known? It was a regular apocalypse of steam and stew, blood and brew that twinned John (the Brawn) McGee, also known as John of the Skiff and John of the Water (from his days on the river), and Arthur (Yankee) Barker, also known as the Pet of Poughkeepsie and The True American—twinned and twined the pair in mortal-izing conflict over who was to be bare-knuckle champion of this godly land.

John came to the pasture like Zeus on a wheel, tossed his hat with the Kelly-green plume into the ring, and then bounded in after it like a deer diving into the lakes of Killarney. His second bounced in after him, Mick the Rat, a stout Ethiopian who, they say, all but broke the nozzle of the God of Water in a sparring meet. The Mick tied the Water's colors to the post as the Yank trundled in, no hat on this one, just the flag itself, Old Glory over his shoulders.

Peeling commenced and the seconds took their stations while the flag was wrapped around the Patriot's stake. Referees and umpires were appointed, the titans shook hands, and yo-ho-ho, off they went. The odds were even at first salvo, but the grand bank of Erin was offering three-to-two on the Water.

ROUND ONE
Both stood up well but the Pet in decidedly the handsomest position. Hi-ho with the left, he cocks the Skiffman amidships and crosses fast with a right to his knowledge box, but oh, now, didn't he get one back full in the domino case and down.

ROUND TWO

The Pet didn't like it a bit. He charged with his right brigade and hooked his man over the listener, which the Brawn threw off like a cat's sneeze and countered with a tremendous smasher to the Patriot's frontispiece, reducing him to his honkies. Said Mick the Rat from the corner, "Dat flag am comin' unfurled."

ROUND THREE

The Patriot came to his work this time with anger at the Mick's funny saying, rushed like a hornet on ice at the Waterman, firing pell-mell, lefts, rights, and whizzers at the Water's nasal organ. Water comes back bing-bing, and we see the claret running free from the Brawn's nostrilations. First blood has been declared for the Pet, which raised the clamor of three-to-one on Patriotism and plenty of takers, including Brawny Boy himself, who ordered the Rat to take a cud of the old green from his jacket and offplay the action. The Water let his bottleman second him while the Rat did his duty at the bank.

ROUND FOUR

The boys came up to scratch, the Pet again for business with vigor from Yankee heaven, pinning the Water boy on the ropes and hitting him at will. What happened to yer brawn, Johnny boy? Oh, it was fearful, and the claret thick as pea soup. Was he gone from us? Hardly. The skiffer outs with an ungodly roger up from the decks of Satan's scow; evil was that punch and it hit the True One in his breadbasket, loosing the crumbs it did, for a great noise came out of the Patriot's bung and he went flat as Dutch strudel.

ROUND FIVE

The Brawn lost blood, all right, but he's a game one. Up for mischief again, he leveled a terrible cob on the Pet's left ogle, leaving Pet's daylights anything but mates, and the blood of the Patriot gushed out like the spout on a he-goat. The Skiffer grabbed the Pet's head of cabbage around the throttle and used every exertion to destroy the Patriot's vocal talent, which we thought a pity, for the Patriot loves to sing duets with his sweetpea, that lovely tune, "I won't be a nun, I shan't be a nun, I'm too fond of Arthur to be a nun." The seconds separated the battlers and it was called a round.

ROUND SIX

Oh, the punishment. The Yankee Pet came up to scratch, erect on his pins, and lit out at the Skiffer's cabbage bag, but an uppercut sent him sliding like a chicken in a blizzard. The Brawn follows with the lefties and righties to the ogles, the smeller, and the domino case, but the Pet won't go down. Tough he was and tough he stayed, but dear God the blood. No quarter now from the God of Water, who goes after the Pet's chinchopper and schnotzblauer, which is a bleeding picture, and one of Erin's poets in the crowd observes, "Don't our John do lovely sculpture?"

ROUND SEVEN

The Patriot came to the scratch in a wobble of gore, both eyes swollen and all but closed, his cheek slit as if by a cutlass, the blood of life dripping down his chest and he spitting up from his good innards. Was ever a man bloodier in battle? I think not. Yet the Pet of Patriotism, a flag himself now—red, white, and blue, and seeing the stars and stripes—moved at the Skiffman, who had contusions of his own, but none the worse for them. And the Skiff let go with a snobber to the conk that put the Pet to patriotic sleep. Old Gory went down like a duck and laid there like a side of blue mutton. A sad day for the Natives, and Green rises to the top like the cream of Purgatory.

We would judge the victory a popular one in this pasture, city, state, nation, and hemisphere, opinions to the contrary notwithstanding. John McGee proved himself a man of grain and grit, and the True Yankee now knows the measure of his own head. For those who wanted more fight, well, more there was—and plenty, too, which the Yankees found to their liking, loving punishment as they do.

A good time was had by all, nobody got killed that we know of, and the nigger carried off John the King on his shoulders.

John McGee, the black man's burden, retired after this fight, claiming the American championship, and rightly so. He left his Blue Heaven only for occasional trips to Boston, New York, and other centers of manly vice to box with Joshua and a few select sparring mates in exhibitions for the sporting crowd. He was heroized everywhere and he approved of such. But in New York (he once told Joshua) he felt kin to all that he saw: the antlike mob of Irish, the Irish political radicals, the city politicians, the gamblers, the brawlers, the drinkers, and oh, those lovely women.

John always said he retired from fighting for the sake of his nose. "No sensible woman," he said, "wants a man whose nose is twice as wide as itself, or that travels down his face in two or three assorted directions."

The power that our hero manifested in galvanizing the attention and loyalty of other men, the magic of his name and fists, generated wisdom of the moment in Manhattan's Democratic politicians. And so they hired John to round up a few lads and fend off the gangs hired by politicians of the Native American stripe, the most vicious and fearsome of these headed by Bill (The Butcher) Platt, whose method was directness itself: invade the polling places in Democratic strongholds and destroy the ballot boxes. But the presence of the newly fearsome John McGee was a countervailing influence, which by dint of bludgeons, brickbats, and bloody knuckles proved the superiority of several Democratic candidates for public office in the great city.

For his accomplishments John was rewarded with the right

to open an illegal gambling house, and assured he need never fear the law as long as there were honest Democratic judges in the world. He began his career with humbleness: three faro tables that catered to gamblers with no money. Perceiving limitations in this arrangement, John persuaded men of foresight to back his expansion, and in a few years owned sixteen gambling hells, including the most luxurious in the city, a Twenty-fourth Street brownstone furnished in high elegance (a taste John had acquired in the mansions of Hillegond and Obadiah), replete with sumptuous dining and endless drink, and featuring a dozen faro tables, two roulette wheels, and private poker salons where John on occasion, or by challenge, played for the house.

I never heard John utter a word on behalf of slaves or against slavery, but as he rose in the world, so did Joshua, working for John as Mick the Rat, as sparring mate, as doorman in the gambling house, and eventually as the most adept of faro dealers, nimble-fingered fleecer of rich men in John's lush parlors. Joshua did this work when he could, but more than half of his time was spent conducting on the Underground Railroad. By the time the war began he had shunted more than four hundred fugitive slaves toward the North Star. He also owned his own policy house a block away from John's faro palace on Barclay Street and had four freed slaves working for him, running numbers.

I spent a fair amount of time with Joshua when I moved to New York. After I broke with Maud on that unpleasant night in her dressing room, I suddenly felt stifled by Albany. The year was 1858 and I had sharpened my writing skills to the point that I felt I could function as an independent. Will Canaday promised to print anything I wrote, I made contact with other editors, and so began a life in New York City. My aim was to work at the *Tribune* for Horace Greeley, a man whose principles seemed as worthy as Will's, and in time I summoned the courage to present myself and my clippings at his office.

"Your dudgeon is admirable," he told me, and so I went to

work on the greatest newspaper in the metropolis. I wrote first
of what I knew well: an interview and reminiscence with John
McGee about his great boxing days. I also used John's connection
to gain access to the dominantly Irish gangs of the Five Points
section (the Dead Rabbits, the Plug Uglies) and write of their
ongoing feud with nativist gangs (the American Guards, the
Bowery Boys). This warfare was a constant in the city, as many
as eight hundred to a thousand young men in deadly battle in
the streets at a given time, and the police helpless to curb it.

I also wrote of Joshua and his former slaves, revealing none
of their identities. I printed slave stories as they came out of
Joshua's mouth:

"Slave named Bandy tried to run away and master slit his
feet.

"Slave named Mandy lost a plow hook plowin' and master
tied her to a tree and whipped her till blood ran down her toes.

"Slave named named Julius was flogged bad for callin' his
master 'mister.'

"Slave named Pompey worked for a man had a wife wanted
a nigger whipped every time she see one.

"Slave named George had a master got hisself into a rage in
town, came home drunk and shot George in the foot.

"Slave named Abram got old and useless but master wouldn't
send for no doctor. 'Let him die,' said master, and old Abram
died with creepers in his legs.

"Slave named Hanson had a master so mean that two hundred
lashes was only a promise.

"Slave named Darius, all he lived on for a year was Indian-
meal bread and pot liquor off boiled pork.

"Slave named Adam ran away and they caught him and tied
him to the ground and whipped him to death.

"Slave named Caroline runnin' stuff up a hill fell down, got
up, kept runnin', and master whipped her, sayin', 'How come
you can't get up that hill faster?'

"Slave named Tucker got punished for goin' to a church meetin' at night. Next mornin' master called Tucker in and whipped him on the head with the butt of the cowhide, got his gun and hit Tucker on the head with the breech, got the fire tongs and hit Tucker on the head with it, got the parlor shovel and beat Tucker on the head it it; then when Tucker went to leave, master got his knife and sliced Tucker across the stomach and hit him on the head with the knife. But Tucker got away holdin' his guts in, ran and walked sixteen miles and found a doctor, and almost died for five days but didn't."

So wrote Quinn.

QUINN, LOOKING STARCHED and fresh in a new shirt and dark-blue dress suit, the only one he owned, wearing also his slouch hat over his day-old haircut, sat in one of the hundred or more rocking chairs on the busy two-hundred-and-fifty-foot porch of the United States Hotel, holding in his lap the Saratoga morning newspaper for today, August 3, 1864, reading a story reprinted from the *Tribune* about the recent battle at Atlanta, the most disastrous of the war for the rebels: immense slaughter by Sherman's army. Quinn also read a letter found on a Confederate soldier captured by Grant. The letter was from the man's brother, a rebel officer, and he wrote: "The capture of Vicksburg and our army last year has proven to be fatal to our cause. We have played a big game and lost. As soon as I am exchanged for a Yankee prisoner I shall leave the Confederacy and the cause for Europe." And under the headline "Democratic Patriotism" Quinn read: "The Democratic leaders opposed the use of Negro troops as an admission that white men of the North could not vanquish white men of the South. This prevented the raising of many thousand Negro troops. But when the government calls up white men through conscription, the same Democrats strive to defeat it, even inaugurating mobs against it. They won't let the Negro go, they won't go themselves, and they claim to be patriotic!"

Feeling the fear and anger rise in him again, Quinn put the paper aside to watch the arrival of three people, affluent parents with two grown daughters, a pair of petted beauties, or so it looked. Their carriage stopped at the hotel stairs and four young Negro men descended to them instantly, one assisting the women, two attending the abundant luggage, the fourth, with whisk broom, sweeping travel dust from the shoulders of all.

Quinn, as usual superimposing Joshua's valiant face on other Negroes, could not complete this picture. He could not imagine Joshua allowing himself even an instant of overt servility, though he'd often worked as a servant. How had the man avoided it? There is a painting of him done by an artist-gambler who frequented John's gaming house, which, thought the artist, captured Joshua from life: standing against a wall in his white doorman's jacket, listening to music being played for John's dinner guests in the next room. There is a smile on Joshua's face, a benign and folksy response to the music, excavating the simplicity of the Negro soul that is so lulled by, so in harmony with, the sweet melodies of the oboe and the violin.

But if anything, Joshua's smile in that painting is a mask of dissimulation, a private recognition that all that exists in this music is the opposite of himself, and that he understands the racial enemy better for having this privileged audience to his pleasures. I have never presumed to truly understand Joshua, but certain things are so self-evident that even the abjectly ignorant are entitled to an opinion, and I therefore aver that Joshua did not aspire to this veranda on which I was sitting, did not aspire to the glut of wardrobe trunks that were being hauled down from the roof of the carriage, did not aspire to join the parade of strutters and predators marching up and down the posh hallways, salons, and drawing rooms of this cavernous hotel, or along the preening streets of the old village, not only did not aspire to own or be owned by such ostentation but despised it for its distance from the reality to which Joshua did aspire: that landless, penurious freedom that was the newborn, elementary glory that followed after slavery.

I saw Joshua in New York not long after John McGee discovered that Limerick, his purebred Irish setter, for which he had paid eight thousand dollars in a public gesture of contempt for the poverty of his early days, had disappeared. The dog was widely known in the city, trumpeted in the gossipist newspapers as the luckiest dog in town, not because it was owned by an affluent world-champion fighter but because a rub of its head had propelled more than a few gamblers into great winnings as they fought the tiger at John's faro tables. John, of course, had invented this story.

When John discovered Limerick's absence from the house, the bedrock of Manhattan trembled with crisis. John sent emissaries into the streets to find him, dispatched Joshua to the police lockup for animals, this being the priority, for stray, unmuzzled dogs were poisoned daily at sunrise and carted to the dump by noon, and owners, if traceable, were fined five dollars for letting a cur run loose in the rabid months of summer. And we were in July. I caught up with Joshua on the street and learned of the impending tragedy as we walked.

"Damn dog don't know when he's well off," Joshua said.

"He run away before?"

"He try. Seem like he need the street, that dog. He ain't no house dog."

"Maybe they already poisoned him."

"May be," said Joshua. "Then look out. John gonna desecrate any cop kill his dog."

We found the dog poisoners taking their leisure, somewhat removed from the doomed bayings that erupted beyond a wooden partition in a warehouse built of failing brick, crude slatwork, and chicken wire. We confronted the sergeant in charge, presented our case, and were led by a rankless lackey to the wire pen where two dozen dogs, most of them mangy mongrels, but among them a fox terrier, a bull, a husky, and a collie, were all leaping and barking their frenzy at us. Limerick was among them, suddenly beside himself with joy at recognizing Joshua.

[251]

"How much it cost to take that red dog outa here?" Joshua asked the lackey.

"One dollar, but you can't take him out without a muzzle."

"You got a muzzle I can buy?"

"Yep."

"How much it cost?"

"One dollar."

Joshua counted the dogs in the pen.

"You got twenty-six muzzles?"

"Yeah. Got a hundred."

"Then we gonna muzzle up these dogs and take 'em all."

"Take 'em all?"

"That all right with you?"

"Whatayou gonna do with twenty-six dogs?"

"Gonna make me a dog house."

Joshua pulled a roll of bills from his pocket to prove his seriousness. Then we muzzled the dogs and turned them loose. With luck they'd find a way to get rid of the muzzles before they starved to death. But poison at sunrise was no longer their fate.

Gordon and Maud arrived at the hotel porch precisely at eleven, the hour of rendezvous, Maud ebullient in a pink frock with matching silk shawl, wide skirt with sweeping train, and her burnished red hair in large, loose curls. Gordon, striding purposefully beside her, looked so brilliantly fresh in his starched cravat, tan linen shirt, claw-tailed coat, and new brown boots that Quinn felt he should return to his own room and find dandier clothes. Having none, he loathed the thought and vowed to become unkempt by midafternoon.

"Ah, you have the newspaper," said Gordon. "I just heard it has an item that must be read."

Quinn handed him the newspaper, and Gordon sat in a rocker and busied himself with print.

"You look like a bouquet of roses," Quinn told Maud.

"How poetic of you, Daniel."

"What do you have in store for me today?"

"Something beyond your imagination."

"Nothing is beyond my imagination," said Quinn.

"Opening day at a brand-new racetrack, you can't know what to expect."

"I thought you might have something more exotic in mind."

"Your old friends John McGee and Magdalena will be on hand. They're quite exotic in their way, wouldn't you say?"

"You're pulling my leg."

"Perhaps later," said Maud. "Do you find Saratoga changed?"

"More crowded, more money, more hotels, more women."

"You've kept busy watching the women, then."

"It seems like the thing to do when you sit on this veranda. Clearly they come here to be looked at."

"Do you like my new dress? It's the same color as the one I was wearing when we met."

"Very nostalgic of you, my dear."

"Nostalgia is not my purpose," said Maud.

"This is vile," said Gordon, rustling the newspaper angrily. "It's a letter. They're referring to your aunt."

"What could they say about her that hasn't already been said a hundred times?" Maud asked.

"It's clearly a threat because of her party tonight," said Gordon. He thrust the paper at Quinn and Maud, and together they read the letter:

Mr. Editor—I would advise a certain aging ex–theatrical performer to keep a sharp eye out today for revelations of what she and her kind mean to this community. We who try to elevate the life of Saratoga are appalled at the degradation she is imposing on our society with her ridiculous social ambitions. We suggest she depart across our borders as soon as possible and

rid us of the repugnant memories of her scandalous life. Courtesans are of the lowest order of mammal, and performing
courtesans who kick up their legs for the edification of the
rabble are a pox on our community.

PURITY KNICKERBOCKER
(Who speaks for a multitude.)

Quinn, deciding the letter and Gordon's response to it were
fatuous and depressing, let his eye roam over the rest of the page,
found an advertisement for hashish candy, exhilarant confec-
tionized: produces the most perfect mental cheerfulness. Also
(remembering Magdalena's five abortions) a medical salute to the
Ladies of America: "Lyon's Periodical Drops! The Great Female
Remedy! But Caution!!! Dr. Lyon guarantees his drops to cure
suppression of the menses, but if pregnancy be the cause, these
drops would surely produce miscarriage and he does not then
hold himself responsible. BE WISE IN TIME."

"That kind of letter is commonplace, just ordinary jealousy,"
Quinn said. "You can't let it bother you. It carries no more weight
than these frivolous advertisements."

"Easy to say," said Gordon, "but they warn of something
coming. They'll try to spoil her birthday party, I'll wager."

"I'm sure Magdalena can take care of herself," said Maud.
"She's as invulnerable as the *Monitor* on things like this."

"But her heart is weak. You know that," said Gordon.

"What's wrong with her heart?" Quinn asked.

"She's had trouble for six months or so. She's collapsed twice
now, but she's doctoring," said Maud.

"I worry she'll be harmed by this business, whatever it is,"
said Gordon.

"Is she joining us here?" Quinn asked.

"She and Obadiah will meet us at the track," said Gordon.

"Has she kept her looks?" Quinn asked.

"And her figure," said Maud.

[254]

"Splendid. She's one of our national physical treasures."

"I agree," said Gordon.

"You do?" said Quinn. "I wouldn't have expected that of you."

"I don't know why not. I'm fond of the whole family."

"As am I," said Quinn, and he leaned over and kissed Maud on the mouth.

"That's a bit familiar, I'd say," said Gordon.

"With reason," said Quinn. "I'm deeply and forever beyond familiar, and beyond that, I'm irrevocably in love with Maud, and I intend to kidnap her."

Gordon broke into laughter and his tall hat fell off.

"How wonderful," he said. "You speak as well as you write. Wasn't that wonderful, Maud?"

"It was wonderful," said Maud.

"Of course you know I mean it," said Quinn.

"Of course you do," said Maud.

"Did Maud ever ask you to kidnap her?" Quinn asked.

"Not that I can remember," said Gordon.

"Good. She asked me, but I was never quite equal to it, and she was a vacillating kidnappee. But now I've decided to carry her off into the night, out of bondage to money, power, and fame, and do arousing things to her soul. Would you like that, Maud?"

"I don't think you should answer that question," said Gordon.

"I have no intention of answering it," said Maud.

"I think it's rather insulting," said Gordon.

"Love is never an insult," said Maud. "Let it pass."

"I'm not sure I like your attitude," said Gordon.

"Oh, you like it, you like it," said Maud.

"I'm not sure I do."

"Are we going to the track or not?" said Quinn.

"We're going," said Maud.

"Having professed love for you, am I still welcome or should I engage my own carriage?"

[255]

"Oh, Daniel, don't be twice a boor," said Maud.

Our triumvirate at this point descends the porch stairs and, settling into Gordon's handsome landau drawn by a pair of matched grays, recedes now, necessarily, into the moving mosaic that Saratoga has become at this hour. The landau moves into a line half a mile long, extending from the front of the hotel on Broadway out past the elms on Union Avenue and onto the grounds of the new Saratoga track. The carriages are a study in aspiration, achievement, failed dreams, industrial art, social excess, tastemaking, advance and retrograde design, cherished fantasy, inept pretension, and more. They are the American motley and they carry the motley-minded denizens of a nation at war and at play. Quinn, aware the Union Army uses up five hundred horses each day of the war, is uncomfortably gleeful to be a part of this many-horsed motley. In his woeful solitude he embraces the crowd, famished for significance that has not been sanctified by blood. Before the day and the night are over, Quinn will observe, speak with, or become friend of, among others en route to the track:

Price McGrady, John's gambling partner in New York City, a faro dealer of such renown that John pays him forty-five hundred dollars per month plus fifteen percent of the house winnings at all faro tables, and who is now in a fringe-topped surrey alongside his lady for today, ready for his horse, Tipperary Birdcatcher, to win the principal race of the day, or, failing that, ready for it to lose, either outcome an exercise in ecstasy;

The Wilmot Bayards of Fifth Avenue, he a horseman and yachtsman, investor in the racetrack with John McGee, and owner of Barrister, a horse that will run in the feature race, Bayard today among the most effulgent presences in the parade, riding in a barouche made in France, drawn by eight horses, and monitored by a pair of outriders who are wearing the silks of the Bayard Stable, gold and green, the colors of money;

Lord Cecil Glastonbury of Ottawa, the iron magnate (and

sympathizer with the Confederacy), in a wine-colored four-passenger brougham, he the owner of Royal Traveler, the horse favored in today's feature race;

Jim Fisk, the stock speculator and financial brigand, in a six-passenger closed coach, the largest vehicle in the line apart from certain omnibuses owned by the hotels, in which the brigand carries five cuddlesome women, all six drawn by six horses that follow behind the German marching band Fisk has hired to travel with him for the week;

Colonel Wally Standish of the 104th Regulars, who rides alone in his two-wheeled cabriolet, proving that the wound he earned in the Second Manassas campaign may have left him with a malfunctional left arm, but that his right is still powerful enough to control his spirited sorrel mare;

Magdalena Colón and Obadiah Griswold, he the carriage maker and principal partner of John McGee in establishing the race-track, and for whom the feature race of the day, the Griswold Stakes, has been named—this notable pair riding in Magdalena's demi-landau with its leather top folded down, she holding the reins of what is known to be the most expensive two-passenger vehicle in Saratoga: Obadiah's masterpiece, gilded rococo in decor, doors of polished ebony, with Magdalena's initials inlaid in white Italian marble on each door; she and Obadiah both eminently visible to all whom they now pass, he entirely in white including white cane and white straw boater, she in a summer dress of gray foulard silk with blue velvet buttons, the dress created in the *postillon* body design with tripartite tail, the new fashion favored by young women with slender figures; and rising from the right side of her straw bonnet the feathered plume of changeable color—gray today—that plume her vaunted symbol of resurrection ever since her time at the bottom of the wild river and which has made her the most instantly recognizable woman in Saratoga, in or out of season.

Along with these, in assorted buggies, phaetons, chaises, coupes, and chariots, come bankers, soldiers, politicians, Kansas farmers and Boston lawyers, litterateurs from Philadelphia and actors from Albany, reprobates with dyed locks and widows so tightly laced that breathing does not come easy, young women with tapering arms and pouting lips, full of anxiety over the adequacy of their *botteries* and *chausseries,* gouty sinners and flirtatious deacons, portly women with matching daughters who are starting their day, as usual, full of high hope that they will today meet the significant stranger with whom the hymeneal sacrifice may at last be offered up—these and five thousand more of their uncategorizable kind all move forward at inch-pace progress into the brightest of bright noondays beneath the sunswept heavenly promise of life at Saratoga.

A quarter of a mile from the track the carriage line intersected with a moving crowd of Negroes singing a song to the music of their own marching musicians, the singing spirited and full, the music rousing, the crowd en route to a celebration (to be marked by song, speeches, and prayer, I would discover in tomorrow's newspaper) of the emancipation of slaves in the rebellious states of the American union, as well as a commemoration of the thirtieth anniversary of the abolition of slavery in the British West Indies. The marchers were singing this:

> *No more peck of corn for me, no more, no more;*
> *No more peck of corn for me, many t'ousand go.*
> *No more driver's lash for me, no more, no more,*
> *No more driver's lash for me, many t'ousand go.*

I observed that the faces of all the marching Negro men brought back, as always, the face of Joshua and his myriad masks of power.

I saw John McGee as soon as we came within sight of the

track's entrance, where all carriages were discharging their pas-
sengers. Here, looking more prosperous and fit than I'd ever seen
him, handsomely garbed in starched white linen, black broad-
cloth, and patent-leather boots, and with a full and perfectly
trimmed beard as black as coal tar, stood the redoubtable God
of Water and Horses, guarding the portal like the three-headed
dog of Hades. He truly did seem to own three heads, so busy
was he greeting and weeding the crowd. Up to a half-dozen
people sought to pass through the gate and into the track proper
at any given time and John knew many by name. He kept up a
steady monologue:

"Ah, there you are, Mrs. Woolsey, lovely day for the
races . . . Mr. Travers, your uncle is upstairs . . . Hold it there,
Dimpy, we'll have no blacklegs among us today [and with a
rough pluck of Dimpy's sleeve, John sent the man back whence
he came] . . . And none of yours either, darling [gently turning
back a painted doll] . . . Ah, we'll all enjoy ourselves this afternoon, won't we, Henry? . . . And welcome, Mrs. Fitz, how's
your mother? . . . You've an escort, do ye, Margie, well, so be
it, but if I find you with your hands in anybody's pocket, I'll
whip your hide and put you in rags . . . Your cousin's horse had
a splendid workout this morning, Mrs. Riley, and I'd play him
in the pool if I was you . . . Throw that hoodlum off the premises . . ." Etc.

John left the weeding of undesirables in the hands of two burly
associates and came to greet us, shook my hand vigorously,
gripped Gordon by both shoulders, then kissed Maud's hand
with tender affection.

"Ah, Maudie girl, there's devilish news."

"Magdalena?"

"There's no news of her except she's a year older. It's the
Warrior. They poisoned him."

"Noooooo," groaned Maud, and she collapsed into herself so
quickly that I grabbed her arm, fearing a fall.

"They cored an apple, filled it with opium, and fed it to him. But he had the good taste to spit it out, and we don't think he was hurt."

"Who did it?"

"Ah, now," said John, "I wouldn't accuse anyone. But I have my notions."

"I want to see him," said Maud.

"I thought you would."

And so John took Maud's hand and led us to his carriage and then across the street to the workout track, where we found Blue Grass Warrior coming off a final lap. The jockey, a Negro lad of about sixteen years, rode him toward us, and when John grabbed the reins the jock dismounted. Maud stroked the horse, which was lathered with sweat.

"Are you all right, baby?" Maud asked the horse, and he dipped his head.

"He's doin' fine," said the jockey.

"I'd horsewhip anybody who'd harm such a beautiful animal," said Maud.

"It's dastardly," said Gordon.

Maud felt easeful after a time, and so we walked toward the stables with the Warrior and watched other horses being readied for performance. The jockeys were about, and the Negro grooms and handlers, and we had close looks at two of the Warrior's competitors: Tipperary Birdcatcher, newly purchased by Price McGrady after a particularly fruitful month at the faro tables, the Catcher being a gray colt bred in Pennsylvania by the Dwyer brothers, the noted gamblers and horsebreeders; and Comfort, a bay filly owned by Brad and Phoebe Strong of Slingerlands, an Albany suburb, she a former Fitzgibbon (cousin to Gordon) and an enduring shrew.

Both animals looked splendid to my uncritical eye, for I had knowledge of horseflesh only at its most general and practical level, and was wanting in the specifics of Thoroughbreds, this an evaluation that could have applied to my entire life: he knew things in general; his specifics lacked direction.

We bade farewell to the Warrior and, for luck, I stroked the centered white rhomboid above his eyes. John led us then on a brief tour of his racetrack, orienting us to the betting enclosure, where we might make bid on the auction pools, past the several reception rooms and saloons where beverages, viands, and oysters might be had, along the colonnade with its thickening growth of crowds, and up the stairs to the covered galleries, where Obadiah and Magdalena awaited us in their front-row seat at the finish line.

My first response upon seeing Magdalena after a hiatus of fourteen years was that she was an evolutionary figure. Age had wrinkled her, of course, and comfort had broadened her, her posterior in particular. Her bosom remained handsome, a somewhat amplified garden of promise and romp, but there was an organic pursing to her mouth line, and her hands were birdlike in their animation. Yes. A bird was what she had become. Had she always been a bird? Possibly. Once a ravenously sensuous Bird of Paradise; now, with that upward cascade of throat, an aging swan with fluttering eye.

"Oh, good," she said when we neared her. "Daniel is here. He's smart about these things. On which horse should we wager, Daniel? Maud's silly animal or the Canadian?"

"My horse is not silly," said Maud.

"I know that," said Magdalena.

"You look splendid," I said to her. "But I'm sorry to say I can't counsel you on this."

"Of course you can't," said Magdalena. "You just got here. You haven't even looked at the program."

"He certainly ought to look at the program," Obadiah said.

"That's none of your business," said Magdalena. "Let the boy alone. You've grown up to be beautiful, Daniel."

"You're very kind," I said.

"One doesn't say beautiful to a grown man," said Obadiah.

"Will you shut your mouth and let me talk? Sit down here by me, Daniel," and I did.

"If you don't bet on Maud's horse," said John, "you'll be wasting your money."

"I heard you tell a woman to bet on another horse, down by the gate," I said.

"Well, you can't have everybody betting on the same horse," said John, and he excused himself to attend to the pool betting, pledging to return and inviting us to join him if we felt inclined to gamble, which I did, believing only in Maud's horse, believing Maud could not lose at anything in the world. John moved off into the crowd, which by the day's peak moment would number five thousand. Bodies filled every seat, seemingly every square inch of space under the covered and roofless galleries. In the open area within the tall fence the crowd was equally dense, the movement to own space on the rail already having begun, the men's tall hats a liability for those to their rear. Women in clusters of finery, their vertical hats also a bountiful obstruction, and women with opera glasses observing the judge, the grooms, the horses, and other women, elevated the day into a vision of royalty and its court of ladies and their courtiers enthusing at races run solely for their relentless amusement. What exquisite privilege! What exaltation, that these animals exist to give us pleasure!

"Where do you keep your horse?" I asked Maud.

"She keeps it at my stables," said Obadiah.

"He didn't ask you," said Magdalena. "You must learn to keep your mouth shut."

"I keep him at Obadiah's stables," Maud said.

"You see?" said Obadiah.

"It's very peculiar," I said.

"Keeping a horse in a stable?" asked Obadiah.

"Will you shut up?" said Magdalena.

"Peculiar that we are all here, and how and why it happened,"

I said. "It's Magdalena's doing. If you hadn't died at the bottom of the river, and if you hadn't accepted Obadiah's invitation to come to Saratoga, we'd all be somewhere else. Of course it's possible, even if you'd *never* crossed the river, that we'd all be here anyway. But that's a fated way of looking at things."

"Daniel is so smart," said Magdalena. "If I were younger I'd steal his heart away."

"Well, you're not younger," Obadiah said.

"Shut up, I know I'm not young. I'm sick and I'm dying and nobody cares."

"Who said you were dying?" I asked.

"It's my heart. It's always fluttering and giving me sharp pains. But we all have to die sometime."

"Don't be morbid, Auntie," said Maud.

"Especially don't be morbid on your birthday," said Gordon. "How old are you?"

"Older than Methuselah."

"You look wonderful," said Gordon.

"That's what I tell her," said Obadiah.

"Shut up. I look like a chicken with its neck wrung."

"Why are you having a party and calling attention to your age if you feel that way?" I asked.

"When one is ill," said Magdalena, "one feels it incumbent upon oneself to say proper farewells to one's friends."

"But what if you don't die after this farewell?" I asked.

"She can do another party next year," said Maud. "It's all very silly. You're in excellent health."

"She's strong as an ox," said Obadiah.

"You shut up about how strong I am. I'm weak as a kitten."

"Did that letter in the paper this morning disturb you?" Gordon asked.

"I don't bother with such tripe," said Magdalena.

"Good for you," said Gordon.

"What did it say?"

[263]

"It was just tripe, as you say," said Gordon.

"I thought so. Did they mention me by name?"

"No names were used. Even the signature was a pseudonym. Purity Knickerbocker."

"They're all cowards," said Magdalena.

"Precisely," said Gordon.

"They said I should watch out for something."

"They implied that," said Gordon.

"Extremely silly. What do you suppose they meant?"

"I wouldn't worry about it," said Maud.

"It's totally ridiculous," said Obadiah.

"It's ridiculous when you open your mouth," said Magdalena.

At this point I decided to maintain my sanity by separating myself from Magdalena's quixotry. I stood up and suggested to Gordon, who was beginning to take on the appearance of a loathsome animal of indeterminate species, that we should go to bid on the race.

"I want to go, too," said Maud.

"No," I said. "You stay and keep your aunt company."

"I want to bid. I want to buy a pool on the Warrior."

"I'll buy one for you," said I.

"*I'll* buy one for you, never mind him," said Gordon.

"I'll buy it myself," said Maud.

"Then go by yourself," I said and I sat back down.

"You're a mule, Daniel," Maud said.

"If I were a mule I'd be in battle at Atlanta," I said.

Maud chose to stay, at end, and Gordon and I walked off like school chums.

"Is it true you're going to run for Congress?" I asked him. I had no need to be sociable with him, but Will Canaday had told me he truly was a man of decent principle, a Unionist, staunchly (though belatedly) for Lincoln—unlike his father, Lyman, who thought Lincoln a tyrant and usurper—and good with the workers at the Fitzgibbon foundries. I thought him a bit too full of himself, but he did have the good taste to pursue Maud.

"I probably will," he said. "The party offered it to me."

"The Republicans?"

"Of course."

"You may find yourself running against John. The Democrats are talking of him as a candidate, too."

"I've heard that. I'm afraid I can't worry about the Irish."

The idea of a man entering into a new career at midlife was strange to me, and appealing. I had thought only of continuity since I began educating myself, and so the idea of a mind change—industry into politics, in Gordon's case—seemed like a mutation of the species; and I date to this moment my change of mind on the word.

All that I had written for Will and for the *Tribune* seemed true enough, but a shallow sort of truth, insufficiently reflective of what lay below. Joshua's life, or John's, or my own could only be hinted at by the use of the word as I had been practicing it. The magnificent, which is to say the tragic or comic crosscurrents and complexities of such lives, lay somewhere beyond the limits of my calling. My thinking process itself was inhibited by form, by the arguments and rules of tradition. How was I ever to convey to another soul, even in speech, what I felt for and about Maud, what grand churnings she set off in my inner regions? How could I know those workings, even for myself alone, without a proper language to convey them? I was in need of freedom from inhibition, from dead language, from the repetitions of convention.

If I had not left my disk at the hotel, I would have taken it out of its sack and studied its mystery. And with that thought I knew that what was wrong with my life and work was that I was so busy accumulating and organizing facts and experience that I had failed to perceive that only in the contemplation of mystery was revelation possible; only in confronting the incomprehensible and arcane could there be any synthesis. My wretched inadequacy in achieving integrity of either mind or spirit after having witnessed so much death, deviltry, and treachery was attributable to this. I had become a creature of rote and method at a time when only intuitions culled from an anarchic faith in unlikely gods could offer me an answer. How could I ever come to know anything if I didn't know what I didn't know?

"Well," I said to Gordon as we neared the betting enclosure, "I hope you're getting used to my plan to kidnap Maud."

"You haven't gone soft in the brain, have you, Quinn? Kidnapping is a serious affair."

"They have to catch you, and I can't conceive of that."

"You're unorthodox, all right. I can say that after hearing you talk at the bazaar. But you know I intend to marry the girl."

"Does she intend that as well?"

"We've talked of it often."

"I don't think Maud is very taken with marriage," I said. "I think she much prefers to live in sin."

"You'd best watch your language, fellow."

"You're totally correct. I was just telling myself the same thing."

We were by then at the center of the exquisite vice of gambling on Thoroughbreds, the auctioneer standing on an elevated platform with a pair of spotters watching the crowd of about three hundred for their bids. Bidding on the pools had been frenzied since early morning at John McGee's local gambling house on Matilda Street in the Spa, but now it was reaching an apex of zeal at the track. As post time neared, a chalkboard gave the bids on each horse in the first pool. And now each horse was being auctioned separately, yet again, the folks with the fat bankrolls raising the bid on their favorites to levels beyond the reach of everyday gamblers. John held all bets, giving the winning bidder a ticket on the horse of his choice, with which he might claim all the money bet on his particular pool if his horse won.

John took three percent of all bets, and so stood to win perpet-
ually and lose never a whit—odds that pleased him quitesome.

There would be two races today, the first and most important
being the Griswold Stakes, named for Obadiah: best two out of
three heats, each heat one mile, carry ninety pounds, $50 en-
trance, purse $1,000 added, for all ages. These were the entries:

Lord Cecil Glastonbury's ROYAL TRAVELER, four-year-old,
   highest pool price thus far $1,200
Maud Fallon's BLUE GRASS WARRIOR, five-year-old, pool price
   $950
Wilmot Bayard's BARRISTER, four-year-old, pool price $600
Bradford and Phoebe Strong's COMFORT, five-year-old, pool
   price $255
Price McGrady's TIPPERARY BIRDCATCHER, three-year-old, pool
   price $180
Abner Swett's ZIGZAG MASTER, four-year-old, pool price $60

By the time Quinn and Gordon focused on the betting the
Warrior was up to $1,100. Quinn bid $1,150 and was topped by
a Negro woman with a fistful of money who bid $1,175. Quinn
went to $1,200, the Negro woman to $1,225, Quinn to $1,250
and quiet. And so Quinn took the ticket, knowing it was madness
to spend so much money. But spending it on behalf of Maud
reduced the madness substantially. Also, the total for his pool
was $3,805. So if he won, as he intuited, he would triple his
money.

"I'm glad you didn't fight me," he told Gordon.

"I wasn't tempted."

"There'll be other chances," said Quinn.

They observed the presence of five-hundred- and thousand-
dollar bills in hands of newcomers bidding feverishly on the next
pool. The two men observed the selling of this last pool before
the first heat and noted Maud's Warrior moving into favored
position, the pool now bringing $1,050 on the Warrior, and only

WILLIAM KENNEDY

$990 on Royal Traveler, the other horses standing more or less the same; and then the pair walked back toward their party, observing the jockeys sitting in wire baskets to be weighed, the horses in the paddock circle waiting to enter the track, and on to the gallery to see the first horse already on the track with jockey up and stewards leading the parade past all connoisseurs and ignoramuses in residency on the subject of horseflesh. The buzz of the crowd was growing in volume, the judges alert in their elevated viewing stands on either side of the finish line, the track a mix of sandy loam and clay, sere and pale now from the long drought. It was blazing noon on this inaugural racing morning of August third, and the five thousand all looked out from their privileged galleries, out from the less-privileged standing area below, and still more looked on from perches in trees or atop tall wagons parked on the periphery of the mile-long track, sandy scrub pines visible in all directions beyond the sea of grass planted in the center of the track's oval.

Looking down from his perch between Maud and Magdalena, Quinn saw the Negro woman he had outbid standing with a group of Negro men and women in their own preserve along the rail's final edge, the woman with an unobstructed view of the race. She and her male companion had been the lone Negroes in the betting enclosure, and Quinn now sought to define her from a distance. Her ample self was singular, to begin with; her aggressive presence here a fact that set her apart from the four million slaves and the half-million free Negroes in this divided Union. How does she come to be here when war rages around the heads of her enslaved kith and kin? Why are any of us here, for that matter? Quinn would take bets that the prevailing evaluation would be that she was a madam. She well may be. Quinn knew such madams in New York, drank in their establishments, knew their girls. But Quinn knew also that the woman could be a gambler on the order of Joshua, an entrepreneur who saw her chances and understood them. She could be the inheritor of a

[268]

fortune left by a guilty white man, or a queen of industry in the great Negro netherworld so little understood by white entrepreneurs. Or was she a mathematical wizard who had discovered the investment market? Well, Quinn had a good time trying to place her in the cosmos, and knew he'd be wrong no matter what he decided, just as no man alive looking at Joshua could imagine his achievement in money and survival skills. Was the woman a sculptress from the Caribbees? A sorceress from Sierra Leone?

Joshua's father, known as Cinque, had been stolen by slavers from Sierra Leone, but offshore from Puerto Rico he led a revolt of slaves on board the ship, killed the captain and mate as other crewmen fled in small boats, then with one sailor's help sailed eight weeks toward America and freedom, landing in starving condition at Virginia, where the sailor had vengefully steered them, and there Cinque and other surviving slaves were charged with murder. But instead of trial, and because of his physical value, Cinque was sold to a planter with a reputation for curbing arrogance. In time Cinque found a woman, sired Joshua, and after an escape attempt was hanged by his feet and whipped until he bled to death through his face, leaving a legacy of rebellion and unavengeable suffering for the three-year-old Joshua to discover.

When his own time came for rebellion, Joshua, who had educated himself in stealth, had no need of murder. He fled from master in the night and made his way north to New York, where he gravitated to the first cluster of Negroes he found, that being at the Five Points, the pestilential neighborhood dominated by the Irish, but where Negroes and Italians, in smaller numbers, also lived and worked in the underworld that that neighborhood was, where every stranger was a mark, and where no human life was safe from the ravagements of the street and river gangs: the Daybreak Boys, the Short Tails, the Patsy Conroys.

Joshua learned rat baiting at the Five Points, learned how to draw blood from bare-knuckle wounds with his mouth, this taught to him by an expert named Suckface, a member of the Slaughterhouse gang, who for ten cents would bite the head off a live mouse, and for a quarter off a live rat. Joshua learned to deal cards in a Five Points dive owned by a three-hundred-and-fifty-pound Negro woman called The Purple Turtle. She, like Joshua, lived on a street called Double Alley, and when Joshua told all this to John McGee in a later year, an enduring bond was forged between them; for John knew the Five Points intimately, had cousins there from Connacht (considered by some the lowliest place in Ireland, although not by the people from Connacht), had been in The Turtle's place often, and for years sang the song of Double Alley and its poetic alias, Paradise Alley.

> *Now Double Alley's our Paradise Alley,*
> *For that's where we learned how to die.*
> *We suckled on trouble and fightin' and gin,*
> *And we loved every girl who was ready to sin.*
>
> *Old Double Alley's our Paradise Alley*
> *For nobody ever got old.*
> *We fought for a nickel and died for a dime,*
> *We knew there was nothin' but having' a time.*
> *Oh, I'd sure love to see the old place in its prime,*
> *Double old Paradise Alley.*

The Five Points harmony, though quitesuch it never was between the Negroes and the Irish, waned perceptibly when the war fever came on. The fight to free the niggers was all idiot stuff to the Five Points paddies, whose principal interest was freeing themselves from the woes that ailed them. And so it happened that many Negroes wisely moved out of Paradise to less hostile quarters. Joshua, by then, was long gone from Double Alley, and by the time the war erupted he'd been conducting on the Railroad for more than a decade.

At a brisk tap of the drum the Griswold Stakes got off with as even a start as ever was. Blue Grass Warrior and Tipperary Birdcatcher led a tight pack by a pair of noses, Barrister and Royal Traveler neck and neck behind the leaders, Zigzag Master two lengths off, and Comfort trailing. So it went until the half mile, when Zigzag made his move and challenged the leading duo, his nose at the Warrior's saddle girths, Barrister falling back after a spent burst of speed, and Comfort trailing. At the three-quarter turn it was a three-horse race, the Birdcatcher ahead by a length, Zigzag's jockey freely using the whip to stay close, and the Warrior no more than a neck off in third, the rest far back and Comfort trailing. At the three-quarter turn it was a three-horse race, the Birdcatcher ahead by a length, Zigzag's jockey freely using the whip to stay close, and the Warrior no more than a neck off in third, the rest far back and Comfort trailing. At the top of the stretch the Catcher lost wind, and Zigzag took the lead by a head, but the Warrior on the outside, attentive to the Negro jockey's whip and whisper, moved alongside Zigzag, and then with a surge of power moved in front by a full length, then two, and in the stretch was going away to win the heat. The results:

Blue Grass Warrior	1
Zigzag Master	2
Tipperary Birdcatcher	3
Royal Traveler	4
Barrister	5
Comfort	6

The betting was scrambled for the second heat, Comfort and Barrister withdrawn by their owners. Grooms started their rub-downs of the horses as soon as they left the track, and a keen-eyed steward, by chance and nothing more, noted that a long white marking in Zigzag's nose had taken a shape different from what it had been at the start of the race; whereupon the over-heated animal was examined and found to have been dyed. Under interrogation, owner Abner Swett professed ignorance. But it was quickly learned he was the brother-in-law of Jeremiah Plum, the patriarch of the notorious Plum family, which was famed throughout northeast Christendom for dyeing stolen horses to prevent them from being identified and reclaimed. Before the day was out we would all learn that Zigzag's record had been fabricated as well, that his true name was Wild Pilgrim, and that he was a four-year-old with so many victories that he would have been at least a co-favorite (at much lower and less profitable odds) with the Traveler or the Warrior had his true history been known. The Pilgrim had beaten the Traveler twice, and so only Maud's Warrior was feared as his competitor on this sunbright noonday, which was why John's investigation into the doping of the Warrior focused on Abner Swett of Watervliet, a man of irregular values.

As the horses were about to enter the track for the second heat, a carriage drawn by a single horse, and another horse and rider behind it, came onto the track from a gate at the top of the stretch, and at moderately high speed they approached the finish line, there slowing enough for the crowd to view them in full detail. In the carriage, an old demi-landau gilded like Oba-diah's masterwork, and with the letters M.C. painted on the door, rode a Negro wearing women's clothing, including an un-mistakable copy of Magdalena's hat with a scarlet plume rising from it, the plume and the Negro waving to the crowd as they passed. Behind him, clad only in long white underwear and a woman's red wig, and riding backward and belly-up in the pose well known to multitudes from newspaper advertisements and theater posters—Maud as Mazeppa—rode another Negro, who also waved at the crowd and showed them his backside, to which was pinned a large green shamrock. Then, with a trick rider's expertise, he righted himself, and the two Negroes galloped down the track and out the gate by the far turn before anyone had the wit to stop them.

In the upper gallery, while the crowd exploded with laughter, Magdalena fell unconscious in Quinn's arms.

Soon after the mockery of Maud and Magdalena, the second heat of the Griswold Stakes was run. Three horses were entered: Blue Grass Warrior, Tipperary Birdcatcher, and Royal Traveler. They finished in that order, the Warrior winning by a length, the Traveler a far third. After crossing the finish line, Maud's horse stepped into a hole in what seemed like a perfectly smooth section of the track, twisted its left foreleg, and broke it. The jockey pulled him up and the Warrior stood with his leg bent and dangling. Track handlers went to him and wrestled him down onto his side atop a tarpaulin; then they strapped him into the tarp and dragged him away. After discussing the matter with Maud, John McGee went to the barn where they had taken the Warrior and personally fired two bullets into the animal's brain.

QUINN AGAIN PERCEIVED inevitable death in the dangling leg of Blue Grass Warrior, just as he had seen it in 1863 during the second day of a week of violence now known as the New York Draft Riots. Rioting was entering into a crescendo on that day as Quinn and John McGee turned a corner onto Ninth Avenue, heading for the house where Joshua was waiting out the riots with another man, a newly arrived fugitive slave.

Quinn himself had arrived only a week earlier, back from the battle of Vicksburg to write his personal tale of that ordeal, and having done that, he rested, sipping lager and communing with other ink-stained wretches at Charlie Pfaff's Cave at Printing House Square about the nuances of war correspondency, literature, and Charlie's German pancakes. Quinn's time spent with the lower orders at the Five Points worked against his need for rest, and a doughty *Tribune* editor tracked him down and assigned him to roam the Five and assess the rampant resentment to the draft, the first list of conscripts having just been released by the federal government.

In the Five Points and other like slums of the metropolis there was all but solid opposition to the war and to the race of people whose plight had brought it about. Also in the Five Points, Quinn found that the Copperhead politicians, great friends all of John McGee, were viewed as heroic figures. Denizens of the Five, "outscourings of humanity, the dregs of Europe" commonly called, abided in harmonious squalor with the city's criminal element, and numbered, in all, perhaps eighty thousand in a city of eight hundred thousand, a statistic with wicked potential.

Given the normal antisocial elements of such a group, its antipathy to the war and to the government waging it, given its natural thirst for vengeance, the balance of social madness, in retrospect, can be viewed as easily tippable with the imposition of a hateful law. Such was the conscription law, drafting men for the first time (volunteers and bounty seekers had heretofore sustained the army's needs), but exempting from service anyone able to pay the government three hundred dollars. We need not elaborate on the crystalline injustice of this to the poor man in general, and in particular to the poor Irishman (a quarter of the entire city was Irish), mired in generational denial and humiliation as he was, and for whom free Negroes meant a swarm of competitors for the already insufficient jobs at the bottom of the world.

And so in the heat of a midsummer weekend in July 1863, while Lee was licking his wounds from Gettysburg, the first polymorphic mob, estimated at ten thousand, drank itself into a frenzy in the greengroceries, the dance halls, and the dives of its choice, then took to the streets with baleful intent: Burn the draft office, burn the *Tribune,* that abolitionist rag, and pillage and destroy all that is not of us.

John and I found that mob as we turned the corner onto Ninth Avenue. The screaming that greeted us was horrendous, a battle already engaged between fifty policemen and the uncountable rioters who, in this moment, were led by a gigantic bare-chested, one-armed man, and at his side a young man I'd seen haranguing a crowd at the Five Points two days earlier. I remembered him at that time screaming anti-Negro invective at a crowd, urging rebellion, riot, revolution, no draft, and concluding with huzzahs for Jefferson Davis.

This younger man now fought like a pit bull, felling policemen with his club and with the force of his rage; and beside him the

[275]

giant flailed outward with his enormous bludgeon, an extension of his Herculean right arm, cracking heads and backs with a vehemence, his own head and body remarkably invulnerable to clubbings by police truncheons.

The mob moved relentlessly forward, the police valiant but unequal, routed and forced to flee for their lives as we watched. I do not know how they found Joshua's house. Perhaps they saw a Negro face in a window, or perhaps a neighbor was aware that Joshua had been there in recent days. But they singled out the house, beat open its doors, and swarmed inside.

"If he's still in there, he's dead," said John.

The howling of the mob grew fiercer, more shrill, a wordless yawp of animal frenzy, the mob hearts all linked now in a single feral pulsebeat as they sensed a quarry and a kill. And then, from a second-story window in the house, a man screamed in triumph words I could not understand, but the mob could, and it responded with a roar. The man gave a signal and the mob obeyed. It moved backward into the street and was rewarded with a Negro (not Joshua) being pitched headfirst out the window, whereupon the mob closed in over him and I saw no more of what was done.

Joshua they brought out the door, his head bloodied but he still able to walk, and at the sight of him John broke into a run and pushed his way toward the center yelling, "Don't kill him!" only to be met by the one-armed giant and his cudgel and dealt such a blow as would have killed two normal men. John fell unconscious, bloodied, dead I thought, and death might have been his lot had not the mob's focus been on the preferred quarry: Joshua. The swarm turned its attention from the dissenter, and I pulled John off the street and toward the basement of the nearest house, found it doorless, black, and empty. I propped John in a corner, and as best I could, tried stanching the flow of his blood. He was breathing, but I dared not move him toward help now, for the sight of that bloody head was too likely to whet the mob's appetite for another kill. And so I was fated to guard the wounded John and watch from my darkness as the mob took its pleasure with Joshua. Here is what they did to him:

> They beat him with their cudgels
> And they stabbed him with their knives
>   and he did not die
> They dropped stones onto his chest
> They dropped stones onto his head
>   and he did not die
> They poked holes in him with sticks
> They roped his legs and dragged him
>   and he did not die
> They gave him to the harpies
> And they opened up his flesh
>   and he did not die
> Then the harpies oiled his wounds
> And they lit him with a match
>   and he did not die
> Then they hanged him from a lamppost
> Lit a fire underneath him
>   and he died

The mob moved on, and so I was able to get help from a family on the block to carry John to a bed; and a woman bandaged his head. Two samaritans cut down Joshua but a fragment of the mob came back and found him on the ground and hanged him a second time. When quiet came upon the street I shinnied up the lamppost and cut him down again. His left hand had been severed. I could not find it. I dragged him into my cellar and left him, then explored the neighborhood until I found a peddler with a pushcart. I rented him for two dollars, but when I told him my purpose he reneged. I threatened him and he went with me. When we got to the cellar, Joshua was gone.

WHEN MAGDALENA COLÓN DECIDED she was about to die for the second time, she announced from her bed that the only way she could die properly was lying by the water under a tree. Her intuition about death came at home at midafternoon, two hours after she collapsed in the gallery in my arms. She summoned Obadiah, Maud, her doctor, and her servants to her bedroom and insisted that someone find John McGee and bring him to her to reorganize the evening. Instead of a birthday party to celebrate her being alive for fifty-five years, what she now wanted was a wake to acknowledge her passing over into lovely death, but held while she was still alive and able to enjoy both sides of existence at the same time.

"You can't have a wake if you're not dead," said Obadiah by her bedside.

"I won't even let you come to the wake if you don't mind your mouth," said Magdalena.

The doctor had diagnosed her condition as palpitation, arrhythmia, and syncope, and ordered her to sip brandy, lie with her head below the level of her ankles, with her clothing loosened at neck and waist, with smelling salts on hand for revival in the event of further fainting, a coffee enema if necessary, and with the utmost ventilation to her room.

Maud entered into a weeping rage at Magdalena's plight, but Magdalena delighted in the attention, ordered her maid to find her a loose-fitting blouse, strip her of all undergarments, daub her face with powder, etch with pale crimson the lines of her lips and the hollows of her cheeks, brush her hair forty strokes, impose upon her throat the pendant emerald Obadiah gave her for her fiftieth birthday, heighten her eyebrows and eyelashes with charcoal, push her feet into her silver slippers, and find a pair of strong men to carry her out onto the lawn beneath a tree, where she might freely breathe her anticipated last. She then sent for me to ask my advice in publicizing her wake, since she wanted all her friends and enemies to come. I suggested a handbill.

"Fine," said Magdalena, "and I also want you to write something about me and how I changed the world."

"How did you change the world?" I asked.

"I have no idea. That's why I want you to write it."

"I'll do what I can," I said.

"Splendid. And you can read it tonight at the wake instead of some poopy old prayer."

I was alone at this point in the day, John off in places unknown, and Oba, as people called him, having donned his at-home costume of dressing gown and thigh-length kid boots, puttering around the servants' quarters. Maud closeted herself in her private reverie, emerging only to check on Magdalena's condition, which was improving. When she collapsed in my arms her face was ashen, but by now she had become sanguine and relaxed and was moving toward death with all her summonable beauty.

I took myself to the library, where Oba's butler bought me Magdalena's half-dozen scrapbooks, thick with newspaper cuttings in Spanish and English. I browsed through them and saw an outline of her life, the topography of a notorious career, the mockery of her first death, and on forward into the social notices of her life with Obadiah. What she wanted me to write, I supposed, was an obituary that would heap glory upon her achievements as performer, as mystic, as hostess; but the very thought of that bored me. If I was to do justice to the woman, I needed to move beyond the barricade of empty facts into some grander sphere—charting, for instance, what I myself found significant: her ability to survive as a solitary woman in a hostile world; her love affair with death; and, most important of all (to me), her nurturing of the incredible Maud, and then imposing that hallowed creature on my life.

The decision I had made so long ago, to live my life according to the word, reached its apogee in the war and then descended into the bathetic dumps of faceless slaughter. Yet in writing about what was worst in this world an unconscionable pang of pleasure dogged my every line. Mine was clearly a life fulfilled by language, and I was coming to see that through that, and only that, could I perhaps in some unknown way gild the eccentric life of Magdalena, or the tragedy of Joshua, or my own thrumming symphony of mysteries. By devising a set of images that did not rot on me overnight, I might confront what was worth confronting, with no expectation of solving the mysteries, but content merely to stare at them until they became as beautiful and valuable as Magdalena had always been, and as Maud now was.

It was in this elated frame of mind that I picked up a pen and set down a handful of words that I hoped would begin the recovery not only of what had been lost but also of what I did not know had been lost, yet surely must have been. I was persuading myself that if I used the words well, the harmony that lurked beneath all contraries and cacophonies must be revealed. This was an act of faith, not reason.

And so, rather than writing Magdalena's obituary, I began to write her story, taking the facts not from her cuttings but from my imagination, where, like a jungle flower, she had long since taken root.

I, Daniel Quinn, neither the first nor the last of a line of such Quinns (of this I was hopeful), would, with the courage false or real that comes with an acute onset of hubris, create a world before which I could kneel with awe and reverence as I waited to be carried off into flights of tragic laughter.

I did not write Magdalena's obituary but I did compose the notice of her death and carried it to town to have it printed as a handbill for distribution thoughout the city. It read:

NOTICE OF PROXIMATE DEATH

The social leader and former international theater star Magdalena Colón Griswold, with all sincerity and affection, invites the visiting and resident citizenry of Saratoga to a viewing of her last remains, so to speak, this evening at her home, Griswold Gardens, on the eastern shore of Saratoga Lake. Her passing will take place on the Griswold lawn, and so, to facilitate the viewing, it is suggested that visitors carry with them either candle or lamp. Dinner and libations will be served, and dancing on the lawn will begin sharply at eight o'clock.

Magdalena had not anticipated anything more than a solemn parade of mourners filing past her, uttering condolences, shaking her mortal paw. But when John McGee arrived he put an end to such thinking.

"We're having a party," he said. "You can't spoil everybody's evening just because you've decided to die." And so the final sentence was added to the handbill's invitation.

The guests began to arrive by seven. Those invited to the birthday were received in the mansion; those invited to the wake were directed to the lawn. John, when present at the mansion, clearly became the man of the house, Obadiah no more than a potty little wisp in the cosmos. John took up the welcoming position at the front gate, just as he had at the track, but now he turned away no one, including known thieves.

"Just stay outside the house," he told the thieves he recognized, "or I'll eat your gizzard for lunch."

Champagne, Bordeaux wines, squab, and lobster were served to the birthday guests; beer, oyster stew, and crackers to the mourners on the lawn. John had ordered a stage built at the edge of the reflecting pool and at seven sharp Adolph Bernstein's orchestra from the United States Hotel began the music of the evening with a Chopin medley. John also asked Jim Fisk to bring his German band to the party, Fisk said he would, and did, and so music was continuous for Magdalena's presumably farewell performance. Milo, the Master of Magic from Albany, performed hat and animal tricks at an intermission, and when the music resumed Milo waltzed with a dancing bear, who was actually Cornelius Gómez, an idiot-savant Mexican dwarf, who told fortunes for a quarter afterward on the veranda.

Magdalena watched it all from her vantage point at the cusp of the lawn's principal slope, Maud beside her dotingly, responding to all her whims, which grew fewer as the line of strangers who came to wish her a pleasant passing grew longer.

"What a lovely idea inviting people to your wake . . . Are you dead yet, Magdalena? . . . When do you die? . . . Will we see it happen? . . . Have a good time in heaven, Magdalena . . . We'll miss you . . . Will there be a party for the funeral, too?"

"You're all such dears to come," said Magdalena. "I hope we don't run out of food. Maud, will we run out of food?"

"No, Auntie."

"That's nice, dear. Keep them moving."

No one mentioned the mockery of the afternoon to Magdalena, this warning passed on to all in line by order of John McGee, who said that if anyone talked of the thing to Magdalena he would break both their legs. Of the mockery, John discovered through informers that the two Negroes were both transient stable hands who had no knowledge of what they were doing and earned three dollars apiece for what they thought was entertainment for the crowd.

Gordon Fitzgibbon grew so pensive and melancholy over the mockery that Maud could not bear his presence and sent him away to elevate her own spirits. She told Gordon to cure himself of gloom and come back to the party in jubilation or else she would have nothing to do with him for the entire evening. Gordon went off and drank gin at the United States bar and returned at sunset with a rakish angle to his tall hat and a crooked smile on his face, the first time Quinn ever noted anything likable in the man.

Gordon arrived on the arm of his cousin Phoebe Strong, whose horse had also suffered humiliation during the afternoon, finishing a ridiculous number of lengths behind the winner. What Gordon did not know, nor did Quinn, was that Phoebe had been the architect and executrix of the mockery, and of the letter penned by Purity Knickerbocker—these facts unearthed by John McGee and his Hawkshaw network of social spies. John told only Maud of his discovery, and so Phoebe arrived at the wake with the serenity of a criminal who has committed the perfect crime.

Humanity arrived in great droves to mourn for Magdalena and grieve in its free beer. The lawn was asprawl with a vast multitude, the night a wash of flickering brilliance from a thousand lamps, lighting up the lawn more brightly than a full moon. John took it upon himself to summon a Presbyterian cleric, who was part of Magdalena's social set, to utter a prayer on behalf of the imminent decedent's soul, but the uniqueness of the occasion thwarted the man and instead he uttered a homily on the therapeutic quality of night breezes. Magdalena lost patience and shooed him away.

"Daniel," she said, "you say a prayer for me."

"No," I said, "I can't do that sort of thing anymore. But I shall write about you as one of the great philanthropists in the entire history of sensuality."

"He's so brilliant," said Magdalena. And then she pulled me to her and kissed me on the lips.

"I envy Maud," she whispered.

"You are the queen of the night," I told her, and she feigned a swoon.

The mourners' line undulated across the entire lawn, and at the level area atop the slope the dancing began.

"I should like to dance," said Magdalena. "It may help me die. I should like to dance with John McGee."

"And so you shall," I said, and we organized the bearers, who carried Magdalena and her chaise longue across the lawn to the dancing area. I summoned John and told him he was wanted. He had never stopped being Magdalena's lover, even after her marriage to Obadiah—their assignations, whenever John was in range, being an open secret, and always conducted on Wednesday afternoons, Magdalena's preferred day of the week ever since a young lover told her Wednesday had been named for the god of poetic frenzy.

And so we danced: Magdalena and John, Gordon and Phoebe, Maud and I, and several hundred others, all waltzing to the music of "Beautiful Dreamer," so very popular at this moment. Seeing her dance I did not believe Magdalena would die. She looked irrepressibly radiant. How could such a vivid creature cease to be?

"I think we should change partners," Maud said, and she broke from me and went to Gordon. "I would like to dance with Phoebe," she said.

"With Phoebe?" said Gordon, stunned.

"With Phoebe," said Maud, and she grasped a reluctant Phoebe in a waltzing position and moved her forcefully away from Gordon, all of us suddenly turned into spectators. But dancing was

not Maud's intention, as she proved by spinning Phoebe around
and ripping her dress down the back. Phoebe tried to turn and
strike Maud but Maud was far stronger and quite ready for the
countering. She then flung Phoebe onto the floor, face down,
and sat on her back. Gordon and another man started to intervene but John stopped them.

"Let them be," said John. "History needs elbow room tonight."

Maud continued ripping Phoebe's dress, and then her petticoat
and fluffy netherings, Phoebe squirming and screaming to the
death, of course, howling for help. I thought Maud must have
lost her reason, and yet her method exuded such control that a
purpose was obvious.

"For heaven's sake, what are you doing, Maudie?" Magdalena
asked, hovering over the struggling women.

"This is Phoebe Strong, Auntie, Gordon's first cousin."

"I know it's Phoebe," said Magdalena. "Of course I know
Phoebe. What are you doing to her?"

"I'm ripping her clothing."

"Yes, but whatever for?"

"She's the hateful bitch who planned the mockery of you and
me this afternoon."

"Phoebe did that? Did you do that, Phoebe?"

"I did and I'm glad I did," said Phoebe between screams.

By this time Maud had ripped the full length of every garment
Phoebe was wearing and as the circle around us grew dense with
interrupted dancers Maud fully uncovered the screeching Phoebe's
buttocks for all to see.

"I thought of asking her to apologize," said Maud, "but this
seemed a superior solution. Do you agree, Auntie?"

"Oh, quite," said Magdalena. "Quite indeed. But you know
that is a most unpleasant sight. All full of pimples and dimples.
Oh, do cover them."

At the roar of laughter Maud stood up, and the humbled

[285]

Phoebe, screaming and crying, clutched her rags about her and ran off toward the mansion. The orchestra took up the music again and the beautiful dreamers of Saratoga resumed their dancing under the stars.

As the evening moved on, four whores who had been the recipients of Magdalena's charities (she supported cyprians, waifs, and actresses) turned up, crying helplessly as they bent to say farewell to their benefactress. Their spirits improved when they saw how well she looked, and after several beers they were all in chorus singing "Father's a Drunkard and Mother Is Dead," which took the evening into a new phase.

The crowd was thinning and the light dimming. Many couples moved through various stages of romance by the shore of the lake, or in the shadowed woods, or in the sanctuary of Obadiah's shrub gardens. Gordon could not stop apologizing for his cousin's behavior, he assuming the guilt himself. But Maud wanted to hear no more of it and she left him to dance with me.

"I think it's getting time now to kidnap you," I said.

"A perfect ending to a perfect day," said Maud.

"I would like to sit under that arch," I said, pointing to the trellis where we had watched Magdalena reveal herself to Obadiah at John's urging. We sat on the benches where they'd sat, the roses on the trellises around us all colored a vivid blue by the dark light of the night sky and the dancing flames of a thousand lamps and candles. And then, for the first time since our rendezvous at Hillegond's house, I kissed Maud. I had felt estranged from her after our meeting on the hotel piazza at morning, but I reclaimed our intimacy with the kiss, my brimming passion organizing my mind in a most salutary way. What flooded back to me was not just every memory, every loving response I'd had to her, but the opening also of an entire emotional landscape that I truly knew must exist somewhere but had never been able to find: the discovery of a new place in which to live.

It vanished as quickly as it appeared, a trompe l'oeil of the imagination, but I knew as long as I had Maud with me I could reconstitute it. I took her by the hand just as Gordon arrived.

"You're monopolizing Maud," he said to me.

"I was about to take her somewhere and make love to her," I said.

"You had better quit that sort of talk, fellow."

"It's more than talk, Gordon."

"*I'm* going to marry this woman," he said.

"I've loved her for fifteen years," I said. "Do you think now that I've found her I'll just walk away from her?"

"Maud," he said, "I want you out of this situation."

"She has a will of her own, Gordon. Why do you suppose she's with me?"

"You're an arrogant bastard," he said.

"And you're an insufferable prig," I said.

I stood up and he rose to come at me, but I merely pushed and he went backward onto the bench. He stayed sitting.

"I'll have satisfaction for this," he said.

"You will," I said.

"Oh, no," said Maud. "Never."

I took her hand and pulled her away and across the lawn, seeing Magdalena in the cradle of John's arms, he walking down toward the shore. We stopped and watched and saw her bearers following with her chaise longue, which they placed at the water's edge along with two large candelabra. John put Magdalena on the chaise in a position that allowed her to look out over the great expanse of water, then sat down on the grass beside her.

A storm was developing on the lake, and in an hour the wind would rise and extinguish most of the candles and the party would end. Tomorrow would be a day of fast and humiliation, called for by the President to rekindle the nation's attention to ending the war. Quinn would contemplate a duel with Gordon and remember Joshua's duel with life and his conclusion about it: "If you lose it's fate," Joshua said. "If you win it's a trick." Quinn would dwell on this and perceive that he himself had changed, that he was forever isolated into the minority, a paddynigger and an obsessive fool whose disgust was greater than its object, who was trying to justify in this world what was justifiable only in another cosmic sphere. There were no explanations that satisfied Quinn, only a growing awareness of dark omissions in his life and a resolute will to struggle with the power the past seemed to have over him: power to imprison him in dead agonies and divine riddles. He would wake dreaming of his disk and its faces, a savage dream of a new order: faces as old as the dead Celts, forces in the shape of a severed hand and a severed tongue that would bring Quinn great power over life.

"You will go to war," the Mexican dwarf had told him on the veranda. "You will live a long life, raise sons, and have a happy death." Quinn believed none of it, believed it all.

Maud did not want to go to her room, or to the hotel, but led the way to an upper floor of the mansion on the side that gave a full view of the lawn and the lake. She tried one door and they were greeted with a privileged vision: Obadiah on his knees, holding aloft the skirt of Adelaide, a parlormaid, and licking the back of her right knee. They moved on and found a room and locked themselves in, and then kissed at such a pitch of passion that Quinn thought his chest would explode, so acutely aware was he that at last he had stolen Maud.

"Slow," he said, and he loosened the dark ribbon that held Maud's dress at the bodice. She removed the ribbon from the dress and tied it around her neck as a choker, and he took her dress from her, then the rest of her garments, and she did the same for him. The ribbon was long and uneven and fell the length of her torso to obscure part of her private hair. Quinn's

[288]

eyes studied her with a wondrous lust and a love that was as limitless as the universe. Maud rolled backward onto the simple iron bed, her legs rising, the ribbon falling naturally between her open thighs, leaving her gift mostly secret. Quinn moved between her legs and gently lifted the ribbon to one side. And then Maud and Quinn were at last ready for love.